The Facilit~~ator~~

by

Tracie Podger

Facilitator *noun*

UK /fəˈsɪl.ɪ.teɪ.tər/ **US** /fəˈsɪl.ə.teɪ.t̬ɚ/

Someone who helps a person, or organisation, do something more easily, or find the answer to a problem.

My heartfelt thanks to the best beta readers a girl could want, Karen Shenton, Alison Parkins, and Rebecca Sherwin—your input is invaluable.

Thank you to Margreet Asselbergs from Rebel Edit & Design for yet another wonderful cover, this makes our tenth collaboration!

I'd also like to give a huge thank you to my editor, Karen Hrdlicka, and proofreader, Joanne Thompson.

A big hug goes to the ladies in my team. These ladies give up their time to support and promote my books. Alison 'Awesome' Parkins, Karen Shenton, Karen Atkinson-Lingham, Marina Marinova, Ann Batty, Fran Brisland, Elaine Turner, Kerry-Ann Bell, Louise White and Ellie Aspill – otherwise known as the Twisted Angels.

I'm dedicating this book to Charlie Fenton of The Book Club (TBC) on Facebook. It's a secret club, full of strange people…I mean, readers. So why am I dedicating it to Charlie? Tracy Fenton gets loads of mentions (she is awesome), whereas Charlie is the quiet, serious one, who doesn't. So I thought it would be nice. In all seriousness, The Book Club #TBConFB□□□□ is a great place for readers and authors to chat and find out about new releases. Check it out. Oh, you can't, it's secret! You'll have to message me for an 'in'.

If you wish to keep up to date with information on future releases, and have the chance to enter monthly competitions, feel free to sign up for my newsletter. You can find the details on my web site:

www.TraciePodger.com

My mission in life is not merely to survive, but to thrive; and to do so with some passion, some compassion, some humour, and some style

- Maya Angelou

Cover design – Margreet Asselbergs, Rebel Edit & Design

Model – Burton Hughes

Photographer – Eric Battershell, Eric Battershell Photography

Formatting – Roses & Thorns

It had been six months since my husband left. Six whole months of self-doubt: wondering what I'd done wrong, self-loathing, and many, many bottles of wine.

I sat at my kitchen table, looking at the documents in front of me. I had started divorce proceedings on the grounds of adultery; something my mum had desperately tried to change my mind on. She wanted me to stay married to stop him from moving on. I wasn't into those kind of games.

There was no going back for me. Scott had been caught red-handed, fucking his assistant over the boardroom table. He'd been filmed, probably with a mobile phone, and *someone* had kindly decided I needed to be sent that clip.

The video had been sent from an unknown number, although I believed it was sent from the recipient of his cock. It had proven very useful when shown to my solicitor. There was no denying an affair. All I'd received from him was a list of reasons why I was such a terrible wife. Maybe, in his mind, that was his justification.

I worked too much. I was a hard-nosed career bitch. I didn't pay him enough attention. She understood him.

I'd laughed at the last one. Since the dawn of time, when a man decided it was perfectly okay to be caught balls deep in someone other than his wife, it was that same excuse, '*she understands me.*'

I played with the thin gold band on my wedding finger as I read through the documents. I wondered at what point it would be suitable to remove it, I wondered why I hadn't already. Maybe I'd save it for when the divorce was finalised. I'd create some sort of event; have the removal of the ring be a symbolic gesture that fifteen years of my life was over.

I sighed. Fifteen years Scott and I had been together. We'd met in school. Now at thirty years old, I was a single woman for the first time ever.

The intercom to my apartment alerted me to the fact my ride had arrived. I shoved the documents into my briefcase, along with my laptop, collected my suit jacket from the back of my chair, picked up my handbag and overnight bag, then left.

"Looking good, Lauren," Jerry said, as I climbed into the back of his very plush Mercedes.

"Thank you, I could do with a little flattery this morning."

Jerry was my boss, owner of a media company in the center of London, and a good friend. We hadn't been friends when I'd agreed to become Head of Marketing at a business he'd just established, that friendship had built over time. He was the most amazing person and a brilliant businessman: a self-made man, who'd stumbled into the online advertising phenomenon before it was even a thing.

He had also been in love with me for years.

"Remember, hold your head up high and keep that smile on your face," he said.

I took a deep breath as I settled into the soft, grey leather seat and his driver pulled away from the kerb.

"I intend to."

It was a Friday morning and we were heading to Hampshire for the company's annual conference, or piss-up, as Jerry liked to call it. But why the need for my chin up and a smile on my face? My husband, soon to be ex-husband, would also be there.

When Scott's affair had been discovered, Jerry had wanted to '*boot the fucker out*,' I recalled as his words. Scott was Head of Development, a job I'd secured for him. The woman he was fucking? His assistant.

"We could always pretend to be together, if that makes you feel better," he said.

I laughed as I patted his leg. "And spoil our wonderful friendship?"

"I can but try," he said, dramatically.

"So, tell me about this new company about to invade us?"

I wanted to change the direction of a conversation we'd had many times. Jerry had confided in me that he had sold part of his business for a *'shit-ton of money'*, he'd said. I was pleased for him, he worked harder and far longer hours than anyone else I knew. It had been something that had come as a surprise, and the deal was done far quicker that I'd thought it would be.

"Well, as you know, world domination has always been my plan."

"Be serious," I said, with a laugh.

"I'm going to introduce them at the conference."

"And what will they bring to the company?"

"Big in telecommunications, shipping, you name it. Owner likes to invest in successful businesses, sit back, and reap the rewards."

"Are they going to have a day-to-day input?"

"There'll be changes, of course, but don't panic, you're a keeper."

"Will you do me a favour? Will you ask reception to leave this for Scott?" I handed him an envelope.

When his affair had been discovered, and I'd gotten over the initial shock, one of the first things I'd done was contact the hotel and ask for my own room. The hotel had been full; we'd taken all the rooms. Jerry had offered me a side of his bed, if I wanted to share the suite I'd booked him. Of course, I declined that generous offer and booked myself into a nearby hotel. It wasn't ideal, but there was no way in hell I was sharing a room with Jerry.

"What is it?"

"Divorce papers. The last lot I posted to him went missing, funnily enough."

Scott didn't want a divorce; neither did he want reconciliation, not that it was on the cards. He'd refused to instruct a solicitor, and I'd been trying to get him to sign the damn papers for weeks.

"I'll do better than that, I'll hand them to him myself. So, plans for tonight?" Jerry asked.

"I have to go to the conference hall this afternoon, and you have a dinner arranged with your new partner. I booked you a table for six o'clock, as instructed. Although why you want to eat that early, I don't know."

"Because I'm always hungry by then. You can join us if you want," he said.

"Jerry, you are a great friend, and I get enough shit because of that friendship. Once they know that I knew of this deal before them, my life will be even more lonely than it is now."

I didn't have 'friends' at work. I'd been working with Jerry since the beginning. He'd asked for my help in marketing his newly formed company, and we became close, with that came the gossip. I'd often wondered if Scott's affair had been a result of his insane jealousy of the relationship Jerry and I had.

"Fuck them, have dinner with us."

I laughed. "No, I've got too much to do, then I want an early night."

"Oh well, your loss," he said, as he took out some papers from his holdall in the footwell and read through them. I did the same.

Chapter Two

"Miss Perry," I heard.

Jerry's driver had alerted me that we were nearing my hotel. I'd been engrossed in my work and hadn't taken notice of the journey.

"I don't like it that you're not staying with us," Jerry said.

"I can't. I can't stomach seeing him laughing and joking with his minions. And the hotel was full when I tried to book my own room."

The car door was opened for me and I stepped out. "I'll ring you later, but see you in the morning," I said.

My overnight bag was handed to a porter and I followed him in. I checked in, collected my key, and headed for my room. I enjoyed hotel stays, and it didn't bother me being on my own. I'd travelled a lot on business; I'd gotten used to eating alone, but as I inserted the key card into the reader, a pang of nervousness hit me.

I'd managed to successfully avoid Scott over the past six months. Whatever communication was needed was done through my assistant and his new one. The previous had *left*. We sat in meetings, avoiding eye contact, and I'd kept it as professional as possible. But I wasn't looking forward to the ball on Saturday evening. I wasn't looking forward to seeing him enjoy himself, while I pretended to.

I unpacked my overnight bag, plugged my laptop in to charge, and decided on some lunch from room service before I headed to the conference centre.

****

The conference centre was theatre style, and capable of housing the employees who'd sit through Jerry's round up of the financial year and plans for the one coming. A large overhead monitor would display his presentation while he stood at a lectern on a small stage. Having been to many of our year end conferences, I knew the employees, those attending for the first time, were in for a treat. Jerry liked to throw in a few jokes, drop the F bomb on a regular basis, and make the experience an overall enjoyable one.

Although the hotel had a room large enough to house us all, it was the theatre style seating that had sold the facility to me. No matter where people sat, they'd be able to see our wonderful leader.

When I was done checking the room, then making sure all the materials I needed were sitting with the front desk, I jumped into a taxi and headed to the other hotel. I made a point of not wringing my hands at the thought of bumping into Scott. I'd been tempted to call ahead and ask if he'd checked in, but didn't want reception notifying him that someone had enquired. He'd know it was me.

"Hi," I heard, and saw Jenny, my assistant, make her way over to me as soon as I entered.

I'd texted her to let her know I was on my way.

"How are we doing?" I asked.

"All okay. Seating plan is done, I put you with Jerry," she said with a wink.

I chuckled. "Thank you. Now, let's find the catering manager."

After a brief meeting to confirm food allergies had been taken into consideration, we met with the event planner and confirmed table layout, the entertainment hadn't pulled out at the last minute, and that they had enough of the wine Jerry had selected for each table.

"Fancy a drink?" Jenny said, once we were done.

"Sure, why not."

We headed to the bar and I hesitated before entering. "He hasn't checked in yet," she said.

I took a deep breath and sighed. "I checked so I could warn you," she added.

"You're a star, you know that?"

"I know you don't want to talk about it, but I can tell you this, pretty much every woman in the company has your back."

That I doubted.

"Jenny, it's not that I don't want to talk about it, I mean, I can hardly avoid it since we both work at the same company. It's more that I

6

want to distance it from work. I don't want it to encroach into how I do my job."

We ordered two glasses of wine and found a corner with two low chairs and a coffee table to sit at.

"I was talking to Penelope, Patrick's assistant. She said that she spat in Scott's coffee after he'd demanded she make him a cup." She laughed as she took a sip of her wine. "Not that we were gossiping about you," she added quickly after.

"It's okay, I hope the fucker drank it."

It actually felt good to drop the career woman façade for a few moments. Jenny looked at me, wide-eyed, I think it was probably the first time she'd ever heard me swear.

"Are you okay, though? This has got to be hard," she said.

"I'm nervous, of course. I haven't been in the same environment as him, socially, for a while. But it's just one night. I'll live."

It was as I finished my sentence that I saw him. A man with blond hair, wearing a white shirt and black trousers, faced reception. He had his back to me, but I'd know him anywhere. I caught movement beside him and my stomach lurched.

"Oh my God, he fucking brought her," Jenny said.

Standing beside Scott was the bitch he'd had, correction, was still having, an affair with. Partners had been invited to join us for Saturday evening; most had opted to leave theirs at home. Was he trying to make a statement?

"What a prick," Jenny said, bringing my attention back to her.

"I think I'll head to my hotel."

"Don't let him drive you out," she said.

"He isn't, but you don't want to see me smack that bitch if she tries to talk to me," I laughed, a fake laugh.

I placed my glass on the coffee table and waited until they'd headed toward the lift. I heard his laughter as he met his colleagues. I saw her hand on his back. My stomach was in knots, I felt physically sick that he would do that to me. That he would bring her to a company

7

event knowing I would be in attendance. Did he hate me? He must have. Before I allowed those tears, that had caused my throat to constrict, to fall, I snuck out.

****

Babe, I just found out. I'm telling her to fuck off. J x

Jerry's text had come through the minute I'd walked through my hotel room door.

It's fine. Let the fuckers think they have one over on me. I will smile and laugh, I might even get drunk and kiss someone ;) I replied.

Let that be me, please? Think on it, how wonderful would it be if he thought you were fucking the boss? Jerry texted.

He already does ha ha. It's fine. Go have your dinner. I'll see you in the morning.

I loved Jerry, as a friend. As much as I knew he was someone I could rely on, someone who would welcome me with open arms, and offer a shoulder to cry on if I needed him, he was still my boss. I loved him, and my job, too much to risk fucking anything up with a drunken kiss, or as Jerry would have it, a night of passion.

I slumped down on the bed and let the tears fall. I was miserable; I thought I'd been doing so well, hiding the anguish, the hurt, and the pain.

I decided to take a long soak in the bath, read a little, and then head down for dinner. I'd booked a table for one; unfortunately it was for seven o'clock. I'd have preferred earlier, there were often less diners looking quizzically at a table for one. I'd done it myself. I'd look and wonder why that person was sitting alone, especially if it was a woman. Had they been stood up?

I dressed in a pair of black trousers and a white shirt. I blow dried my hair and piled it on top of my head. I sat and applied my makeup; although dining on my own, I would still make an effort. I grabbed the very high, patent heels I'd bought to wear with the slinky evening gown at the ball and slipped my feet into them. I would wear them to break them in a little.

I ate a simple meal of steak and salad, only recently having found my appetite again. I guessed the only one good thing to have come out of our break-up was the loss of weight. Nothing like a good drama to help shed the pounds, Mum had told me.

I took my Kindle from my bag and read a little. It distracted me from the glances and showed the curious diners I had prepared to be alone; I hadn't been stood up. When I could stand it no more, I asked for my coffee to be taken to the bar. Instead of the empty nook I'd spotted while walking into the dining room, the waiter placed my coffee on the bar. The nook, sadly, was occupied. I climbed on a stool, intending to drink the coffee then head for my room.

"All alone?" I heard. I looked up to see the barman polishing a glass and standing in front of me.

"I have a conference, The Marriott was fully booked," I said.

"How about a drink to go with that?" he said.

"Why not. What do you suggest?"

"I don't see you as a brandy drinker, port isn't good with coffee. So, how about a whiskey?"

"I don't generally drink whiskey," I said.

"Try it."

He set a short, heavy cut glass on the bar, placed a couple of ice cubes in it then poured a measure of whiskey. I picked it up and smelled first. It wasn't as harsh as I was expecting. I took a small sip. There was a faint hint of orange, smoked and aromatic. The liquid warmed my mouth and throat.

"Mmm, that's nice, what is it?"

He showed me the bottle; the label meant nothing to me. "It's a Glenmorangie Signet," he said. That meant even less.

"Have the lady try a Redbreast Twenty-One year old," I heard, said in a low, smooth, American accent.

I turned towards the voice. Standing behind and just to the side was a man who initially took my breath away.

"May I?" he asked, gesturing to the stool beside me. I nodded.

9

He undid the button of his suit jacket, removed it, and placed it over the back of the stool. He then sat; he didn't need to climb like I had. He rested one foot on the metal rung, the other stayed put on the floor.

For a minute I was speechless, and not entirely sure why. He turned to me and smiled. There was something about him; he was confident but it was more than that. I couldn't put my finger on it.

The barman had placed two glasses on the bar; it was only then that I found my voice.

"Thank you," I said.

"Tell me what you taste," he said. I watched as he brought his glass to his nose and inhaled, all the while keeping eye contact with me.

I raised the glass to my lips, inhaled before tipping it and allowing the liquid to coat my upper lip. I took a sip.

"It's sweet but spicy," I said.

He smiled, displaying perfectly straight white teeth. "Anything else?"

"It's smooth, silky," I said, and then took another sip.

"It's a fine whiskey, one of my favourites," he said.

"I'm not really a whiskey drinker," I said.

"So, tell me, why are you sitting here all alone?"

"That's direct," I said, with a laugh.

"I'm a *direct* kind of man," he said.

Had it been anyone else, I think I would have bid a goodnight and left. I was curious as to what it was that kept me sitting there; that had me talking. I told him about my job and the conference I'd organised.

Before I realised, I'd finished the whiskey, and my coffee. I hadn't stopped talking and he'd hardly said a word.

"I'm sorry, I've talked a lot. Let me get you a drink," I said.

"I've enjoyed listening to you, and I'll get the drinks."

Without even looking up at the barman, he gently tapped the bar beside his glass and it was refilled without question.

Power: that was the word I'd been looking for when he'd first sat beside me. The man exuded power. A shiver ran over me and I chuckled.

He narrowed his dark, very dark, brown eyes at me. "Something funny?"

"No, just a shiver, made me giggle."

"It's a pleasant sound, Miss…"

"Oh, I'm sorry, I'm accepting your drinks, and I haven't introduced myself. Lauren, my name's Lauren," I said.

I expected him to announce himself, he didn't, and for some reason I didn't ask.

"Are you here on business?" I asked.

"I am." Again, I thought he might reveal what business, but he didn't.

"From America?"

"No. I live here now, Lauren. Well, in London." It was about the most I'd learned about him in the time we'd been chatting.

He turned sideways on his stool; I did the same until we were facing each other. He had one arm resting on the back of his stool; the other held the whiskey glass on the bar. He was clearly a fit man. I could see muscles bulge under the white shirt he wore, and ink. He had tattoos down one arm, extending onto his hand. He caught me staring at his hand and I felt my face flush. I picked up the glass and raised it to my lips, initially to hide the discomfort I had begun to feel. It wasn't that he made me uneasy, but certainly nervous. I tilted the glass and looked over the rim at him. He stared at me, intently.

"Where from, in America?" I asked.

"Is that important?"

His answer took me aback. He smiled; his voice was still low, seductive, even.

"I guess not," I said.

"That was rude of me, wasn't it?"

"A little, but if you don't want to tell me that's fine."

"Then, I apologise."

He didn't give me an answer though. Instead of doing what I should have, thanked him for the drink and left, my curiosity was further piqued. I liked the mystery of him. There was something quite refreshing about having a conversation with an exceptionally good-looking man and not knowing a thing about him.

We continued to talk, well, he continued to ask questions and I answered. I'd tuned out the voices that floated around the bar. It was as if no one else existed, just us.

I watched as he took a sip from his glass, and then licked his lips so slowly my breath caught in my throat. But it was his eyes, or rather the way he stared at me, that had me wanting to clench my thighs together. He'd roam my body, as if mentally undressing me, before bringing his gaze back to mine. Maybe it was the whiskey, maybe it was loneliness, but all of a sudden a powerful need hit me. I wanted him. I didn't know him, and I didn't want to.

"Are you happily married?" he asked.

I twisted the thin gold band I wore on my finger but I didn't answer.

"I don't think you are. You wouldn't have been sitting, alone, in a bar for…" He consulted his watch. "Three hours talking to me."

I didn't have an answer, well I did, but not one I was prepared to give to a stranger. I gently slid from the barstool.

"Do you want to take me to bed?" I asked, surprising myself.

I was thankful that I held my clutch to stop my hands from shaking.

"Yes." He laid down the glass of whiskey and the ice tinkled as he did.

Brown eyes stared at me; eyes that failed to conceal mischief.

He stood, towering over me. He slowly slipped on his jacket, closed the buttons before taking my hand in his and leading me to the lift.

12

He didn't speak as he retrieved a card from his inside pocket and inserted it into a keypad.

The lift ascended beyond the numbers listed and opened to a foyer. He took the card from the keypad and walked to an oak door, the only door in the corridor. The click as the lock disengaged was only marginally louder than my heart hammering in my chest.

He opened the door, swinging it wide, then stepping aside to allow me to enter before him. I walked into the penthouse suite.

"Can I get you another drink?" he asked.

I nodded; my mouth was too dry to form words.

I watched him stride to a cabinet. I heard the tinkle as ice was placed in glasses and then the splash of liquid. He returned with two crystal cut glasses and handed me one.

"More whiskey," he said. His voice was low, husky.

I took a sip, welcoming the burn as the liquid hit my lips, my tongue, and gently slid down my throat. I cursed the ice as its noise gave away how much my hand was shaking. He took a step closer, then another. He reached up and trailed a finger down my cheek, then over my throat.

"You have for as long as it takes you to drink that whiskey. After that, if you are still here, there's no turning back," he said.

I raised the glass to my lips once more and downed it in one. My eyes watered. I glanced to the side of me, reached out, and placed the empty glass on a coffee table. I then stood tall and stared back at him. His lips slowly formed a smile, a very wicked smile.

"I don't know your name," I said, quietly.

"Neither do you need to. Think of this as just one night with a stranger, one night to fulfil your fantasy."

I didn't think sex with a stranger had featured high up on my list of fantasies, but the heat coursing through my body and the throbbing between my legs told me otherwise.

Chapter Three

For a moment there was silence. He sipped his drink and stared at me. He was so close I could smell his musky scent.

"Did he betray you?" he whispered.

At first I was unsure what he meant. It took me a moment to understand.

"Yes," I answered.

"And you feel, what?"

Even if I didn't want to, I answered; I couldn't stop myself.

"Worthless. Inadequate. Lonely."

He placed his glass on the coffee table next to mine. He reached up with his hand and pulled the pins from my hair, letting it tumble around my shoulders. He ran his fingers through it.

"Then I'll show you that you're not any of those things."

I wasn't sure how my legs were keeping my body upright. They were visibly shaking. I tried desperately to measure my breaths, but when he reached for the top button of my shirt and undid it, my heart raced faster.

"Are you nervous?" he asked.

"Yes. I…I don't make a habit of doing this."

"Good. I like nervous."

He closed the gap between us, using his hand to lift my chin until I was looking up at him. He leaned down slightly, and I closed my eyes, wetting my lips. I expected to feel his on mine but he gently ghosted them across my jaw, tilting my head to give him access to my neck. The feel of his lips on my skin, his breath as it tickled, had all but caused my legs to give way. I reached up and gripped the lapels of his jacket, simply to steady myself.

I felt his lips curl into a smile; he was pleased with my response. He placed small kisses down my neck, pulling the collar of my shirt away. Then he trailed his tongue back up to my jaw.

He stepped away and that action caused me to open my eyes quickly.

Without a word, he shrugged off his jacket. "I'm enjoying the taste of you," he said.

I couldn't find the words to answer that. Yet again, I was taken aback.

"Undo your shirt," he said.

I raised my hands, trying hard to disguise the shake, and unbuttoned.

"Slower," he said.

I kept eye contact as I did what he'd requested. When I'd undone all the buttons, I let my arms fall to my sides. I watched as he loosened his tie, pulling it through his collar. He rolled it around his hand before stepping back towards me and placing it next to his glass.

He trailed his fingers down either side of my neck, across my chest, and parted my shirt. I watched him lick his lips as he stared at my breasts. There was something very carnal in what he did, and it had my stomach clenching further. He pushed the shirt from my shoulders until it fell to the floor.

Goosebumps raised my skin, following the path his fingers made as he very gently ran them across the cups of my bra. He reached around and unclipped it, sliding the straps from my shoulders. Everything he did, every movement he made, was controlled: measured to elicit the desired response. I swallowed hard, convinced that he'd heard me.

I opened my mouth to speak; the silence was beginning to overwhelm me. Before I could, he placed one finger over my lips.

"Shush," he said. "No talking, just feel."

He reached for his whiskey and dipped his finger in the glass; he then ran that finger over my lips. Before I had a chance to catch the drip, he'd placed his hands in my hair on either side of my face and kissed me. No, he devoured my mouth. It was as if his kiss had sucked the air from my lungs. His tongue took control of mine; his hands gripped my hair. I clung to him, my hands fisted his shirt. I couldn't stop the moan that seemed to have risen from the depths of my stomach, leaving my mouth.

I was gone, totally gone. My head spun and it wasn't from the alcohol, it was him. Just his kiss had me wanting to come. I crossed my legs, trying to clench my thighs tight together. He let go of one side of my head, ran his hand down my side, and having to bend slightly, he slipped his hand between my thighs and pushed my legs apart again.

He pulled his mouth from mine. "When you come, it will be either over my fingers or my cock, or in my mouth."

My jaw fell open; I heard it click. He smirked and raised his eyebrows. He reached down, undid the button, then the zip of my trousers, they pooled around my feet. I stepped out of them, and once again, he took a step back. His gaze leisurely trailed from my breasts to my black lace panties and then down to the high heels. He nodded, as if approving.

"You have an awful amount of clothes on," I said.

"So undress me then," he replied.

I lifted one leg to remove my shoe.

"Leave them on," he said.

I reached up to undo the buttons on his shirt, pulling it from the waistband of his trousers. He offered me his arms and I unbuttoned the cuffs, one at a time. As he had done to me, I slid the shirt from his broad shoulders, having to reach up to do so.

I let my hands slide down his very toned stomach, so toned every ab was defined. I undid his trousers. As I did so, he kicked off his shoes. I decided to be brave. I placed my hands on his hips and slowly lowered to a crouch, pulling his trousers down as I did. He wore tight black shorts, and I had to catch the words before they spilled from my mouth at the sight of his erection. His cock strained against the cotton, a small damp patch had formed as it wept precum. I ran my hands down his shins, removing his socks then slowly stood.

"Turn around," he said.

"Why?"

"Turn around," he repeated, slower.

I did. I heard the shuffle as he kicked his clothing away. I felt the gentlest trail of his fingers down my back, and again, my skin puckered at his touch. He grabbed my hair in one hand, angling my head so he could kiss across my shoulder, pushing my head forward so he could kiss the back of my neck. I reached behind me, placing my hands on his thighs; I needed the support.

He pressed his body against mine, or maybe I'd leaned back into him, by that point I wasn't sure. I could feel his cock pressing into my lower back. Even in heels, he was a good foot taller than I was.

One arm snaked around me, his hand covered my breast and he dragged his palm across my nipple. The roughness of his skin set mine on fire, figuratively of course. Heat raced over me.

I'd begun to pant, finding it difficult to disguise my laboured breathing. I could feel the wetness between my thighs, and I wanted his fingers, his cock, or his mouth.

"Do you like these?" he asked, as he slid his hand down my stomach to the top of my panties.

"Yes."

"Shame."

With that, he ran his fingers around the waistband to my hip, and in one fluid movement, he'd ripped them from my body. The movement caught me by surprise, and I stumbled sideways slightly. He held my hips. When I'd steadied myself, I felt his hand run over my arse, slide between my thighs and over my opening, just once. He gently slid his hand back again. I tensed as he ran his wet finger between my arse cheeks. I heard him chuckle.

"You're so wet," he said.

"I…" Again, I was unsure how to reply.

"Tell me your fantasies, Lauren. If you could do anything right now, what would it be," he whispered in my ear.

"I…"

"You said that already."

He slid his hand around my waist, lower and lower. His other hand reached around and cupped my chin; he forced my head up to look at him while his fingers circled my clitoris.

I moaned out loud and closed my eyes.

"Open them, look at me," he said. His voice had taken on a huskiness.

"Answer me."

"I don't know, I can't think," I said, as his fingers stroked and teased my clitoris faster.

I gripped his thighs and moaned again.

"Think."

"To be fucked by you, a stranger," I said, crying out at the same time.

"I like your choice of words, Lauren. I love to fuck, hard."

My name rolled slowly off his tongue and seduced me. His words had me moaning out loud, had my stomach clenching with the need to come, had a flush creep up my chest and neck, and my nipples were so hard that they hurt.

"Oh, God," I cried out. He chuckled.

I wanted to come; I wanted to feel his fingers inside me. I let go of one of his thighs and covered his hand with mine; I pushed his fingers lower towards my opening. He pulled it away. I let my head fall forward and my chin rest on my chest. Before I'd even caught a breath, he lifted me from the ground and carried me to his oversized bed. He laid me down

"I don't fuck in hotel beds, normally. But for you, I find myself wanting to make an exception."

He stood beside the bed and removed his shorts. His cock sprang free. I tried not to, but I couldn't stop staring.

He crawled onto the bottom of the bed. He ran his hands down my legs, removing my shoes and tossing them to the floor. Then he crawled up my body, holding himself above me on his arms. He lowered his head, and kissed down my chest before taking a nipple into his mouth. I gripped his hair as he sucked, as he bit. I arched my back off the bed, feeling his cock against me.

He released my nipple to tend to the other one. I'd never before experienced the stomach clenching and thigh trembling that I was at that point, using just his mouth, his tongue, and his teeth.

My wet skin chilled when he lowered himself, kissing down my stomach. I released my grip on his hair when his tongue found my clitoris. I didn't have time to prepare. When he forced his tongue inside me, I came. It took me by surprise and I screamed out. He held his hands over my hips, forcing me to keep still when all I wanted to do was arch my back. I covered his hands with mine and clawed at his wrists.

Sweat beaded on my upper lip as wave after wave of heat, of static, ran over me. I could feel the wetness seeping from me, rolling down towards my arse. He lapped and sucked, he moaned and the vibrations caught my clitoris, sending more shockwaves through me. His fingers dug into my skin, painfully, yet they only heightened every sensation that was causing my nerve endings to fire off electrical impulses. I found out that day, it wasn't a myth. Light, stars, whatever the fuck they were, flickered behind my closed eyelids.

I couldn't catch my breath, my heart pounded inside my chest so much I could hear the rush of blood as it passed my ears to feed my brain.

It was as he moved away that I finally opened my eyes. His chin glistened and he licked his lips. He kept his focus on me as he crawled back up my body.

"Lick," he said, bringing his chin close to my mouth.

I cupped my hands around his face and licked every single drop of my cum from him. My tongue felt grazed by the stubble covering his chin. I loved the roughness of it. I loved the roughness of him, period.

He reached over to the bedside cabinet and withdrew a condom from the vanity kit housed in the drawer. Without a word he tore open the packet and rolled it down his cock. He positioned himself over me, and taking one hand at a time, he raised them above my head. He held both wrists in one of his hands. With his other, he slid it down my thigh and under my knee, raising it; I wrapped that leg around his waist. Before I had a chance to do the same with my other leg, he pushed inside me.

I closed my eyes and cried out as my muscles, which hadn't been stretched that much in, well, forever, burned. He stilled, waiting for me to relax. When I opened my eyes to look at him, his stare bore straight through me. He moved, slowly at first, grinding his pelvis against mine, rotating his hips slightly, causing a sensation inside me that I'd never experienced before. I tightened my legs around his waist and tilted my hips. I wanted him deeper.

He upped his pace, pounding into me so hard and so fast, my body jolted up the bed. My overly sensitive skin prickled as another orgasm built. I moaned out loud until I heard myself scream. That second orgasm was like a freight train hitting me right at the core. My stomach muscles tightened, my body shook, and still he kept going. My wrists hurt from being pinned to the bed, and my head spun. I felt dizzy as I lost control. He fucked me through the most intense orgasm of my life.

He slowed his pace while he watched me come down. Sweat glistened on his chest and on his shoulders. I longed to lick that from him. I wanted to run my tongue up his stomach, inhaling his scent. Before my brain had registered, he had pulled out of me.

"On your knees," he said, resting back on his heels.

I struggled to sit; he flipped me over using my hips. He pulled at them until my arse was in the air, and I propped myself on my elbows. He entered me again. My hands gripped the bedding. I lost track of time, I lost count of how many times he had made me come. With his cock pounding inside me, he reached under and teased my swollen clitoris. I wanted to sink into the bed, and every time my legs shook too much to hold me up, he held my hips, physically lifting and holding me in position.

The sound that left his lips was guttural, a growl so deep it could have only come from the depths of his stomach. It was primal. That sound alone caused a shiver to run up my spine, causing the hairs on the back of my sweaty neck to stand on end. His fingers gripped tighter, enough to ensure I'd be bruised as he came.

As he lessened his grip on my body, I slumped face down on the bed. I rolled to my back and looked at him. He had his head flung back, his eyes closed. I could see him taking deep breaths in through his nose, exhaling slowly through his mouth. After what couldn't have been a full minute, he brought his head forward and looked at me. He didn't blink, at all, but a slow smile crept over his lips. I'd held my breath, unsure of his reaction at first.

"Fuck," I said.

"Fuck, indeed."

I giggled, that turned into gentle sobs. I felt wrung out.

He climbed from the bed, pulled the condom off, and deposited it in the bin. He sat on the edge beside me. He reached out with one hand and tenderly brushed my hair from my face.

"I take it you're done?" he whispered.

"You're not?"

"No, I want to fuck you all night. That was a warm up."

"Oh."

He laughed as he pulled the covers from under me and climbed in. I shuffled over giving him room.

"Rest for a little while," he said.

I closed my eyes, promising myself I'd open them again in ten minutes. I just needed enough time for the residual ache from multiple orgasms, something that was new to me, to leave my stomach.

When I opened my eyes and glanced at the digital clock on the cabinet beside me it was five o'clock the following morning.

Fuck, I thought.

I gently turned my head towards him. He was lying on his stomach, his head facing away from me. His arms were under the pillow that he rested on. The sheet was been pushed down low on his hips revealing a muscular back.

Fuck, fuck, fuck, I thought, again.

As gently as I could, I slid from the bed. My legs felt weak and my thighs were coated in my tacky cum. I grabbed my trousers from the floor, pulling them on; I stuffed my bra in the pocket and put on my shirt. I grabbed my shoes and bag then crept to the door. I winced at the sound of the click as I opened it and stilled. I heard him shuffle but nothing more. I closed the door gently behind me and rushed, barefoot, for the lift. I kept my finger on the call button, praying it would arrive empty and quickly.

When the doors slid open, I breathed a sigh of relief as I stepped into the empty carriage. I pressed for my floor, and as the doors closed, I turned to look into the glass wall.

"Fuck," I said, aloud.

I had dark circles under my eyes from mascara that had run. My hair was a tangled mess, my lips slightly swollen. In my haste to dress, I hadn't done the buttons of my shirt up correctly. I ran my fingers through my hair, wet the tips of my forefingers and dragged them under my eyes.

The lift doors slid silently open on my floor, and I hesitated before stepping out. I listened for any noise. When I was confident I was on my own, I made that walk of shame to my room.

I opened the door, stepped in and closed it. The adrenalin I'd been running on left, and I slumped against the door.

"Good Lord, what the fuck did I do?" I said.

I wanted to giggle; I wanted to cry. I'd had sex with a stranger, someone I'd met in a bar at a work conference. How fucking cliché was that?

I held my hand over my mouth to stifle the giggle/cry.

When I felt the strength return slightly to my legs, I walked into the bathroom. I stripped and turned on the shower. I could smell myself; I could smell sex. I stepped into the shower cubical and just stood under the jets of water.

"Oh my fucking God," I said.

I wasn't sure whether I should be shocked or applaud myself. Whoever he was, I'd had the best night of sex ever. Scott could never, in a million years, have produced that many orgasms, that intensity, or kept it up for as long as he had. Then I remembered his words, '*that was a warm up!*'

"Oh no," I said. I cringed as I remembered that I'd fallen asleep on him.

I scrubbed myself clean, washed my hair, and wrapped one towel around my body and one around my head. I made myself a cup of tea and crawled under the bedcovers. I sat and drank, and I thought. Just the act of thinking about the night, of thinking about him, had my clitoris throbbing.

A wave of sadness washed over me. I brushed away the thought that I'd never see him again from my mind. He hadn't wanted me to know who he was. That in itself meant the evening was just what I'd told him I'd wanted: one night of sex with a stranger. He'd fulfilled a fantasy, one that hadn't been in the forefront of my mind initially, but had proven to be quite exciting and so totally out of character. I sipped my tea until eventually I did giggle, and then laughed out loud. I wouldn't feel any shame; I was a single woman, who did what tons of single women did. I had an amazing night.

Chapter Four

I was dressed, hair styled and makeup on, when room service brought breakfast to my room a couple of hours later. Was I hiding? Probably. The thought that I might bump into him at breakfast had crossed my mind. I wanted to save him, and me, that embarrassment.

I sipped my coffee, ate my pastries then collected all I needed for the conference. I opted for the stairs, again, not wishing to bump into him while travelling down from his floor in the lift. I scuttled across the foyer and into the back of a waiting taxi. I breathed a sigh of relief as we pulled away.

In one way, I wished I'd left him a note, to thank him for the smile that I could not keep off my face. I was ready to fight the world that morning. I had a secret and knowing that, was a powerful thing.

"You look very happy," Jenny said, as she met me at the conference centre.

"I'm a morning person," I replied.

"Urgh, anyway, I got you a coffee," she said, as she handed me a takeout container from Starbucks.

"Thank you. Right, let's get started."

We unboxed the brochures we'd had delivered and placed one on each seat. I connected my laptop to the lectern and ran through the presentation Jerry was to deliver. I checked that the microphone worked and I could be heard, speaking at normal levels, all the way at the back. Jenny had given me a thumbs up as confirmation. I made sure to tape down any loose wires and charger leads I could find, I didn't want Jerry falling over.

"I'm going to head to the hotel. I need to check with the event manager, there were a couple of changes to be made to the seating plan. You stay here and greet everyone. I'll be back as soon as I can."

She smiled and nodded. She placed her hand on my arm and squeezed. She'd seen right through me. "I'll keep a place, just there, front row, closest to the door, for you."

I didn't want to be there when Scott arrived. I'd do my utmost to avoid him.

"Thank you."

I grabbed my handbag and left the conference centre. I didn't hail a taxi; instead I walked to the nearest coffee bar and queued for a fresh drink. I took out my phone and sent a text to Jerry, letting him know we were ready to go. I stood in the coffee shop, near the door, sipping from the cardboard cup and watched to see if any of my colleagues came in. Thankfully, no one did and when I thought it was time, I quickly headed back.

Jenny was standing by the auditorium door. "I was about to call you," she said.

"Got held up, sorry."

We walked in, the lights were lowered and we took our seats at the edge of the first row.

I tuned out when Jerry started with his presentation. I'd heard, and read it, many times. In fact, I made it. My mind wandered to the previous evening. I recalled every single minute, from being in the bar to sneaking out in the early hours of that morning. I relived every breath of his on my skin, every touch.

"Will you sit still?" Jenny whispered.

I looked at her, wide-eyed. I'd been so engrossed in my night, I'd been wriggling on my seat.

"Sorry, uncomfortable, that's all."

The presentation was scheduled to last about four hours; we'd timed it. Afterwards, the staff had a few hours to relax, use the gym or spa, before the evening event started at seven o'clock.

I checked my watch, Jerry was bang on time, and I smiled, knowing what was coming next.

"So, folks, that's about it. Bored you shitless yet?" he said from the lectern.

A ripple of laughter followed. No matter that he could jest, everyone there had the respect for him to not heckle or call out, and I was pleased about that.

"I have an announcement to make. As some of you know, I've been in talks with various companies over the past year, looking to build our communications division abroad. I'm pleased to announce that I've taken on a partner, someone who has the capability to help me realise my dream. Remember, world domination and all that shit?" Another round of laughter followed.

"You'll all get to meet him this evening, but I'd like to welcome Mackenzie Miller."

"Oh my God," Jenny said.

"Oh my God," I said, at the exact same time.

"He's fucking hot," she added.

I covered my mouth to quell the nausea as I watched the stranger from the previous night walk to the stage, climb the steps and shake Jerry's hand, and then smile. I sunk a little in my chair. Although he scanned the room, his eyes didn't settle on me. I racked my brain, had I said which company I worked for? I'd told him I was here for a conference, but there could be others. I prayed there were others.

"Thank you, Jerry, for that welcome," he said.

"Oh, that voice," Jenny whispered.

As Mackenzie placed his hands on the lectern and his shirtsleeves rose, I saw the scratch marks on his wrists.

"I feel a little sick, I'm going to sneak out," I said.

She looked at me. As quietly as I could, I slid from my chair. Instead of heading to the door beside me, I crept alongside the tiered seating to a door at the rear. I knew it led to a corridor that connected back to the foyer of the centre. I'd been given the tour.

When I'd exited the building, I flagged the nearest taxi and headed back to my hotel.

I knew Jerry would be mad, I'd tell him the same as I had Jenny: I genuinely, at that moment, felt ill.

My heart pounded as I lay on the bed in my room. I could feel a headache coming on. I reached above me and switched off the lights. My phone beeped in the bag I'd thrown onto the bed.

"Shit," I said, as I reached for it.

You okay? J

Sorry, migraine, give me an hour?

Okay, but call me if you need anything x

I hated lying to him, but luckily I'd suffered with migraines in the past, it was a stress related thing. I didn't want to even begin to imagine what my stress level was at. I groaned as I lay back down. I closed my eyes, hoping I could get an hour's sleep, not because I was tired, but because I didn't want to think.

It was a knock on the bedroom door that woke me. I blinked a few times, waiting for my vision to come back into focus after I'd switched on the light. I crept to the door and looked through the spy hole, then breathed a sigh of relief that it wasn't him. I opened it.

"You okay? You look like shit," Jerry said as he walked in.

"I was absolutely fine then got hit with a massive headache. I'm so sorry, did I miss much?"

"I don't know if you managed to meet Mackenzie or not."

"No, I left as you introduced him. I'll introduce myself tonight."

"He's staying here if you want to join us in the bar. I'm going to grab a drink with him now."

"You go. It's okay. I'm sure you've got tons to talk about. I need to shower and get ready for tonight."

"Is it him, has he upset you?"

I wondered which 'him' he was referring to. "I can still throw the bitch out," he said.

"No, it's fine. She's obviously his partner. A little crass to bring her but others have brought their partners. Mind you…"

I grabbed the folder from my bed. I hadn't thought to check whether he'd added a plus one for the meal. I hoped he hadn't. I sighed when

27

I saw that he had. Jenny must have missed it when she did the final head count. I pulled out the table plan. We had one cancellation on Scott's table, fortunate for him but a shame in that we could seat her.

I called over to the event manager and asked her to change the name card.

"Should have left it, had the bitch standing there not knowing where to sit," Jerry said.

"Then I'd be laughed at for doing something petty. It's fine; go have your drink. Let me get rid of this headache so I can enjoy this evening."

"I should have fucked him off," Jerry said.

"Go, I'll see you later. And congratulations, that was a great presentation."

"Of course it was, one of my favourite people wrote it." He laughed and gave me a wink as he left.

I made a cup of tea and settled in the large armchair in the corner beside the windows that overlooked a small garden. I read for a while and sipped my tea, trying to calm my nerves. There was no ducking out of the evening event, and I realised I would be sitting at the same table as 'him.'

His name hadn't been on our list, just 'guest' of Jerry. We never knew who that guest would be. Sometimes he'd bring a 'friend' to an event, other times his mother, who I loved. There was a little part of me that was sad that he hadn't settled down, found a woman to share his life and wealth with. But I guessed, that wealth was why he chose to keep his circle very small and his bed empty.

I'd tried not to, but I continually checked my watch. I was hoping time would slow down, it didn't. With an hour to go before I had to arrive, earlier than the rest to ensure the room was set out as expected, I ran the bath. I pinned my hair up, not wanting it to get wet.

I washed, climbed out then wrapped a towel around me. I sat at the small dressing table and applied my makeup. I knew it was a dumb thing to do, but I bought all new: new makeup, new underwear, new dress, and new shoes. I'd had my hair cut. I wanted to walk into that room looking stunning, or as stunning as I could. I wanted to show Scott what he'd thrown away. As I stood in front of the wardrobe and inspected the red floor-length silk dress, with a slit up to the thigh, I cringed. There'd be no hiding in that.

I styled my hair, dressed, pulled on the shoes, and picked up my clutch. After taking a deep breath, I left the safety of my room and took the lift down. I crossed the foyer and waited for the doorman to flag down a taxi.

When I arrived at the venue, I headed straight to the ballroom. Waitresses were still scuttling around doing last minute preparations. The DJ had set up in the corner and was standing by the bar, drinking.

I found my table and placed my clutch on my seat. I was sitting to Jerry's left, 'guest' to his right. I had thought to move myself but then, if I was directly next to Jerry, it wouldn't be so easy for him to talk to me.

And I had Fred, who manned the security desk at the office, next to me. No matter what the occasion, the old man was always invited. Jerry wouldn't allow any member of the team, regardless of position, to be left out. He always sat at Jerry's table and I was thankful. He would keep me entertained, for sure.

****

"Would you like a glass of champagne?" I was asked.

The waitresses were ready, standing by the door to hand out glasses of bubbly as the guests arrived. I took one from a nearby tray and thanked the waitress. When I heard Jerry laughing in the doorway, I turned my back, pretending to be inspecting something on a neighbouring table.

"Lauren, babe," he called out; I inwardly cringed at the term of endearment.

I straightened my back, jutted out my chin, and turned. I caught the look of amusement on Mackenzie's face, at least that was something. I was expecting shock, amusement was better than that I guessed. I smiled and walked over; there was no avoiding it.

"Mackenzie, I'd like you to meet my head of marketing, Lauren Perry. She'd be my right hand man if she had agreed. Been with me since the beginning."

He held out his hand, I reached for it, trying not to look surprised as a pulse of electrical current ran between us.

"It's a pleasure to meet you, Lauren, again," he said.

I saw Jerry raise his eyebrows. "We met in the bar, last night, I hadn't realised he was your guest," I said, by way of an explanation.

"It's a pleasure to meet you again, too, Mackenzie," I said.

"Can I get you a drink?" Jerry asked. I raised my still full champagne flute.

"Whiskey for me," Mackenzie asked, ensuring Jerry had to leave for the bar, I assumed.

It was when I found myself alone with him that the nerves kicked in.

"You ran off," he said. "Well, you fell asleep, then ran off."

"Yes, sorry about that. This is very awkward," I replied.

"Why?"

"Why? You're sort of my boss now."

"And?"

"I'm not sure how it works in America, but sleeping with your boss isn't really the thing to do here."

"We did more than sleep, and I don't care how you Brits operate."

"Look, please, I get enough stick from my *colleagues,* who think I have more than a friendship with Jerry. Can we just forget what happened? And what with my…"

I didn't finish the sentence. "No to your question. And you were going to say...?"

"My husband, soon to be ex-husband, is our head of development, Scott Perry."

"Ah, the one who brought the *bitch,* as Jerry so politely calls her. I understand now."

"One whiskey," Jerry said, interrupting us.

"I'm going to check on a few things, you know where you're sitting?" I said.

"No, where?"

I sighed, "There." I pointed to a round table, centre of the room.

"What if I don't want to sit there? I'm all on display," he said.

"Jerry, you've spent your life wanting to be on display. Now, don't stress me out, that is where you're sitting."

"Feisty, I like it," Mackenzie said.

"Ah, she loves me really," Jerry replied.

I patted his cheek. "You wish. Now, please, excuse me?"

I placed my glass on the table and walked away to the sound of their laughter. I had no idea how my legs managed to carry me straight to the toilets, but they did.

I walked into a cubicle and locked the door. I lowered the toilet seat lid and sat. I'd only just gotten my breathing under control when I heard a couple of women come in.

"Did you see? Scott brought his girlfriend," one said. The other chuckled.

"Must be awkward."

"Doubt the ice queen cares, she's got Jerry and that fucking delicious hunk at her table."

At that I stood, flushed, although there was no need, and unlocked the door. I walked straight to a washbasin and smiled at the women's reflection in the mirror.

"Have a wonderful evening, ladies," I said, as I pulled a paper towel from the pile, dried my hands, and left the room.

I didn't know what to do or where to go. We were being called in for dinner, and it was the last place I wanted to be. I swallowed back the tears. At least I had confirmation of the nickname I'd been given; I'd always suspected it would be something to do with the cold.

I walked back into the dining room with my stomach churning and a fake smile on my face.

****

I made it through dinner, thanks to Fred. He only stopped chatting to take the occasional mouthful of food or sip of wine. Jerry had tried to include me in his conversation with Mackenzie. I answered when required to, smiled and laughed when appropriate, but otherwise tried my hardest not to make eye contact.

When the plates were cleared and coffee was poured, Jerry leaned towards me.

"This is really hard for you, isn't it?"

"Huh?"

"Being here with Scott and the bitch."

"A little, yes."

"You know, it's okay to drop the act. You don't have to be tough all the time."

"And let them see me affected? No way."

He smiled and nodded. "Do you want anything from the bar?"

"I'll go, what did you want?" I only offered for one reason, I'd be left alone at the table.

"No, you're officially off duty now."

I laughed at that. "I'm never off duty," I said.

"Maybe you should be. It's okay to be professional. It's okay to be fucking amazing at your job, but it doesn't need to consume you and sometimes you let it."

Jerry's comments surprised me. Okay, so he swore constantly, he never wore a suit to work, he was 'one of the lads' sometimes, but he always worked hard. He didn't stop working. All I'd ever done was follow his lead. He paid me well, and I wanted to be worthy of that.

"I own the company, Lauren. Even if for totally selfish reasons, I work harder than anyone, because one day, I'll reap the bulk of the benefits. That doesn't mean you have to match me, minute for minute," he said, as if he'd read my thoughts.

He stood and left the table. I felt Mackenzie's stare, and when Fred decided he'd had enough of my company, I had no choice but to acknowledge him.

"Did you enjoy your meal?" I asked.

"Yes, although, no matter how long I've been here, I still can't get used to the way you guys eat." He moved seats to be next to me.

"Eat?"

"With your forks, you hold them upside down."

"I have no idea what you mean," I said.

"You eat this way…" He reached for a stray dessert fork that hadn't been cleared away and held it in his hands. "We eat this way."

I watched his fingers slowly turn the fork over. I wasn't watching the 'fork,' I was imagining those fingers on my body.

"Has Jerry introduced you to anyone?" I asked, needing something to distract me from my thoughts.

"No, he's a little, what was that word I heard, scatterbrained?"

I laughed then, relaxing a little. "Yep, he is."

"You know, I think you would be better as his second in command, or whatever he wanted you to be. From what I've seen so far, he really can't function without you."

"I don't want that, I like what I do. And I think his assistant does a good enough job."

To make a point, he said, "The assistant I'm yet to meet? The assistant who is yet to introduce herself and offer to help me meet the team?"

"Fair point. But I guess she feels she's off duty tonight."

"And you're not?"

"No. I organised all of this. I have to keep a clear head to ensure it continues to run smoothly and everyone enjoys themselves."

I stood and smoothed down my dress. His eyes travelled from my face to my… I wasn't going there with that train of thought. However, I was sure I heard him inhale deeply.

"So, how do I introduce you?"

"Mackenzie Miller, it's my name. Or Mr. Miller when we get to your husband," he said, with a smirk.

Oh fuck! When I'd offered to introduce him to people, it wasn't because I wanted to spend more time with him; it was so I was working, doing something to distract myself. I hadn't factored in coming face to face with Scott.

"Let's start with him," he said, standing and doing up his jacket button.

"I…"

"Get it over with, Lauren." The friendliness had left his voice. His face had hardened a little.

"I'm sorry, I don't think…"

He stepped closer to me. "Did you feel *worthless, inadequate, lonely* last night?" he whispered.

I found it hard to breathe.

"No," I said, cursing that my voice had risen.

"How did you feel?"

"Good."

"Good isn't a feeling. I'll ask you again, how did you feel?"

"Sexy, confident…"

"Then think of last night. Your pupils have dilated, Lauren. Your heartbeat has increased. You're reliving those feelings; keep it. You look sexy as fuck in that dress, do you know what I'd like to do right now?"

I shook my head; my mouth had dried.

"Rip it from your body and fuck you into next week. Now, introduce me."

He stepped away and raised one eyebrow at me. I coughed and reached for a glass of water, took a sip, picked up my clutch, and then pushed my shoulders back.

I hoped my shaking legs weren't noticeable as I walked across the room towards a group of people. I could hear Scott laugh and watched as she whispered something in his ear. He turned to face me as I approached.

"Mack, it's great to have you on board," Scott said, reaching out his hand for a shake.

Mackenzie ignored it and looked towards me.

"Scott Perry, Head of Development." I looked at Scott. "Scott, it's Mr. Miller."

"Oh, erm, Mr. Miller, it's good to finally meet you," Scott said.

Mackenzie, finally, reached out and took Scott's hand. They shook.

"I've heard a lot about you, Scott."

"All good, I hope," he replied with a nervous chuckle.

Mackenzie didn't answer. Inwardly I was doing a fist pump.

I introduced him to the three other heads of departments. He asked each one about their role within the company and assured them he'd take some time to sit with each and discuss his involvement.

I couldn't fail to notice the stare from *her*, and I thought, if I looked hard enough, I was sure I could see drool.

Mackenzie placed his hand on my lower back, static coursed over my skin.

"Miss Perry, we have a schedule to discuss, shall we?" He over emphasised the *Miss* as if it were a statement to not acknowledge my husband.

As we were about to leave, I heard, "Isn't she just in marketing?"

The bitch had spoken. Mackenzie looked at her. "No, Miss Perry is my eyes and ears on the ground, so to speak."

Without another word, we walked away. I kept on walking straight out of the room, taking longer and longer strides until I found myself at the front entrance. The porter opened the door for me and I stepped out, into the cold.

I had my hand on the taxi door, opening it, when I felt him step up behind me. He reached over and shut the door.

"The lady doesn't need a ride right now," he told the driver.

I spun around, stumbling as my heels caught. He took hold of my elbow and propelled me into the shadows.

"Thank you! Fucking, thank you, for that!" I said, not bothering to disguise the level of anger in my voice.

He didn't speak, but I wanted to slap the smirk from his face.

"You've just fucked up my job." I said.

"Say that again?"

"Say what?"

"Fuck, say it again."

"Fuck you."

The smirk turned into a smile.

"It's been fucking hard enough working with that lot of shits, you've just made it one hundred times worse for me."

"Why do you care?"

"Why do I care? Really? You need to ask that question? You fucking walk into that bar, seduce me with your fucking eyes, now you've ruined my career."

I sagged, the entire fake ice queen façade left me, and I sat on the low, cold wall behind me.

"I seduced you with my eyes?" He chuckled as he spoke.

"Don't laugh at me, Mackenzie."

"I just wasn't aware my eyes had those capabilities. I would have assumed it was my mind that I used to seduce you."

"Play on words," I mumbled.

"Your career isn't ruined at all. In fact, it's just starting. I have plans for you."

"You don't own the fucking business, only part of it. I decide what I do, not you."

"Finally, we see the Lauren with some balls. I do own the business, I own the majority shares."

"What? I'm going," I said.

I stood, hoping it was just the cold and not a damp wall that had my arse frozen.

I stepped around him and caught the eye of the porter. "I need a taxi," I said. He nodded and stepped out into the road.

Mackenzie stepped beside me. "You can get your own taxi," I said.

A car pulled up and he reached forward to open the door for me. I slid into the seat and cursed as he climbed in beside me.

"Chewton Glen, please," he said to the driver, giving him the name of the hotel.

I refused to look at him; I kept my gaze on the side window. I fished around in my clutch looking for my phone. I swiped my finger across the screen, pretending to check for messages. I didn't have any; no one was missing me. I threw it back in.

The taxi pulled up and I opened my door. I climbed out and walked straight through to the lift. It annoyed the hell out of me that he matched me stride for stride.

I jabbed at the call button, again refusing to acknowledge his presence. When the doors slid open, I stepped in and pressed for my floor. He didn't present his key card to allow him access to his floor.

I knew he was looking at me, I could feel it. I kept my gaze on the digital dial watching the numbers.

"Interesting, isn't it?" he said, mocking me.

"I'm resigning, first thing Monday," I said.

"No, you're not."

"You don't get to tell me what I can and can't do."

"I won't allow it."

"Allow it? Fuck off."

I heard him chuckle and he took a step closer. I could have sworn I heard him hum, or growl, or something. A noise emanated from him.

"You get off on that, don't you?" I said, as the lift came to a stop and the doors slid open.

"On what, Lauren?"

"Me swearing at you."

He held out his arm to keep the lift doors from closing, effectively blocking my way.

"I get off on seeing a confident woman. I get off on seeing the fire in your eyes and the confidence you think you don't have, seep from your pores. I get off on seeing someone whose body shook with fear just a short while ago, stand up to me. And, yeah, you have my cock fucking hard."

I turned towards him. I tried and I failed to stop my gaze lowering. I tried and failed to not take a sharp breath in when I saw his erection straining against his trousers. I pushed his arm down and walked away.

"We're not done yet, Lauren," I heard him say.

My hands shook as I inserted the key card; my legs shook more as I stumbled through the bedroom door.

"Jesus Christ," I said, as I sat on the bed.

Chapter Five

I didn't sleep well at all that night. I tossed and turned, frustrated and angry. Who the fuck did he think he was? I cursed him, and Jerry, although I wasn't sure it was entirely his fault.

In the morning, I showered and grabbed my pad. I wrote out my resignation. I could type it up and then email it.

I ordered breakfast from the room service menu and sent a text to Jerry.

What time are we leaving?

Whenever you're ready, I'm bored. Came his reply.

I'm just eating then I'm happy to leave.

Okay, give me ten.

I finished my breakfast, packed my overnight bag, and made my way to reception. I checked out and walked out of the hotel. It was a bright day, although chilly, and I pulled my wrap around me.

Jerry was standing by his car, Mackenzie beside him. They were talking and at first hadn't noticed me. Jerry's driver stepped forward to take my luggage and placed it in the boot.

"Here she is," Jerry said with a smile.

"Good morning. Are we ready?" I asked.

"Sure." He turned to Mackenzie. "So, I'll see you on Monday."

Mackenzie nodded. I held out my hand to him. "Mr. Miller, it was a pleasure to meet you."

He took my hand, slowly closing his around it. "The pleasure was all mine."

I pulled my hand away and climbed into the car. It was a minute or so before Jerry joined me.

"Well?"

"Well, what?"

"What do you think of him?"

"I think he'll do wonderful things for your company, Jerry."

"By that, I take it you don't like him."

"I don't know him. He's a character, for sure."

"I think it's that Italian American thing. He's a bit gangster, isn't he?" he chuckled.

"Maybe, anyway, what are you doing for the rest of the day?" I asked.

"Chilling, want to chill with me?"

"I've got plans, sorry."

I wanted to ask how Jerry had met him, but I wouldn't allow my curiosity to build. I wanted to get home, put on some sloppy clothes, and watch shit TV, on my own.

"How much of the business does Mackenzie own?" I asked.

"Sixty percent, that wasn't the original deal. I hate to lose control, but it was that or nothing, and you know what? I kind of like the idea of letting go of the reins a little. It's hard doing it all alone."

I wasn't sure if that was a stab at me or not. Right from the beginning, Jerry had wanted me to stand alongside him. He'd even offered to give me shares, because I'd been with him from day one, but I knew nothing about business. I didn't want to get bogged down with the admin of it all. I liked being creative, I liked coming up with ideas to promote the company. I liked working *in* it and not *on* it.

"It's been, what, ten years? You deserve to sit back a little," I said.

Ten years we'd worked together, both straight out of education. Although we had attended the same college, we hadn't known each other then. We'd met in a bar, he'd spilled his drink on me, we got chatting, and the rest, as they say, is history.

"Yeah, but I'm only thirty, not retirement age yet," he said, with a laugh.

"Is there something else you want to do? Maybe play a little golf?"

"Golf! Yeah, can you just see those stuck-up fuckers allowing me on a golf course? I'd walk around with a cigarette in my mouth, swearing."

"Mmm, maybe not."

"Another ten years, and then I'll sell out completely, travel a bit."

"When was the last time you had a holiday?"

He had to think. "Fucking years ago."

"Take a holiday then."

"I might. These skinny legs haven't seen the sun for a long time. I can just see me and Mum sitting on a beach in the Caribbean." He gave me a wink.

It occurred to me then, like me, Jerry didn't seem to have many friends. He'd forgone life in the pursuit of a successful business. I only hoped the payout had been worth that.

"I'll see you Monday then, and thanks for the ride," I said as I climbed from the car.

I put on a load of washing, grabbed a meal from the freezer to defrost, and changed into jeans and a jumper. The apartment was chilly, so I wrapped a blanket around me and curled up on the sofa. As predicted, there was nothing worth watching on the TV, so I scanned through Netflix to find a movie.

****

It was with trepidation that I entered the office on Monday morning. Maybe I was overthinking the sly glances thrown my way, or imagining the whispers behind hands. For the first time ever, I felt very uncomfortable.

My stomach turned every time I heard the lift ping, alerting me that someone had arrived on my floor. I wasn't sure whether Mackenzie would even visit that day. I hid myself away in my office, only leaving to grab a cup of coffee, and only when I thought the coast was clear. Jenny had offered to do a lunch run for me, which I'd declined. My stomach was too knotted to eat.

I hated the tension, I hated that I allowed that tension to grow as each hour passed. It was only when I noticed the clock on wall showing five that I began to relax. Jenny popped her head around the door to wish me a goodnight, and as each person started to leave, the automatic lighting dimmed.

I preferred to work late. If I could bring myself to do it, I'd start later in the morning and work into the night. It was peaceful and an escape from a lonely apartment. I sighed as I recalled Jerry's words. Maybe I needed to get a hobby, or a life, something that took me out of the office and focussed my brain on fun.

I closed down my laptop and packed it away in my briefcase. As I did, I chuckled bitterly. I even took my work home.

I stood by the lift, not watching the direction of its travel. When the doors slid open, I entered and pressed for ground. A tear formed in my eye and when I blinked, it slid down my cheek, followed by another. I didn't bother to wipe it away, nor did I notice the lift start to travel up one floor.

The doors slid open, and as I had my head bowed, all I saw was a pair of black brogues. I looked up, straight to the face of Mackenzie.

"Lauren, are you okay?" he asked, concern laced his voice.

"Of course, why shouldn't I be?"

"Because you're crying."

I raised my hand and brushed the tears away.

"Is there any point in saying I have something in my eye?"

He stepped into the lift, too close to me for comfort. The doors closed, but neither of us pressed for ground.

Before my brain could register, he raised a hand and used his thumb to wipe under my eye.

"You have smudged mascara," he said, gently.

"Thank you, ground?" I asked.

"Why are you crying?" he asked.

"Maybe because I'm sad today?" I tried to keep the sarcasm out of my voice; he was my boss after all.

"Why are you sad?"

It was always questions with him. He rarely volunteered any information, just asked a lot.

"My husband left me, I've been humiliated by him. My colleagues are whispering about me and avoiding me like I have some contagious disease. I should resign but I can't bring myself to. I'm tired. Take your pick."

"Then I'll have to do something to cheer you up, won't I?"

We had arrived on the ground floor and he took hold of my wrist. I was thankful it was the hand holding my briefcase, so he couldn't take hold of that. He pulled me along as he walked to the entrance. Fred stood, but we ignored him as we passed.

"What are you doing?" I asked.

"Wait and see."

He hailed a taxi and refused to speak anymore until one arrived. He gave the driver an address before opening the door and ushering me in.

"Where are we going? I have to go home. I want to go home," I said.

"Later."

"Not later, now."

He turned on his seat to face me. Once again, I saw that steely gaze and a look of determination on his face.

"So tell the driver to take you home," he said, challenging me.

I didn't want to go home, I didn't want to go with him either. I didn't know what the fuck I wanted to do.

I didn't reply, and with a smug look, he settled back in his seat. We continued the journey in silence.

It wasn't long before we pulled up outside a set of iron gates. Behind them was a stunning modern house, in front of Hampstead Heath. Mackenzie paid the driver, and taking hold of my wrist again, he opened his door and pulled me gently along the seat to join him. I watched as he entered a code into a keypad beside the gate and set in a brick column. The gates swung open and he strode up the drive. I was power walking to keep up with him.

He took a set of keys from his pocket and opened the front door to his home.

"I shouldn't be here," I said.

"Why?"

"Quit with the questions," I said.

"Okay. Yes, you should be here because I brought you; you had little choice, since I didn't tell you where we were going; I've only brought you here to feed you ice cream, in the hope it will cheer you up." He took a breath after his rather long sentence.

"Ice cream?"

"Ice cream."

The man totally fucking baffled me. On one hand, we had the powerful, intensely staring, devilishly handsome, fucking amazing in bed Mackenzie. Then on the other, we had the grinning idiot, still devilishly handsome, still amazing in bed, wanting to feed me ice cream Mackenzie!

"Ice cream," I said, shaking my head.

He took the briefcase from my hand and placed it on a consul table in the vast hall. I had no choice but to follow him through to an even vaster kitchen. He gestured to a stool tucked under a breakfast bar.

I watched him shrug off his suit jacket and roll up his shirtsleeves. My mouth watered at the sight of his forearms. One was tattooed; both were muscular. I don't know what it was about his forearms, but I felt a pang of want right at my core.

"We have…" he started to say, as he opened a large stainless steel freezer.

"Chocolate chip, white chocolate, salted caramel, pecan, gin and tonic…" he frowned at that one. "Strawberry and…" He looked over to me with a smirk. "Very vanilla."

He stared at me, expectantly. "So?"

"Salted caramel," I said.

"I like that you like salted," he said. I ignored him.

He pulled two tubs from the freezer and placed them on the bar in front of me. He then walked to a drawer and retrieved two spoons.

"I'm surprised you know your way around a kitchen," I said.

"Why wouldn't I?"

Again, another question.

"Don't you have help?"

"Help? No. I like to cook, I spend most of my time in this room, and I like ice cream before dinner."

"Obviously this is your house then," I said.

"Obviously." He opened the lids of the ice cream tubs, pushed one towards me then handed me a spoon. "Eat."

Watching him lick ice cream from a spoon, while keeping his gaze on me, had that pang at my core resembling an explosion. No matter what he did, it was erotic, seductive. It was a game he played very well, I was sure of that.

Or maybe it wasn't. Maybe he was simply a seductive individual. From what little time we'd spent together, he clearly knew what he wanted from life and took it with both hands.

"You play a good game," I said, eating a spoonful of ice cream.

"Game?"

"The seduction game."

He laid down his spoon and smiled. "It's not a game, Lauren."

"Oh, okay, let me guess, it's *who* you are," I chuckled.

"No. When I said it's not a game, I meant, I don't *play*. I'm deadly serious."

My hand paused halfway between the ice cream tub and my mouth. I was sure my mouth might have even stayed open. He reached over and wiped his thumb under my spoon to catch the ice cream that was about to drip. I watched, unable to take my eyes away, as he placed his thumb between his lips and sucked. Yes, he was deadly serious all right.

"Why are you trying to seduce me?" I whispered.

"Because I want to, because I can."

Was I that desperate, naïve? Scott had been my only boyfriend, lover, and husband. I was totally out of my league with Mackenzie.

"I think I should go," I said. I laid my spoon on the bar and replaced the lid of the tub.

He stood and waited for me. I was a little disappointed that he hadn't immediately tried to stop me. But then, I wasn't playing games either. He frightened me. Not that he was scary, but because I was unsure of the feelings coursing through my body. My clitoris throbbed, my heart hammered in my chest, my skin felt electrified. My head was telling me to get the fuck out of there.

"I'll drive you home," he said.

"I can catch a cab."

"Not from here you won't. Not so sure the local committee would allow such a lowly carriage to tarnish the neighbourhood."

I followed him to the front door, where he grabbed his keys and a small black gadget. He handed me my briefcase and locked the front door behind us. Instead of walking straight to the gates, we headed around the side of the building to a garage. He pressed a button on the black gadget and the garage door started to rise.

"Black or red?" he asked.

"Red, why?"

When the garage door had opened sufficiently, I saw two cars: one black and one red. Two identical sports cars, the make of which was beyond my knowledge of vehicles, stood side by side. I heard a beep, saw indicators flash a couple of times, and heard car doors unlock.

He gestured with his hand that I should walk to the passenger door; it was the only one on that side of the car. He opened it. How I managed to lower myself as much as I needed to slide into the seat, without my skirt rising to my waist, was beyond me.

I waited until he was settled into the driver's seat. "What car is this?" I asked.

"Aston Martin, DB9," he said. "Very British."

"Very *James Bond*," I replied.

"There's that, as well, I guess. Now, address?"

I wasn't sure I wanted him knowing where I lived. "Canary Wharf," I said.

"Big place, Canary Wharf, I have offices there. Any particular part I should arrive at?"

Fuck, he had offices near where I lived!

"Providence Tower, I can direct you once we are closer," I said.

"I know where Providence is."

He started the engine and whether it was because we were in a confined space or not, the engine roared, a deep throaty roar. It reminded me of the sound he made when he'd come. I shivered when that thought came to mind.

"Cold?"

"No, I'm fine."

The voice of his satnav startled me; I hadn't expected it to come on since he knew the route he had to take.

"You have an American satnav," I said, not sure why I found it amusing.

"I miss the accent."

"How long have you been here?"

"A few years. I know Americans here, of course, so I don't really need that to give me my fix."

"Is there, like, an ex-pats community?"

He laughed. "No, mainly a few American business associates. We do a lot of business in your capital."

"What do you actually do?"

"Besides unsuccessfully seducing you?" He looked over and smirked.

I wasn't sure about the *unsuccessful* part. I could feel the wetness in my panties.

"I'm a venture capitalist, I guess that is the technical term. I invest in businesses, then when the time is right, I sell them and pocket the dollars."

"Do you intend to sell us out then?"

"One day. Jerry isn't in for the long term. And when a business is profitable, at its peak, it's criminal to hold on to it."

"It's criminal to sell it and potentially put employees out of work."

"Who said anything about putting people out of work? I find buyers that want to take the business to the next level. That in itself ensures employees are secure. Besides, I'm a businessman, Lauren, not a charity."

"Wow." I wasn't sure what other answer to give. I kept my gaze firmly ahead and my mouth closed.

"You think I snuck in, persuaded Jerry to sell me his business, with the intent of making you all unemployed? He sought me out."

I refused to engage in any further conversation with him. We drove the rest of the way in silence.

As we pulled into the underground car park of my block, I released my seat belt and reached down in the footwell for my briefcase.

"Now you're pissed," he said.

"No, disappointed. I'm not sure I like you very much."

"Really? Because from where I'm sitting, I think that's a lie."

I turned in my seat to face him, hoping he'd see the indignation on my face.

"Your body betrays you, Lauren," he said, with that fucking gravelly voice that had my stomach clenching again.

"Fuck my body…"

"I'd like to," he said, interrupting me.

"I meant; I don't care what my body *tells* you. My mind thinks differently."

"Then it's your mind I have to work harder on. Have a good evening."

Had he just dismissed me? He had, he'd fucking dismissed me!

I climbed from the car and slammed the door behind me, wincing at the sound, and too scared to look back to see if I'd shattered a window or something.

I stomped off, realising I was heading in completely the wrong direction but not wanting to turn around and pass him again. I kept going, rounding a corner and then waited with my back to the wall. I heard the engine roar and echo around the half-empty car park. I waited until that roar became distant and I knew he'd left. Then I walked back the way I'd come and up the stairs.

"Fucking prick," I said to myself, as I huffed and puffed up four flights of stairs.

I should have taken the lift, or maybe, I needed to get a little fitter.

I slammed the door of my apartment once I'd entered, and then felt silly. There was no one to hear or see my tantrum. I threw my briefcase on the kitchen table. As I did, I saw a small white card poking from the side pocket. I pulled it out.

Printed in black was his name and underneath a mobile phone number. No company details, nothing. I hadn't noticed him slip that in the pocket and wondered when he'd actually had the time to do so. I flipped it between my fingers. Part of me wanted to tear it up; part of me, the part I was trying to control, was pleased.

"Well, Mackenzie Miller, maybe two can play your game," I said. "I need a hobby."

Chapter Six

The rest of the week passed uneventfully. I didn't see Mackenzie in the office at all. I'd asked Jerry when he was due back in and received raised eyebrows and a smirk. What was it with men and their smirks? According to Jerry, he was out of town, on business.

I'd been pleased when Friday came around and did something I hadn't done for a long time. I left work on time. I arrived home, stripped off my suit, and stood under the shower. I had a date with Netflix and a takeaway. I'd just pulled on a pair of PJ's and wrapped a towel around my head when I heard a knock on my door. I stood for a moment. No one should be able to get past the front door without the code or calling up.

It has to be security, I thought.

I opened the apartment door, and then cursed myself for not checking the spy hole. Mackenzie was standing there in jeans and a shirt, open at the neck, and with the fucking sleeves rolled to his elbows, tempting me with those forearms. He held two bottles of wine.

"I wasn't sure what you liked, red or white," he said.

"How…?"

"Oh, forgive me." He placed both bottles in one hand, the necks between his fingers and held out his other hand for a shake. "Mackenzie Miller," he said.

I frowned but couldn't stop the twitch of a smile. I took his hand and gave it a firm shake.

"Lauren Perry," I replied. "Like the champagne."

"Laurent Perrier, close though, and just as nice on the tongue," he said.

I laughed and shook my head. "So, red or white?" he asked.

"Red." I took the bottle from him and closed the apartment door.

I covered my mouth to stifle the giggle. I was thirty years old and giggling like a schoolgirl. I gave it a minute before looking through the spy hole. I couldn't see him, but I could see the bottle of white on the floor. I stupidly opened the door to retrieve it. He stepped out from just beside the door.

"That was rude," he said.

"Yep. Funny though."

"Hmm, not sure. Are you going to invite me in?"

"Before I do, how did you know where I lived?"

"I dropped you off here, remember?"

"How did you know what door number?"

"I own the company you work for, therefore I own the personnel records too."

"I'm not sure I'd agree that you own them. Don't you have such a thing as the Data Protection Act in America?"

He shrugged his shoulders. "If we do, then I regularly breach it."

I swung the door wide and gestured with my arm for him to enter. I'd play along for a while.

"You didn't call," he said.

"Was I supposed to? Are you expecting me to come running to you all, 'seduce me, Mackenzie? I'm a weak woman who needs a romance novel Dom.' Well?" I'd used a childish voice to emphasise the point.

"No, I'm not attracted to weak women, they break too easily. I'm impressed with your knowledge of a romance novel Dom though."

I huffed as I walked to the kitchen with the two bottles of wine. I held one up then the other. He pointed to the red.

"Although, maybe I should put you over my lap and spank that tight ass of yours," he said.

"In your dreams."

"For now."

Again, that fucking clenching started at his words. I'd need to do something about that. Maybe if I did some sit-ups, I'd have better control of my stomach muscles and could stop it from happening.

I handed him a glass of wine and took a sip of mine. It was a lovely wine; I hated to guess at the cost.

"Have you eaten?" he asked.

"Not yet."

"There's a great Chinese locally, we can order in, if you don't want to do your hair."

I'd forgotten about the towel wrapped around my head. Vanity had me grabbing it and pulling it away. I ran my fingers through the tangled mess of hair. Again my body betrayed me when my stomach, the one that hadn't stopped clenching, grumbled loud enough for him to hear.

"Takeout it is then," he said, as he pulled his phone from his jeans pocket.

Before I had a chance to protest, he had the phone to his ear and was talking. He hadn't even asked me what I wanted.

It's all a game, I thought.

I placed my wine on the counter and grabbed two plates and some cutlery. I cleared the table of my briefcase and handbag and set it. He took a seat, twisting the wineglass stem between his fingers. I sat opposite him. At first we didn't speak.

"I owe you an apology," he said.

"You do. And don't give me the, 'I misunderstood you' crap."

"I'd never insult your intelligence with that. I think you understand me only too well."

"So?" I took a sip of my wine.

He furrowed his brow. "You said you owe me an apology, where is it?" I asked.

Under the table my legs shook at my audacity. No matter what, he was still my boss.

He smiled. "You intend to make me work for it, don't you? Lauren, we started off on the wrong foot. I don't regret one minute of spending time with you, fucking you, but I apologise for everything else."

I chose to ignore the first part of his sentence.

"I accept your apology." I raised my glass to his.

"I like this Lauren," he said.

"This Lauren?"

"Already you've changed. In just a week there's a spark, a light in your eyes."

"Maybe I'm just done with bullshit."

"I'm glad to hear that. Because I have a proposition for you."

I was interrupted from asking what the proposition was by a knock on the front door.

"Dinner," he said.

"That was quick, and how did they get in?"

"I took the chance that you might be hungry and pre-ordered."

He hadn't answered the second half of my question. He rose and opened the door. He returned quickly with two white plastic bags.

"I do hate the British fascination with plastic bags," he said, as he set them on the kitchen counter.

"Why?" I asked, as I unpacked tinfoil containers.

"Bad for the environment."

His answer surprised me. Only a week ago he was telling me how he liked to buy a business, sell it for a profit, that he wasn't a charity, and was unconcerned about the employees of said business. He didn't seem to be the type of person concerned about the environment. But then, I had to remind myself; I didn't know much about him at all.

We sat and ate, drank wine and chatted. He was evasive on his past, family, and businesses. It was as I cleared away the plates and stacked the dishwasher that the atmosphere changed, became highly charged with electricity. He'd been relaxed, or had certainly given the impression he'd been so.

Then I saw the physical change in his body. He'd tensed so slowly that I was able to see every muscle contract. If I could see inside him, I'd watch tendons tighten and ligaments shorten. I'd watch every vertebrae twist and move as his spine became rigid. The one thing I wanted to do, but had no way of, was to be able to read his mind. He was closed, his features devoid of emotion, his eyes dark.

I didn't like the change in either him or the air around us that sparked with tension. I took my time to pour more wine and set the dishwasher on. I was deliberately slow as I filled the jug with fresh coffee and kept my back to him as the kettle boiled.

I didn't need to look to know he'd silently left his chair and was standing behind me. His musky aftershave wafted around. His hands appeared in my line of vision as he placed them, at either side of my body, on the countertop. He was close; enough to have me push up against the kitchen cupboards to keep a semblance of distance and respectability.

"You've spent the whole evening asking questions. Now it's my turn," he whispered, as he ran his nose up the side of my neck.

I tried not to react. "You've spent the whole evening avoiding answering those questions. Maybe I'll do the same."

"But I don't need your words, Lauren, to get the answers."

His breath ghosted the sensitive skin just under my ear. I wanted to turn and push him away, but I didn't. It was just a game, right?

"What turns you on, Lauren?" he whispered. His mouth was close to my ear.

"I'm not going to answer that," I whispered back.

"My voice does, I can see that."

"How?"

"Your skin is reacting, every word I utter causes goosebumps, just here," he said, as he ran his nose the length of my neck.

"I'm cold," I said.

His deep throaty chuckle had the hairs on my arms stand on end, let alone goosebumps.

I gripped the countertop to stop myself from leaning back onto his chest. I wouldn't give in, no matter what he did.

"You're an arrogant fuck," I said.

"Hmm, I'm not sure I'd agree. Arrogance suggests superiority, yet I worshiped your body."

"Oh, please." I dragged out the word 'please.'

"I made you come, three, four times?"

"What changed, Mackenzie? Which version of the man are you really? The one I just dined with, or this one?"

"I'm whichever one is required at the time."

"You need therapy."

"I have it, right here." His lips closed around my earlobe, and he sucked it into his mouth.

"I'm not qualified," I said, desperately holding back the moan that wanted to replace my words.

"Then I'll train you," he said as he released my earlobe.

"I have a job, I don't need another."

"Do you know what I'd love to do?"

I shook my head, although I had half an idea.

"I'd love to shove my cock down your throat to stop your smart words."

I spun around quickly but he didn't move away.

"How dare…"

Before I could finish my sentence, his mouth was on mine. He took that small step closer until his body was flush with mine. His tongue forced its way in, demanding control. I raised my hands and placed them either side of his head, and I pushed. I wasn't strong enough.

Again my body betrayed me, my tongue tangled with his as if it had a life of its own. I'd wanted to flatten it, deny him any response other than an open mouth. I couldn't.

My hands slid around his head, my fingers tangled in his short dark hair. I gripped and pulled. He didn't react. I couldn't bring myself to pull it from the roots, to hurt him in the hope he'd give back the mouth he'd taken prisoner. I didn't want to.

It was his moan that had me finally kissing him back with the same level of passion. Instead of pulling his head from mine, my hands pushed it closer. I needed to gain control; I needed to turn the tables. I needed to up my game.

He breathed heavily through his nose. I could feel his erection as he ground into me. I was so aroused by his *assault;* I could smell myself. I'd never been kissed so passionately; I'd never had my blood boil, my heart pound, by a kiss before. But then, I'd never encountered anyone like Mackenzie.

I had my eyes closed when his kiss changed, became gentle, when he pulled his head back a little until he was gently sucking on my lower lip. I opened them when he finally stopped.

He didn't smile; he didn't smirk. Whereas before his face was emotionless, then it wasn't. Despite his dark eyes, I could see his pupils dilated with lust. I felt overwhelmed by him, by the emotion I seemed to be able to provoke without knowing how or why.

"What do you want from me?" I whispered. I was no match for him.

"Everything. I want you to experience everything. I want you to feel worthy, more than adequate, and to know you're not alone."

He took a step back. I watched his chest rise and fall as he regulated his breathing to get it back under control. He raised a hand and I flinched slightly, not knowing why. He ran the back of his fingers down my cheek.

"So hot," he said. I was hoping he was referring to the flush that burned my skin. Or maybe I wasn't, I didn't know.

"What turns you on, Lauren?" he asked again.

"You."

"Even when you don't want to be?"

"Even when I don't want to be."

"Will you do one thing for me?"

I didn't answer, nor nod, or shake my head.

"Write down your fantasies."

"Why? Why do you need to know that?" It was a question he'd asked me before.

"Because."

"I think you need to leave." I didn't want him to, I wanted him to pick me up and carry me to the bedroom, strip me of my clothing, and fuck me like he had before.

"I will, but only because you and I are not finished yet. Write those down for me."

Without another word, he turned and walked out of the kitchen. I heard the front door open and softly close. I counted to twenty, in my head, before my legs gave way, and I slid down the cabinet to the floor.

I raised my shaking hand; my fingertips gently touched my still tingling lips.

"What the fuck are you doing to me?" I whispered.

Tears rolled down my cheeks, but I wasn't sure that it was in sadness. I was wrung out, for sure. I was an emotional wreck, but had been before Mackenzie Miller made an appearance.

I wasn't sure how long I'd sat on the tiled floor. My phone beeped to let me know I had a text message. I stood and winced as my knees ached. My phone was still attached to the charger on the kitchen counter. I reached for it.

Do you know how hard it is to drive a high performance sports car with one hand down your pants? Mackenzie

"How the...?" I shook my head. First thing Monday, I'd be having words with Personnel.

I typed.

Since I don't possess a cock, I guess the answer is no. Drive carefully.

It was with a smile that I changed 'unknown' to his name in my contacts.

I poured myself a large glass of water, turned off the kitchen lights, and headed for my bedroom. I pulled down the blind and climbed into bed. I picked up my Kindle and just held it. I'd intended to read but I couldn't see the words. My mind was filled with him, his scent, his words, his breath, and his touch. Everything about him consumed me. I liked it.

****

I woke late the following morning; my night had been filled with the eroticism that was Mackenzie Miller. I couldn't recall the dream, but judging by the wetness between my thighs, I assumed it to be good. I slid my hand under the waistband of my pyjama bottoms and my fingers circled my clitoris. I closed my eyes and thought of him. I brought every minute detail to mind. His dark eyes and hair, the way the muscles on his forearms had flexed when he tensed. I pictured him with his hand down his *pants*. His strong fingers wrapped around his cock, massaging himself.

I heard his whispers in my head; I felt his breath against my skin. I was transported back, I recalled the way he humiliated Scott, for me. I relived every moment I'd spent with him until my body shook, and I moaned out loud as an orgasm washed over me. It was neither as powerful or as fulfilling as the ones he'd given me, but it was enough to dull the ache between my thighs.

****

I was half tempted to Google why someone would be interested in another's fantasies but was too frightened to see the results and have that in my search history. I thought of his request while I showered and dressed, and as I sipped my tea and ate my toast. If it had been anyone else who had asked me, the word 'pervert' might have sprung to mind, but there was something about him that said he had plans. It was all part of the game.

If I were to stand a chance of winning this game, I'd have to think hard. There didn't appear to be any rules, other than fucking with my head. One minute he'd been a normal guy, sharing a meal and a bottle of wine, the next: predatory and challenging.

I was sure he was a little fucked up in the head, perhaps more than a little. No matter what, he was beginning to intrigue me.

I walked into my bedroom and opened the wardrobe door. Black, grey, more black; it was devoid of colour. I smiled, although shopping wasn't one of my favourite things to do, maybe it was time for this 'ice queen' to thaw.

I checked my watch and decided to head to Westfield's. I'd avoided visiting the 'largest shopping centre in the U.K.' according to its advertisement, until then, not wanting to be surrounded by people invading my personal space. I was a woman on a mission. I forbade myself from picking up anything dark or dull. No muted tones, no pastels even.

By the time I'd arrived back home, I had bags of colourful clothes and a couple of new pairs of shoes. I didn't remove the black suits. When the game was over, I had no doubt I'd be back to wearing them. I simply moved them to one side and hung red, green, blue, and purple alongside them.

The last bag that I emptied was from the chemist. I pulled out a box of condoms and placed them in the bedside cabinet, just in case.

I chuckled as I sat on the bed. Whatever this game was, it felt liberating, empowering even. I'd found I wasn't slumping my shoulders so much; the tension in my neck wasn't as noticeable. I was answering back, standing a little taller. So what if great sex was a by-product?

When I thought back on the last few months with Scott, I guess somewhere along the line I'd begun to feel a little downtrodden. Maybe instinctively I'd known, maybe I just hadn't wanted to face up to it. We hadn't had sex in months, in fact that could have been a year. We didn't go out alone, together. If anything, we were really just flatmates, except he was the one having all the fun.

I picked up my phone. Was it the norm to text my boss on a Saturday afternoon? But then, we'd crossed that 'should not have been crossed' boundary the first night we met.

I've been thinking. It's a little perverted to want to know a stranger's fantasies, don't you think?

I waited with bated breath for a reply. I knew what I was doing: baiting him, but for the first time in a long time, I felt alive.

Ten minutes, then twenty minutes passed before he finally replied.

I sucked your cunt, Lauren. I'd hardly call us strangers. And I'm offended by your accusation.

Oh shit! Was I offensive? I sat there with no idea how to reply. I reread his text. It surprised me to notice that I wasn't disgusted by his choice of word. Had anyone else used the 'C' word, even within earshot of me, I'd cringe; tell them off for being so crude. But not him, and I wondered why.

I'm sorry. I didn't mean to offend.

I'd pressed send before I thought about what was going on. In fact, I had no real idea what was going on at all, but had I just played straight back into his hands?

I asked you to do one thing for me. Now I'm asking for another. Trust me.

Trust him? I didn't know him. This 'stranger' had bowled into my life. I'd spent an amazing night, doing something I'd never done before; sex with a stranger, then found out he was my new boss. I'd thought back. Had he known who I was?

I don't know you.

My name is Mackenzie Miller. If my father is to be respected, you need to add 'the second' to that. I was born in South Carolina, moved to LA late teens. Google me.

Google him? Why the fuck hadn't I done that earlier? I grabbed my laptop. Thankfully there weren't that many Mackenzie Millers in South Carolina or LA. His father was involved in manufacturing back in the 1970's. I found an old college photo; Mackenzie had played football, American football. There was a report detailing how he was about to turn pro before being injured in a car crash that had resulted in the death of his friend. Fuck! That must have been a painful time, both physically and mentally.

He was as good-looking in his teens as he was an adult. I could imagine the cheerleaders fawning all over him, or maybe that shit just happened in movies.

I found lots of articles about his business dealings. Some where he was accused of shutting down companies and putting people out of work, others where he'd saved the day. My understanding of a venture capitalist was someone who came into fledgling businesses and financed them; obviously what he did was a little more involved, or I had it wrong.

One thing that did surprise me was his date of birth. Mackenzie was ten years older than I was and due to celebrate his forty-first birthday.

I shut down the laptop for fear of being tempted to get some work done. I'd promised myself I was taking a weekend off, no matter what.

I decided to take another cup of tea and sit on my balcony. It overlooked the Thames, and on a bright spring day, the river traffic was high. I watched the boats motor up and down. As much as I loved living in London, I did long for a walk on a beach, or a stroll through a forest. Feeling a little nostalgic, I called my mum.

We chatted for an hour, she told me about her neighbours, the relatives I didn't really have a great deal to do with, and how my brother was doing. It was always with sadness when we spoke about Sebastian. He'd decided to take a ride on his motorbike one day; he was just a teen when his world was altered in such a dramatic way. He was hit by a truck, paralysed and left brain-damaged. It wasn't his fault, and for that reason only, he received a substantial pay out that allowed Mum to move to the coast in a specially modified bungalow to care for him.

He loved being by the sea, and I felt a pang of guilt that I hadn't visited for a month. Mum would hold the phone to his ear and I'd talk to him. He'd reply with gurgles but it made him happy to hear my voice.

****

I'd decided to take a walk the following morning. I took the path alongside the river, leaning over the railings every now and again to watch the activity below. No matter what time or day of the week, London was busy. I watched couples holding hands, others swinging children between them. I watched individuals sitting on benches, chatting and laughing into their mobile phones. My earlier cheerfulness was a little dulled. Other than Mum, I didn't have anyone I could do that with. I couldn't sit on a bench and call a friend to laugh with. I'd immersed myself in Scott and my job. Watching those people made me realise how isolated and lonely I was.

I wasn't concentrating when a car pulled alongside me. I'd been so focussed on containing my misery, I hadn't heard the purr of a powerful engine.

"Lauren," he said.

I looked around as Mackenzie climbed from his car, the black one that time.

"Hello," I said.

"What are you doing?"

I looked at my feet, brought one up, replaced it, and then repeated the process with the other. "Walking, it's called."

He laughed. "Wait there, let me park up." He slid back into his car and drove off.

Should I wait? Of course I fucking would. I took a seat on a bench and raised my face to the sun. I closed my eyes, letting my skin soak up its rays. A few minutes later he was back. He sat beside me and I smiled at him.

"Are we doing that thing? What was it you called it? Walking?" he said.

He stood and held out his hand. It was with a little trepidation that I reached out for it. We walked hand in hand.

"So, is this what you do on a Sunday morning?" he asked.

"No, believe it or not, this is the first time I've walked this path since I've lived here."

"What did you do then, in your spare time?"

I hesitated before speaking. "Whatever Scott decided he wanted us to do."

"Sounds boring."

"It was."

"So now you have to find yourself, don't you?"

I stopped and looked at him. "Why do you say that?"

"You've spent your whole life with one man. I guarantee you lost yourself somewhere along the way. I also guarantee that coffee in your cupboard was his favourite, and the wines in your rack were the ones he'd chosen."

I couldn't speak at first. He was absolutely right.

"See, there is no need for words where you're concerned. Your expressions tell me everything I need to know. Come with me."

He led the way through a maze of buildings until we reached a small shop, tucked away under an imposing office block. He pushed open the door and allowed me to walk in first. The smell that hit me had caused me to stop, mid-step. Mackenzie collided into my back.

I laughed and continued to walk forward. The wonderful scent of fresh coffee wafted around. I looked left and right, every available place was filled with jars and jars of coffee beans. Each had a little chalkboard underneath with details of the bean, strength, and origin.

"Mackenzie," I heard. A man walked from behind the counter with a tea towel in his hands.

"Ed, busy?"

"Of course. What can I do for you?"

"I'll have my usual, and this lady needs to experience what you have on offer."

"Ma'am, let's start with strength," he said to me.

I shrugged my shoulders. I either bought Scott's favoured brand of instant, or whatever was the first my hand reached on the supermarket shelf. I'd never visited a coffee shop before.

"Let me get some blends together and you can taste, decide what you like," Ed said.

"What do you think I should buy?" I asked Mackenzie.

"I'm not going to answer that. You're going to choose. You're not swapping one's man preference for another's."

I walked around the shop, reading and inhaling deeply the different aromas. A hand on my hip brought my attention back and to the tray of small coffee cups that had been placed on the counter.

"Taste each one," Ed said. "Take a sip of water between."

I lifted the first cup to my mouth. I didn't drink my coffee black usually but took a sip. It wasn't as hot as I'd have made at home. I did as instructed and took a sip of water between. As I progressed up the line, the coffee became stronger, more aromatic, and smoother.

"Well?" Mackenzie asked.

"I like them all," I replied with a laugh.

I started at the beginning again. Mackenzie leaned against the counter. He held in his hand a small espresso cup, just the way he drank his coffee affected me. Everything he did was slow and measured. I watched from the corner of my eye as he closed his eyes and inhaled before each sip. He clearly appreciated his coffee.

"I still can't decide," I said.

"Then choose three, first, middle, and last," he said.

He nodded to Ed, who gathered three jars and measured out coffee into small brown paper bags. He stuck labels on the front and placed them into a paper carrier bag, then handed it over.

"How much?" I asked, as I fished into my jeans pocket for my debit card.

I saw Ed look over to Mackenzie, who just smiled.

"On me," Mackenzie said.

"Thank you."

"Can you give her some proper cups and a cafetière," he added.

Ed pulled a boxed set from a shelf.

"I have cups," I said.

"You have mugs, not the same thing. To appreciate coffee, it should be in small doses."

I accepted the second carrier bag and we left the shop.

"I could have paid for that myself," I said.

"I'm sure you could have, but why, if you don't have to?"

I caught him subtly check his watch.

"I guess I should head home," I said, giving him the opportunity to leave.

"I was hoping you may have time for lunch."

"I thought you'd have to go, sell businesses and all that."

"It's Sunday, I don't sell businesses on Sunday, just one of my little rules." He gave me that smirk again.

"Why were you here?" I said.

"I didn't say I didn't work, I just don't sell."

"I'm not sure I'm dressed for lunch," I said, looking down at my jeans and Converse.

"You don't need to be. Come on," he said, not giving me an opportunity to reply as he strode off.

I jogged to catch up. We walked into one of the many underground car parks and towards his car. He clicked a button on his key fob, and I saw the boot rise slightly. He placed my purchases in, shut it, and then walked to the passenger side to open the door for me.

"You didn't pay for the coffee," I said, as I lowered into the seat and not entirely sure why that thought had just come to me.

"I own the shop, Lauren."

He shut the door and walked to his side. "You know, I don't think I'll ever truly get used to being in the wrong side of a car and on the wrong side of the road," he said, as he climbed in.

"How do you know it's the wrong side? Maybe it's the right side, and you've been doing it wrong all this time."

"I don't do things wrong."

"Ever? I don't believe that."

Once the barrier rose, we pulled out into the waiting traffic.

"I do things that don't have the result I was hoping for, but never anything wrong."

"Why? How do you know what's right if you don't make mistakes?"

"I make mistakes, but that's not what you asked. I don't choose to do anything wrong. Like I said, if it doesn't work out, that's a problem, not a wrongdoing."

It was a twenty minute drive before we pulled up outside a small bistro nestled in a back street. It didn't seem the kind of place I'd expect him to dine at, but then, he hadn't done anything so far that I'd expect.

I wasn't sure he was even legally parked as he turned off the engine and climbed out. He opened my door, held out his hand to help me, and we walked into the restaurant.

"Do you own this as well?" I whispered while we waited to be seated.

"No, I just like the food. I eat here a lot."

The restaurant wasn't busy and we were quickly shown to a small table. Mackenzie pulled his chair away from being opposite to me and rearranged it to the side. Only the corner of the small table separated us. We were handed menus.

A jug of iced water was placed on the table and two glasses of white wine. I hadn't ordered any wine. A waiter stood waiting to take our order, not giving me enough time to even read through the whole menu.

Mackenzie chose a rare steak with sautéed vegetables. Because I wasn't given a chance to decide, I chose the same.

"So," Mackenzie said, as he slid one glass of the wine slightly towards me.

"So, what?"

"Did you think on what I said, in my text?"

I took a sip of wine, so I didn't rush into an answer.

"I'm just not sure why you want to know, and why you can't see how awkward this is."

He sighed and I wasn't sure if it was in frustration or not.

"You have been stuck in one relationship forever. The woman I met in the bar was scared, lonely, and unsure of herself until she discovered she was wanted. She willingly walked into my room, stripped naked, and let me fuck her. Okay, she fell asleep before we'd really gotten going, but the eyes of *that* woman, the one acting out a fantasy, were alive. For that few hours, she came to life; she became empowered. She wanted something and she took it."

He'd been speaking in that low, gravelly voice I heard when he was aroused and knew he was reliving every moment, as was I.

"Acting out a sexual fantasy isn't empowering. Becoming a successful single woman is," I said, a little breathless.

"And how do you do that in what is a predominantly man's world, Lauren?"

"I don't have to use sex to do it."

"It's not about using sex, it's about being confident enough to know what you want and to take it."

I wasn't sure I saw the comparison between work and sex. I wasn't sure about the 'taking it' part, either.

"You are the only female head of a department. All the colleagues on your level are men. Do you socialise with any of them?"

"No, I don't socialise with anyone from work."

"Because you've been so focussed on being the good wife, correct?"

"Yes."

"And where did that get you?"

His comment stung. I hadn't realised I'd leaned my body closer to his while we'd been talking, until I sat bolt upright and a gap appeared.

"That hurt, Mackenzie," I said, deciding to be truthful.

"It was supposed to. Use that hurt, focus on it here." He placed his hand on my lower stomach.

We fell silent as two plates were placed in front of us. I picked up my cutlery and began to eat, not making eye contact with him. I tried hard not to, it was the most inappropriate place, but I started to think about fantasies. It was something I'd never really considered before.

"I don't know that I have any. Although, it was exciting to do what I did that evening, in the bar. It was something I'd never done before, but I don't have a list of *bedroom* achievements to meet," I said quietly.

"All women, and men, have fantasies, Lauren. We all have a, 'try before I die' list. I imagine as a teenager you lusted over a movie or a pop star, am I correct?"

"Yes."

"Then that was a sexual fantasy."

"Can you stop saying that word, *sexual*?" I asked, looking around as I did.

"The restaurant is mostly empty, no one can hear me. Does sex, or talk of it, embarrass you?"

I had to think before I answered. I used the excuse of taking another mouthful of food.

"Over a meal, yes."

"Liar." He placed his cutlery on the table. "You need to unlock that box, up here," he said and tapped the side of my head. "Let yourself be free, for once, without the confines of your Britishness, without that ridiculous notion that you can't be a *sexual* creature, who likes to take and give pleasure. You'll find it very liberating."

Of course, he drew out the word, 'sexual.'

Was I frigid in my thinking? I'd had sex, plenty of times, but I guessed for the most part, it was just the good old missionary position, with very little experimentation.

I finished my meal in silence.

"Shall I take you home?" he asked. I'd been aware he had been staring at me the whole time.

"I think that's best. I think we've already crossed a boundary that we shouldn't have."

"You had no idea who I was, you did nothing wrong."

"Did you know who I was?"

"Not at first, only when you told me about the conference."

"Yet you still wanted to…"

"Yes," he said, cutting off my sentence. "I'm not your *boss* as you keep saying. I own the company you work in, that's all. Rationalise it."

He stood and took out his wallet; he placed a few notes on the table and waited for me to join him. I followed him to the car.

I wanted us to hit every red light, to crawl in traffic, or be stationary at road works, but for the first time, the London streets we drove along were fairly quiet. We arrived back in Canary Wharf way quicker than I wanted. I'd told him I wanted to go home for one reason only; I was scared. Not of him, of my reaction to him.

He pulled into the car park and into a parking bay. He switched off the car and turned slightly in his seat. I hadn't spoken the whole journey.

"Talk to me," he whispered.

I looked straight ahead.

"I liked it when you held my arms above my head and I couldn't move," I replied.

"You liked being restrained?"

"Yes."

"How did it make you feel?"

"I…I couldn't move, you could have done whatever you wanted."

"And that turned you on? How would you take that to another level?"

"I'm not sure. I've read about it, in books, I like the thought of it."

He opened his car door and walked around to mine. The soft click of the lock disengaging echoed and I stepped out. He took hold of my hand and silently we walked to the lift. We hadn't spoken a word as we travelled up to my floor, nor as we walked through the apartment door. It was only as we stood in the hallway did he speak, one word that had my skin prickling and my blood pumping around my body.

"Bedroom?" he said.

I led him to the room I'd slept alone in for the past few months, to the room I'd shared with another man. I stood in the middle and faced him.

"Naked, now."

I undid the buttons of my shirt, slid it from my body. I popped the button on my jeans, lowered the zip and wriggled them down past my hips, kicking off my Converse as I did. I tried to sexily remove my socks, but that was beyond my capabilities, and I found myself hopping from one foot to the other.

I unclipped my bra, removed it, and then my panties. I stood before him completely naked, in the middle of the afternoon. I wanted to giggle; daytime sex wasn't something I'd done for a long time.

I watched him undo a few buttons of his white shirt then pull it over his head. He stepped towards me, unbuckling his belt as he did. I watched as he pulled it through the loops so tantalisingly slow.

"Turn around," he said.

When I did he took my wrists and bound them together. He picked me up and carried me to the bed, laying me down on my front. I twisted my head so my cheek was flat to the pillow. I felt the bed dip as he climbed on the end and then with his hands around my ankles he spread my legs. He'd hardly touched me, but I was ready to combust. I felt his tongue run along my calf, circle behind my knee, and slowly up my thigh. It crossed my backside and back down the other.

He shuffled further up the bed with his knees between my legs, keeping them apart. I felt his finger trail ever so gently down between my shoulder blades. Then across my backside, drawing circles on each cheek.

"Do you like this?" he asked.

"Yes," I whispered.

His finger dipped between them, over that place that had me tense, until they slid down between my thighs.

"Can you feel how wet you are?" he said. I could only nod.

Too slow for my liking, he trailed his fingers over my opening, circling my clitoris. I closed my eyes, absorbing the sensation. He pushed two fingers inside me, hooking them to stroke and tease. I moaned. My body throbbed at his touch, hummed for more.

"You want me to do whatever I want, don't you?" he said.

"Yes." I was beyond more than one word answers.

"I'm going to fuck your ass," he said.

I tensed, and then panic set in. I tried to wriggle away, he kept his fingers inside me, stroking. He placed his other hand on my lower back holding me down.

"Not now, Lauren," he said, then chuckled.

"Not ever," I replied.

"Never say 'not ever'."

He began to slide his fingers in and out of me. He slid his free hand under my hip, finding my clitoris that throbbed as he teased it, coaxing me into an orgasm.

Before I'd had a chance to come down, he moved to one side of me, held my hips and gently rolled me over. He resumed his position between my thighs. With his hands at either side of me, he lowered his head and took a nipple between his teeth. He flicked the hardened nub with his tongue then sucked it into his mouth. I arched off the bed, pushing my breast further into his mouth.

He palmed the other one, roughly squeezing until I cried out. It wasn't a cry of pain though. Pleasure coursed through me. I missed his hot mouth on my skin when he pulled his head away.

"So you like being restrained, I can work with that. What else?"

He kissed my stomach gently; his tongue drew circles across my skin.

"I liked when I was on my knees," I said.

"These aren't fantasies, Lauren. Think. Delve deep into your mind."

"I…" I had to pause as his tongue trailed through my pubic hair and stopped just short of where I so desperately wanted him to be.

"I want…"

"You want what?" His tone of voice was demanding.

He swiped his tongue over my opening, just the once before pausing again. I could feel his breath on me and it was torturous.

"Challenge me, Lauren. Give me your dirtiest, darkest, let me see if I can achieve that for you."

My stomach lurched at his words. So this was what it was all about? His tongue lapped at my clitoris.

"I want to feel what it's like to be with another woman," I said.

His chuckle reverberated, causing a shock wave over my clitoris; his tongue delved inside, rewarding me for saying something that had taken me by complete surprise. Until that moment, I'd never thought of sex with another woman. I wasn't even sure where that had come from. But I smiled, one point to me, I thought, that was something he couldn't do to me.

His tongue brought me to another orgasm, a powerful one that ripped through my stomach, produced primal sounds from my chest and beads of sweat on my forehead.

He wasn't about to let up though. He reinserted his fingers, his teeth gently clamped against my clitoris, and his tongue flicked the then overly sensitive nub. I drew my heels towards me, raising my hips. I wanted harder, deeper, and faster.

"More," I said, noticing the huskiness in my own voice.

Three fingers teased and stroked. My brain was firing off electrical impulses so fast my body couldn't keep up.

"Fuck me, please," I said.

"No. You give me more," he replied.

More? I wasn't sure what it was that he had done to open that box in my mind, but the words tumbled out. I told him I wanted to have sex in public; I wanted that thrill of the possibility of being caught.

With his fingers inside me, his mouth on my clitoris, and the thoughts running through my head, I came for a third time. I know I cried out, over and over. I know I could feel tears run down my cheeks; and I know I must have fallen asleep immediately after, again.

I woke to darkness outside. I was lying under the covers, still naked and with a sticky residue between my thighs. My wrists were unbound, although my shoulders reminded me they hadn't been for a while by the ache.

I looked around the room; Mackenzie had gone. I swung my legs from the bed and found them surprisingly stable. Naked, I stepped from the bedroom into the hallway. The apartment was quiet and I knew he'd already left. A pang of disappointment hit me until I checked my watch. It was nine o'clock. I must have slept for hours.

I walked to the kitchen needing a glass of water, which I carried back to the bedroom with me. I picked up my jeans and fished out my phone from the pocket.

You left. I typed and then sent to Mackenzie.

His reply was almost immediate.

You were sleeping so soundly, I didn't want to disturb you.

I'm sorry I fell asleep. I sent.

Don't be. I like that I can produce that level of arousal that it exhausts you.

Not being overly familiar with multiple orgasms, I wasn't sure if my need for immediate sleep was normal or not. There was no fucking way I was Googling that for an answer. I decided on a shower, although it was with reluctance. Keeping the scent of my orgasms on my skin was a reminder that he had been there. His hands, his tongue, had given me more pleasure than anyone before. I smiled, thanking my stars I was only thirty, and I'd have many years of that level of pleasure.

It was as I stepped into the shower that I crashed, emotionally. I didn't *have* him; I didn't *have* any time other than what he offered. What we were doing wasn't a relationship, it was just sex. I showered, picked up my phone and walked into the kitchen to fix a snack.

So, I guess you *are* a sex therapist after all. I typed and then pressed send.

Not so much a sex therapist, call me The Facilitator.

The Facilitator?

I'll lead you to that place you want to be. I'll make your dreams a reality.

Holy fuck! I prayed he didn't mean what he'd said. I hoped I'd just totally overthought the fact I'd told my fantasies. What would he do with them?

"Stop being an idiot," I said to myself.

He couldn't do anything I didn't want him to do, could he?

Chapter Seven

I scanned the wardrobe deciding what to wear. I was a changed woman; well I was trying to be. I'd had three, no four, orgasms over the weekend, and I intended to do exactly what Mackenzie had suggested. I was going to shed the *old* Lauren and embrace the new.

I selected a pair of black trousers and paired it with a red shirt and red high heels. I let my hair hang loose, and after applying my makeup, I left for work. I was aware of the glances from men I received and I liked it. For once, I didn't keep my head bowed; I looked up. I stood tall and I walked like a woman with a purpose.

"You look hot," I heard Jenny say as I entered my office, a half-hour later.

"I'm thawing out," I said with a laugh.

"About bloody time," she called after me.

I even sat back in my chair and raised my feet to my desk as I read through some notes on a new media marketing campaign Jerry wanted to investigate.

"Fuck me," I heard. Looking up, I saw Jerry standing in my doorway.

"I thought we'd had that discussion before?"

He laughed. "I like," he said, sweeping his hand towards me.

I shook my head and I lowered my feet.

"What can I do for you?" I asked.

"Other than the usual, what do you think of my plans?"

We spent a half-hour discussing his ideas, and I made notes, promising to have a full proposal for him, with costs, in a couple of days.

As much as I didn't want to, I checked my messages and emails on a frequent basis during the day. I'd hoped for a message from Mackenzie. I tried not to be disappointed when I hadn't received one on either. I put him to the back of my mind and continued my day.

"So, I don't think, in the year I've been working here, I've seen you in anything other than a black or grey suit," Jenny said, as she strode into my office.

She'd brought a coffee with her, and I winced at the taste of instant. It also reminded me that Mackenzie still had mine in the boot of his car.

"A new me, Jenny," I said.

"Good. Me and Sally are going to a new wine bar that's just opened around the corner after work, if you want to join us?"

Jenny had never invited me to join her after work, and her and Sally going out together surprised me.

"Sally? As in, Jerry's Sally?"

"Another lonesome. We need to make a club, I'm on my own, she's on her own, and you, well, no one knows whether you're *really* on your own or not," she added a wink after that comment.

Sally was Jerry's very efficient and elderly assistant. Not someone I would have paired with Jenny nor the wine bar type.

"Yes, I will. Why not?"

"Come on then."

I checked my watch not realising it was already five. Of course, for Jenny it was the end of the day. I packed up my things, and she used my phone to call Sally. We met her in the foyer, and I think she was as surprised to see me, as I was her.

Because the wine bar had just opened, it was fairly empty. We found a booth and ordered a cocktail each.

"We're off duty, aren't we?" Jenny asked.

"Sure are," I replied.

"Okay," she took in a deep breath, as if preparing herself to ask a difficult question. I froze, wondering what she was about to say.

"You and Jerry, have you ever…?"

I relaxed, then laughed.

"No, never. He's a really good friend. I've been with him since day one."

I then told them about our first meeting, where he'd spilled his drink on me me.

"I know what people think and even now, being single, it's not somewhere I'd go. I cherish our friendship," I said.

"I'd do him," Jenny said. "But now we have the delicious Mackenzie." She sighed as she took a sip of her drink.

"I'd do Mackenzie, although, I'm not sure my sixty-year-old body would be up for it," Sally said.

I couldn't help but laugh out loud and it felt good. It felt good to sit, drink with a group of women, and laugh.

"Would it bother you that he owns most of the company?" I asked.

"No, it's only a problem if it all goes tits up, I guess," Jenny replied.

"It makes me pissed off that people think you can't have a relationship with someone at work. If you're professional enough, I mean, look at you and Scott," Sally said.

"I spend most of my time avoiding him, Sally. It's hard work. I have to sit in a meeting with him tomorrow, and I'm not looking forward to that."

"You'll be fine, especially if you make sure you dress to kill," Jenny said.

"I'm so glad that bitch has gone though. I never liked her," Sally added.

Sally liked everyone, usually. "If she had stayed, I'd have left," I said.

"Jerry wouldn't allow that, he booted her out the minute that video was seen. She's a tart and he, sorry to say this, has always been a slimeball," Sally said.

I laughed again. The feeling that other women understood what I had gone through, that they had my back, was a new feeling.

"You know, for a long time I've felt very alone. I know what people at work think of me, and I wasn't trying to be aloof deliberately. I just wanted to work hard and prove myself," I said.

"Fuck what anyone says, it's jealousy. Yeah, they talk about you. You're the only woman up top and best friends with the boss," Jenny said.

"You do like to call it as it is," Sally said with a laugh.

"No other way. Up front and honest, best policy," she replied.

We drank a few more cocktails, laughed a lot, and staggered out to get taxis. I hadn't done that for years, not since my college days. I smiled all the way home.

The trouble with alcohol on an empty stomach was that it affected the brain way more than it should. I'd kicked off the high heels and decided I needed water to help sober me up. I sat at the kitchen table sipping from a bottle and thinking back over the weekend. I chuckled.

"It's a game," I said. "Just a game." My voice hitched mid-sentence.

Was it though? I wasn't sure anymore. Maybe he was just a perv. I giggled some more as I thought of him getting himself off on what I'd said. I cringed at the same time. Was I just a tool to entertain him? I'd played straight into his hands, I'd told him things I shouldn't have. I felt the tears pool in my eyes.

"What a sad fuck!" I shouted. My words echoed back, reminding me there was no one to hear, no one to listen.

The other trouble with alcohol on an empty stomach was that it blurred reality; it made the recipient do dumb things. Dumb things like sending a text.

I'm a little drunk. I just wanted to say something. I sent.

A little drunk is okay, what do you want to say? Came Mackenzie's reply.

Fuck You. I giggled as I pressed send.

Is that a request? How, Lauren? How would you fuck me?

You play a good game; want to tell me the rules? Make it an even playing field.

For someone a 'little' drunk you sure are articulate. And I told you; I don't play games.

Are you mocking me?

No, Lauren. Go to bed. Was his reply.

Had I not dropped the phone, and the action of reaching down for it had my head spin, I couldn't have been held responsible for my response. I stumbled into the bedroom and fell onto the bed. Wasn't this the part where he was supposed to come barging in, having miraculously obtained a front door key? Or the part I find out he owns the building and security waves him past? Or the part where he rips off my clothes and makes mad, passionate love to me?

That's what happened in my books, why couldn't it happen in real life?

****

"Oh, fuck," I groaned, reaching for my phone to stop its alarm.

I'd patted the bedside cabinet not able to find it. With only one eye open, I realised it wasn't there.

"Shit," I said, as the previous evening started to replay in my mind.

Cocktails, lots of cocktails, no food, and then…Oh no!

Despite the banging in my head, I'd swung my legs from the bed and walked to the kitchen. I used my foot to sweep the phone from under the table and cursed at the cracked screen as I crouched to pick it up.

I scrolled back through my text messages. "Oh, fuck," I said, again.

I filled a glass with water and opened one of the drawers grabbing a blister pack of pain relief. I swallowed down two, set the kettle to boil, and took the glass of water to the bathroom. Hopefully, a shower would sort me out.

I nearly screeched when I saw myself in the bathroom mirror. Black mascara lined the underneath of my eyes. Red lipstick stained not only my lips but also the skin around them. My hair was a tangled mess. I was still dressed in the previous night's clothing that were crumpled and creased.

I stripped and stepped into the shower. I soaped myself, head to toe, and washed away the previous night's excess. As I stood and selected what to wear, I gave myself a mental slap on the arse. I would not feel guilty about going out and getting drunk, nor would I feel apologetic for sending daft text messages.

****

"Good morning, Jenny," I said, as I passed her desk.

She wore dark glasses. "You're chirpy this morning," she said.

"Lightweight," I teased, as I continued to walk to my office.

I switched my phone to silent and placed it in a drawer, I didn't want to be tempted to check it.

I got on with my work, surprising myself that I wasn't that far behind from taking a weekend off. Maybe I wasn't as overloaded with work as I'd made myself believe.

I'd worked through lunch and it was late afternoon that my stomach started to protest.

"I'm just popping to the sandwich shop, do you want anything?" I asked Jenny as I passed.

"No, I've eaten."

The sandwich shop was next to our office block, it wasn't somewhere I visited regularly, but it was close enough to grab a quick bite to eat. When I returned Jenny beckoned me over.

"You have a visitor," she whispered.

I looked towards my office, the door was shut and the vertical blinds covering the glass wall were obscuring any view in.

"Who?"

"Mr. Miller," she said, then raised her eyebrows. "And your meeting today was cancelled."

"What does he want?"

"Coffee, for two, and a packet of Advil."

"Maybe he has a headache. Best not keep him waiting," I said.

My stomach churned as I placed my hand on the door handle, and I took a deep breath in as I opened the door. He was standing with his back to me, looking out over the London skyline.

"Lock the door, Lauren," he said.

"Excuse me?"

He slowly turned. "Lock the door, a simple request."

"No. This is my office."

He strode towards me. "Then take the risk of your assistant walking in and seeing me make you come."

My jaw fell open. "What the…?"

I hadn't finished my sentence before his mouth was on mine, and I was pinned to the door. I fumbled around me and found the lock, not that I wanted to *obey his command*, but because I would have been fucking mortified had she walked in.

His hands dragged my skirt to my waist. I grabbed them to stop their ascent. He kept his hands where I'd stopped them but didn't release my skirt. He pulled his mouth away slightly and before I could shout at him, he spoke.

"Trust me," he whispered.

My words flowed back; *I wanted that thrill of the possibility of being caught.*

"Trust me," he whispered again.

I let go of his hands, and while he continued to look at me, he raised my skirt to my waist. I saw him smile as one hand ran over my silk stocking top. He placed his hand between my thighs and the heat of his palm transferred through my panties. He gently drew his fingers back and forth.

"Your team is sitting no more than four or five metres away," he said. It was all I could do to nod.

I'd felt the heat that started to build as he teased. I felt the wetness that started to soak into my panties. When he did too, he gave that half smile that showed the mischievousness in his face.

I let myself relax slightly as he pushed my panties to one side and stroked across my opening. I closed my eyes and let it happen.

"Shush, they'll hear you," he said.

I hadn't been aware of the moan that must have left my lips when he inserted two fingers.

He stroked inside me, teased and pinched my clitoris, and all the time I had to bite down hard on my lip to keep quiet. He stood slightly to one side of me, his pelvis pushing into my hips. I could feel his erection, and I reached down, placing my hand over him. I heard him take a sharp breath in as I squeezed and used my palm to rub over the bulge in his trousers. I matched his pace, and when he moaned; I knew he was close.

I placed my other hand on the back of his head, pushing his face towards mine, and kissed him. I forced his lips open with my tongue, I demanded, and I got. His fingers worked me faster, bringing me to my orgasm. The fact I couldn't make a sound heightened the wave of heat that flowed over me, intensified the static that coursed over my skin. If I hadn't been kissing him, I'm sure I would have cried out. I continued to rub my palm over his cock until I felt him shudder slightly and his body tense.

When he withdrew his fingers from me, he placed them in his mouth and sucked them clean. If I hadn't already come, I think I would have then.

I startled at a knock on the door. Wide-eyed I looked at him. He took a step back and I shuffled my skirt back into place, taking large strides to reach my desk before perching on the edge.

Mackenzie opened it. "Thank you, Jenny," he said.

Leaving the door open, he turned and walked towards me, holding two small cardboard containers of coffee.

"Real coffee, not the shit you have here," he said.

"Thanks, Jenny," I said, calling over his shoulder. She was standing in the doorway admiring the view as he walked away from her.

She chuckled as she pulled the door closed and left.

"Fuck, that was close," I said, as my body sagged.

"No, that was perfect timing."

"You sent her to get coffee? You knew what time she was coming back?"

"Sure. What's the point in experiencing the thrill of nearly getting caught, if you don't nearly get caught?"

"And what would have happened if I hadn't come?"

"You would have spent the rest of the afternoon frustrated, I guess," he replied, as he took a sip of his coffee.

"Or I could have just given myself an orgasm after you left?" I said, smirking at him.

He did that half smile thing again and raised one eyebrow. "You'll make yourself come while I watch, next time."

"Are you sure there will be a next time?"

I felt a little shitty when I saw him blink rapidly a couple of times. Maybe he wasn't as cocky as I'd thought.

"That will be entirely your decision. You can always stop me."

"I wasn't so sure about that earlier."

"You just say no."

Trouble was, I didn't think I was capable of that. I was enjoying the 'trysts,' the surprise, not knowing when he'll show up or what will happen. It was escapism and exciting, it had my heart racing, and my brain scrambled. He had my body humming with anticipation.

"I have a meeting, one I tried to cancel but couldn't," he said, as he drained the small cup of coffee.

I nodded, expecting him to turn and leave. Instead he took a step towards me, brushed a piece of hair away from my face and tucked it behind my ear. He gave a soft kiss to my cheek and then he left.

It was a couple of minutes later that I heard a knock on my office door.

"It's open," I called out.

Jenny came in holding two mugs of instant. I hadn't the heart to tell her that since being introduced to the real stuff, I wasn't sure I could drink it, but I took a sip anyway.

"So?" she said.

"So, what?"

"You're still with us?"

"I don't know what you mean."

"He had meetings with all the heads today. The gossip mill is churning, people are scared for their jobs."

"He didn't mention anything about people losing their jobs. He's getting to know everyone and see exactly what they do, that's all. It's quite normal," I lied.

Had he been in the building all day and it was just my 'turn' to be seen? I'd have liked to think he'd made a special effort.

"And here are two of my favourite ladies," I heard, as my office door opened. The only person who never knocked, and rightfully so, was Jerry.

"Mmm, that smells nice," he said. I handed him my coffee.

"Jenny, if you want to head off a little earlier, you can," I said, wanting her out of my office.

"Cool." She rushed from the room.

"You okay?" Jerry asked.

"Sure, what can I do for you?"

I sat in my chair and he took the one opposite. "So, Mackenzie wants to buy me out, completely."

"He does? Why?"

"He thinks I've taken it about as far as I can. He thinks he can do wonderful things if he merged this into one of his companies, or words to that effect."

"How do you feel about that?"

"I'm tempted, to be honest. Remember you asked if I have any other ideas? Well, I think I'd like to take some time out and think up new projects."

"You don't feel he's manoeuvring you out, do you?" I said.

"No, he was quite upfront, told me if I wasn't interested nothing would change."

"Who would run the company? It's not like he can do it day-to-day."

"Have you seen his 'right hand man'? Mind you, I guess you wouldn't have. Fucking stunning."

"His right hand *man* is stunning? Something you want to tell me?" I said with a smile.

"His right hand *woman* then. I'd bang her in an instant, but I don't think she'd go for me."

I shook my head. "And that's why, my friend, you are single. You don't *bang* anyone. So he has a female alongside him."

"I met her a couple of months ago. Gabriella. Even the name gives me a hard-on."

"Jerry!"

He laughed as he rested his feet on my desk, scattering my perfectly piled paperwork.

"I'm glad you took the weekend off, I keep telling you, you work too hard."

"It was refreshing. Want to know something? I don't work all the time because I'm busy, it's to relieve the boredom. I'm stuck in an apartment, on my own for two days, it gives me something to do."

"You only have to call me."

"I'd love nothing better than to ring you and we go out for a meal, as friends. But I know you'll try to hit on me and ruin it," I said gently.

"Fair enough. You know I am kidding when I do that shit, right?"

"Oh, that makes me feel a whole lot better."

"You know what I mean. Dinner, tonight? I promise I won't hit on you."

"You promise?"

"Scout's honour."

"You were never in the Scouts, but yeah, why not?"

"Good. I'll give you a shout when I'm done. Maybe we'll both leave on time."

I settled back and continued with work. I needed to organise a meeting with an advertising agency, but if Jerry was going to sell out, perhaps I should put everything on hold.

****

"Where are we going?" I asked as I climbed into Jerry's car.

"Simpson's In The Strand. They've got a great cocktail bar."

"I'm not sure I can stomach cocktails," I said.

"Yeah, what did you do to poor Sally, she was a shower of shit all day."

I laughed. "I think we drank a little too much on an empty stomach."

Despite the early hour, the restaurant was busy. It was the first time I'd had the opportunity of dining at Simpson's. It was classically designed, all dark wood and chandeliers. We ordered our meal and I opted for water instead of wine.

"So, what are you going to do?" I asked, referring to Mackenzie's offer.

"I think I'm going to take it. Will you come with me, in whatever I do next?"

I paused before I answered. "I guess it depends on what you do. If I were you, I'd take a break first, before you decide. You've worked, what fourteen hour days, every day of the week, for how long?"

"Too long. Maybe I'll take a couple of weeks' holiday somewhere."

"Jenny said Mackenzie met with all the heads today, I think some are wondering if they're going to lose their jobs."

"If he merges then it's possible, I guess. I'd feel a little shitty about that," Jerry said.

"You can't. They've been paid well, ridden the ride, so to speak. You have to think about yourself."

"If I take his offer, I want to make sure your job is secure," he said.

"Jerry, don't even worry about that. It's time to think about you, no one else. I'll be fine, whatever happens."

Inside a pang of anxiety started to rise. I could only afford the apartment because of my salary. Although Scott had been on the same pay grade as me, it had been my savings that had been used for the deposit. Which reminded me of something.

"You did give Scott the divorce papers, didn't you? I haven't heard anything from my solicitor."

"I did, the bitch took great delight in telling me she'd have him sign and return them."

"I wonder if they'll stay together." It was more of a thought than a question.

"I doubt it, he was seen out with another woman a couple of nights ago."

"Really? What a shit."

"Don't feel any compassion for her, but yeah, a total shit."

We had both opted to forego starters and our main meals were placed on the table. For a little while, we ate in silence, comfortable enough in each other's company to not have to make small talk.

"You know, you look so different to just a couple of weeks ago. What really happened?" Jerry asked.

"If I tell you, you have to promise me it won't go any further. I'm trusting you, Jerry."

"I promise."

"I met someone. Well, it's not a relationship, I don't actually know what it is."

"Sex, it's just sex, tell me I'm right?" he said with a laugh.

"It's just sex."

His mouth hung open. "I was kidding. Wow. Good for you, at least one of us is getting some."

"I've never done anything like this before, but it makes me feel, I don't know, liberated."

"And what else?"

"And shitty, slutty."

"You know, it's only women that think they can't have a relationship that's just physical. If you know that's all it is, and you don't want more from him, then so what? It's okay to have fun, Lauren."

"I know, but it's more complicated than that."

"Any relationship is only as complicated as you make it. Relax, have fun, go with the flow, fuck Scott out of your system," he said, laughing.

"I think that's what I'm doing."

"Then I'm jealous of this mystery man. Do I know him?"

"No. I don't think anyone knows him." It wasn't a lie; Mackenzie Miller was a mystery.

"If it makes you feel good, Lauren, and it keeps that smile on your face and your eyes bright, then it's not a bad thing. Just be careful that you don't let feelings get in the way."

We continued with our meal, and as much as Jerry kept the smile on his face, it didn't reach his eyes. I felt bad, but I had no one I trusted to talk about what was happening, and after this afternoon, I needed to talk.

"That's the problem, sometimes I like him, and other times I don't. It's all a game, exciting, but a game nonetheless."

"Does he want a relationship with you? Like, dates and all that?"

"I don't think so. Although, we've been out for lunch."

"If it's bothering you, stop it."

As if it was that easy.

"That's the problem, I don't really want to."

"Then quit moaning and just enjoy it," he said with a smirk.

I shook my head and laughed. We sat and chatted some more about work, about what holiday Jerry was to take, and the fact that he wanted to take his mum with him. We laughed and I enjoyed my time with him.

"I need to get home," I said. Whether it was the drunken night's sleep the previous night or an orgasm mid-afternoon, all of a sudden, I was tired.

Jerry paid the bill, waving away my insistence on contributing, and we headed out to his waiting car. He'd never learned to drive and living and working in London meant he hadn't had to. But it was nice to not have to suffer the tube. His driver dropped me off home and I took the lift to my apartment collecting my mail on the way.

Leaving the mail on the kitchen table, I headed for the shower. It was while I was sitting with a cup of tea that I opened the pile of letters. There were bills, and then there was a letter from the solicitor. My hands shook when I read that Scott wanted a division of assets organised before he signed the divorce papers. He wanted half the equity of the apartment, pensions, and savings. My savings.

He'd brought nothing to the marriage. I was always the careful one, squirreling away money, even from my days doing a paper round. Why the fuck should he be entitled to any of it? Surely they'd have to take into account it was my money that put down the deposit. There wasn't enough equity to buy another apartment in London, especially in Canary Wharf. Prices had skyrocketed, and sadly, I'd bought when property prices were at an unusually high peak. I'd hoped to sit on the apartment for another few years before having to sell.

If he took half my savings, half the equity, I'd barely be able to afford a one-bedroom apartment in the suburbs. As for my pension?

Why the fuck should he be entitled to half of that? Was I entitled to half of his? Didn't one cancel out the other?

My great evening had soured. I threw the letter on the table and headed for bed. As I lay there, I tried to calculate. The banks were on their knees, getting a mortgage was near on impossible. Then a thought hit me. Was this all the bitch's idea? I wouldn't let her get one penny from me.

Sandra, her name was. She'd been the only real friend I had. We'd been in college together, and even back then it was clear she was in love with Scott. She'd often flirt and I wondered why I'd kept her as a friend. But back then, I was overconfident in our relationship, I guessed. When Jerry employed Scott, she soon followed. I hadn't twigged at the time; I hadn't been suspicious at all. She'd followed him around from job to job. Now I knew why.

As I lay, a more worrying thought hit me. If Scott lost his job because of the merger, he'd be more desperate for money.

Chapter Eight

I didn't see Mackenzie for a few days, and in one way I was glad. I spent hours on the phone with my solicitor and hours more moaning to Jerry. His solution was to get Scott bumped off. If only. I was going to be asked to complete a form with my savings and assets, but the solicitor assured me, she'd make sure the apartment deposit was taken out before any division.

It was towards the end of the week that I finally heard from him.

Hi, I'm out of town, in LA actually. Family issues. I have a birthday party to attend next weekend that I'd like you to accompany me to. Mackenzie's text had said.

I'm sorry to hear you have family issues. And that sounds lovely, thank you.

I remembered that he was due to celebrate his forty-first birthday but couldn't remember when. It hadn't sounded like it was his birthday party.

You'll need a change of clothes. We'll be away overnight.

Oh! Did that mean we'd be staying in the same room together? Other than the first night, we hadn't actually slept together and that hadn't been intentional. Had I not fallen asleep, I'm sure I would have been doing the walk of shame a lot earlier than I had.

Okay, if you can just let me know the dress code that would be great.

Dressy for the Saturday evening, casual for Sunday.

Well, at least that gave me an excuse, or maybe it was a curse since I hated shopping, to purchase a new dress.

****

I waited until the Sunday afternoon before venturing to the shopping centre again. I'd thought it wouldn't be as busy then, but it appeared a Sunday afternoon stroll with screaming kids around an exclusive shopping centre was all the rage. I ducked into a couple of the more upmarket stores and browsed. I'd rather spend a few hundred pounds on a dress and shoes than have to part with half to Scott. A couple of thousand pounds later, and shell shocked, I walked out with a gorgeous purple halter neck dress, matching shoes, and a new clutch.

Mackenzie had said dressy, not black tie, so I'd opted for mid-calf, which I believed would cover all bases. When I got home, I tried the dress on again. I loved the way it hugged my curves, although the front of the dress may have been considered a little raunchy. I hoped the party wasn't going to be full of old men. There were two strips of material that extended from the waist to fasten behind my neck. Those two strips of material left enough of a gap between them to expose my stomach and chest.

I made a list and added tit tape to it. I booked hair and nail appointments for the Friday before.

I willed the week to fly by and it did. Although, the closer it got to Friday, the more anxious I'd become. I hadn't heard from Mackenzie at all. I toyed with sending him a text or even calling him. I didn't know what his family issues were, perhaps it was something serious and he'd forgotten about the party. I decided to pack my overnight bag, just in case.

I hated just sitting around waiting, but I wasn't going to chase him. I had to remind myself we didn't have a relationship, and even if one was on offer, I wasn't sure it was what I needed right then.

By the time it had gotten to nine o'clock that Friday evening, I'd resigned myself to the fact he had either forgotten or something major was keeping him away and unable to text.

I tried my hardest not to feel pissed off. I kept reminding myself that until I knew, I couldn't allow the sense of disappointment to overwhelm me. I opened a bottle of wine and poured myself a glass. I decided to waste some time watching a movie and curled up on the sofa.

I was halfway through, not really watching, a shoot 'em up film when the intercom buzzed. Not expecting anyone, which made me chuckle as I *never* expected anyone, I was slow to respond. It buzzed for a second time. I rose and pressed the speaker button.

"Hello?"

"It's me, can you open the door?"

Thankfully, the intercom came with a camera. The voice was distorted and not immediately identifiable. I saw Mackenzie looking directly at the camera and I buzzed him in. I gave it a minute then opened the front door as he exited the lift.

"Hi," I said. "You look really tired, are you okay?"

"I literally just got off a plane, came straight from the airport."

I held the door open to allow him to walk in. "I was watching a movie," I said, not sure he'd want to know that.

"Sounds good."

"Can I get you a glass of wine?"

"That sounds better."

His answers were clipped, he obviously wasn't about to explain his silence, and it wasn't my place to push. I poured him a glass and he followed me to the living room.

"I can start it again if you want," I said.

"What it is?"

I gave him the title but since I hadn't been concentrating, couldn't tell him the plot. "I've seen it, carry on from where you were."

I curled up in the place I'd vacated and he sat beside me, but with enough of a gap to make me edgy. Something was clearly off.

Within a half-hour he'd drunk the glass of wine and was asleep. Jet lag must have gotten to him. I switched the movie off and gently slid from the sofa. I took off his shoes and slowly raised his legs onto the footstool. I didn't want to disturb him, but the angle at which he had fallen asleep, meant he was going to have a stiff neck when he woke. I pulled a throw from the back of the sofa and covered him with it.

I watched him for a moment. The stubble around his chin was a little longer, and I wondered if that was simply because he'd let it grow or not taken care of himself as well as he usually did. Even in sleep, his brow furrowed as if he had the weight of the world on his shoulders. I left him sleeping and headed for my bedroom.

I pulled on a tank top and shorts and climbed into bed. Maybe I should have woken him; perhaps I should have offered him my bed. I tossed and turned to get comfortable.

It was some hours later that I felt him join me. He slid into the bed behind me and pulled me into his chest. He curled around me without a word, and I fell back to sleep.

****

"Good morning," he said when I woke. He was dressed and standing with a cup of coffee.

I shuffled up into a sitting position. "What time is it?" I asked.

"Eight, just past," he said as he consulted his watch. He held out the mug.

"Remind me to get your coffee from the car. It's been in there for days."

I took a sip, although coffee wasn't my normal morning drink. "Will it still be okay?"

"Sure, if not, we'll just get more."

He sat on the side of the bed. "I'm sorry I didn't call or text. I had some family drama to deal with. It messed up my mind."

"That's okay, I got a little worried. About you, not about the weekend."

"Talking about this party, we leave in an hour," he said with a smile.

"I bought a card, you'll have to tell me whose party it is."

"No need for cards. I paid for the party, that's enough of a gift."

He stood. "I found pastries," he said, as he left the room.

I placed the mug of coffee on the side and headed for the shower. I tied my hair in a bun on top of my head to save it from getting wet. It didn't appear we had the time for me to wash and blow dry it. Once showered, I pulled on some underwear, jeans, and buttoned up a shirt. I grabbed a jumper, some socks and my Converse, and then headed to the kitchen.

While I sat at the kitchen table eating a pastry, I pulled on my socks and shoes.

"Where are we going?" I asked.

"Sussex Coast. I thought we could stop for lunch, there's an old pub in Rye, then relax for a couple of hours before the party."

"Sounds like a nice idea, thank you for inviting me. Do you have to go home for clothes?"

"No, I have enough clean from my trip."

We chatted throughout the journey, but once again I noticed that evasiveness when I got too personal. He hadn't mentioned the family drama and I didn't ask. He was happy to talk about his businesses but anything else had me feeling like I was intruding. Once again, I questioned exactly what this *thing* was that was going on between us.

We stopped at The George Inn, an old pub in Rye, for lunch. Although I'd visited Rye before, I'd never been inside that pub. It was quaint, with little annex rooms and open fireplaces. I learned it was also a hotel and vowed I'd return to stay there one day. I could picture myself curled up on one of the sofas in the little nooks, reading in front of an open fire with a glass of wine.

Once lunch was done, we continued our journey to the hotel.

The hotel we arrived at was a large manor house, set in beautifully manicured grounds. Mackenzie pulled the car to the front entrance and popped a button for the boot to open. A porter collected the bags and loaded them onto a trolley. We followed him in to reception, where Mackenzie handed over his car keys to allow them to park it. He checked us in; it was as he'd collected the key and we started for the lift, I heard his name being called.

"Gabriella," he said, and I watched the broad smile he'd given her spread across his face.

"I wasn't expecting you this early," she said in an American accent as she strode over.

Jerry was correct; she was stunning. Tall, blonde, manicured, and I was immediately thankful when she caught sight of me and smiled some more.

"Lauren, it's great to finally meet you. I'm thrilled you're able to join us tonight," she said. I detected a Southern accent.

I stepped forward and held out my hand, she ignored it and pulled me into a hug, I laughed.

"Thank you for inviting me," I said, once she'd released me.

I wondered what kind of conversation Mackenzie had with her, she'd said *finally* as if she'd been expecting to meet me before then.

"You look exhausted," she said to Mackenzie.

"I am," he replied.

"Go and rest, we're not doing business this weekend. It's all about me," she said, exaggerating her accent.

"Yes, Ma'am," he replied. It made my heart flutter to hear a slight Southern twang appear in his accent when he spoke to her.

"You hear that, Lauren. He sure knows who the boss is," she said and then winked.

"She's about the only woman on earth capable of kicking my ass," he said.

I laughed. It was another side to Mackenzie I hadn't seen before and I enjoyed their banter.

Gabriella left us and we continued towards the lift. "I really like her," I said.

"I guess we have that same relationship you and Jerry do. Good friends and we work well together."

Not that I should have, but I felt a sense of relief when he'd told me they were just good friends. There was no way I'd be able to compete with her. That thought though, pulled me up short. I shouldn't even have been thinking that way.

"She's your right hand man, so Jerry tells me," I said, once the lift doors closed behind me.

"She is, has been for many years. I couldn't function without her."

"And it's her party?"

"Yes, although don't mention her age, she'd stab me if I told anyone."

I laughed out loud. "How old is she?" I whispered.

He leaned towards my ear, cupping his hand around his mouth, not that there was anyone else in the lift to hear.

"Forty, but do not say I told you that."

"You're kidding me, she doesn't look a day older than I do."

Either I'd had a hard life or she had phenomenal skin, or a great plastic surgeon. She didn't have a wrinkle on her face, her skin was perfectly clear, and her eyes bright.

"It's that Southern gal thing. They don't sit in the sun, take care of themselves, and she has good genes. You should see her mother."

We had arrived at our floor, which had only two doors. Mackenzie checked the number on the key card and headed for one. He opened it and allowed me to enter the suite. The porter had obviously arrived before us as, when I walked into the bedroom to investigate, our bags were laid on the bed.

I unzipped my suit carrier, taking out my dress to hang immediately, fearing it would be wrinkled if I left it in there too long.

I heard Mackenzie on the phone so decided to continue to unpack. I looked at his suit carrier, should I unpack for him? I unzipped and took out a suit, a white shirt and tie, and hung them up; I'd leave him to do the rest. I wasn't sure how comfortable he, or I, would be with me rifling around his underwear and toiletries.

I stood and looked around the room. The large, ornate bedstead that dominated the room blended well with the fairly modern interior. On each corner were wooden posts, beautifully carved. I took my toiletries into the bathroom. If there was such a thing as shower envy, I experienced it then. The shower was the width of the room. There was no door and it had a small wooden bench, although why someone would want to sit, I didn't know, a huge showerhead and jets protruded from the wall.

I placed my toiletry bag on the counter that housed two sinks and walked back into the bedroom.

"I do believe I have shower envy," I said, as I walked back into the living area.

Mackenzie was sitting on the sofa with some papers on his lap.

"It's pretty neat, isn't it?"

"You've stayed here before then?"

"Of course. I ordered champagne," he said, not expanding on when he'd visited the hotel.

A knock at the door interrupted any further conversation. Mackenzie opened it and allowed room service to lay a tray containing an ice bucket, champagne, and two fluted glasses on a consul table. He thanked them, signed the docket and, once they had left, opened the bottle and poured only the one glass.

"Are you not having one?" I asked, expecting him to hand me the glass.

"Take off your shirt," he said.

"Why?"

"Because I asked you to."

He took a sip of the champagne. I unbuttoned my shirt and removed it.

"Take off your bra."

"Are you going to ask me to remove each item of clothing individually?"

"You'll find this more erotic if you kept your mouth shut."

I blinked, rapidly, a couple of times. I wanted to call him out on his comment, but he did that thing with his eyes, the stare that had me rooted to the spot. I removed my bra.

"Jeans."

I slowly slid them to the floor, in as provocative a manner as I could, dragging my socks off at the same time. I'd play along.

"Panties."

I hooked one finger either side of the white lace and very slowly lowered each side. I kept my gaze on him while I lowered them to my knees, then let them fall and stepped out of them.

He stood and looked at me, his gaze raked over my body. Finally he took a step towards me, taking a sip of the champagne. He held the cold glass against one of my nipples. The shock to my body had me yelp. He held it there and his eyes challenged me to move away. I didn't. When he removed the glass my nipple was numb, he lowered his head and sucked it into his mouth, full of the champagne he'd taken earlier. The warm liquid thawed my frozen skin. I gasped at the painful tingling as my nipple came back to life.

He repeated the process with the other one, and I was thankful my overheated skin had warmed the glass slightly.

"Bedroom," he said.

I turned and walked into the room. He motioned with his head for me to climb onto the bed. He placed the glass on the table beside it and pulled his shirt over his head. He fished in his jeans pocket and placed a condom next to the side. I was a little disappointed there was only the one. He lowered his jeans and his cock sprang free, he hadn't worn shorts. He picked up the glass and sat astride my thighs. Silently he tipped the glass slightly until the cold liquid dripped onto that hollow at the base of my throat. He dribbled the champagne over my chest, down my stomach, and eventually poured the contents over my pussy.

The cold liquid, as it hit my clitoris, had me gripping the bedsheet. More so when he lowered his head and lapped it up.

"Holy fuck," I whispered, as his tongue circled, licked, and his mouth sucked.

When he was done, he trailed his tongue the length of my body, lapping up the champagne, finally coming to rest on my throat. I pushed my head back, giving him access.

99

"No more foreplay, I need to fuck you," he whispered against my skin.

I was ready; I was always ready for him.

He tore the condom packet open and quickly rolled it down his cock. Before I had a chance to react, he'd pushed inside me. I wrapped my legs around his waist and he fucked me hard, holding himself above me on his arms.

"I've wanted to do this for a while," he said through gritted teeth.

I tilted my pelvis, forcing him deeper. I wrapped my arms around his back and dug my nails into his skin, raking them down his back as my stomach knotted and heat flushed over my body.

I tried to hold back my orgasm, but it rolled over me, causing me to tense and cry out. He fucked me faster through it. It was only as I was coming down from the high that he gave in to his. It had been short, but oh so sweet.

Mackenzie didn't pull out of me immediately. He gently lowered himself to me and I held him. I liked the feel of his body against mine, the stickiness of the champagne, and his sweat. He nestled his face into the crook of my neck and gave a gentle kiss before rising again and pulling out of me. I felt the void he'd left, not only inside my pussy, but also inside the whole of me.

"An appetiser," he said with a smirk.

He walked naked to the bathroom, removing the condom as he did.

I heard the flow of water as he turned on the shower, and then he called out to me. I smiled as I rose from the bed. He was standing under the jets, his hair already plastered to his forehead. I stepped under, and for a while, he just held me, my back to his chest as water cascaded over us. For that moment, for those few precious seconds, it felt like we had more of a relationship than two people who fucked.

I will not fall for him, was the thought that ran through my head.

I'd begun to think I might not have a choice in that.

****

I sat at the dressing table after drying my hair, applying my makeup, and watching him in the mirror as he buttoned up his shirt. He gave me a wink when he caught me staring. Once I was finished, I unwrapped the towel I had been wearing, and pulled on a black pair of panties, then walked to the wardrobe. He watched me take the dress from the hanger and slip it on. He walked to stand behind me, pushed my hair to one side as he fastened the halter neck. He smiled at me as he planted a gentle kiss on my exposed shoulder.

Something had changed; there had been a shift within him. The brusqueness was gone and had been replaced with a gentleness.

"Ready?" he asked. I ran my fingers once more through my hair, loosening the curls and nodded.

We took the lift down to a ballroom. He was immediately greeted the minute we stepped through the door. He kept his hand on my back and introduced me to everyone that stopped to talk to him. I lost track of names and their relationship to him. Some were colleagues, others were businessmen, and a few were friends of Gabriella's. A waitress stopped in front of us, and he took two glasses of champagne, handing me one.

I spotted Gabriella across the hall. She smiled, broke away from her friends, and walked towards us. She greeted me first with a hug, then kissed Mackenzie on the cheek.

"Happy birthday," I said.

"Thank you. I see you already have drinks, I made sure to have some nice whiskey behind the bar for you, Mackenzie," she said.

"Good. I'll indulge after dinner," he said.

"You saw the guest list, I take it?" she asked.

"I did."

She smiled and nodded, but her comment left me concerned. Mackenzie didn't return the smile.

"You relax, enjoy your evening. I'll behave," he said.

She patted his cheek before leaving. I looked at him.

"I'm not fond of her brother," he said, by way of an explanation.

"Okay. Do you want to mingle? I'll be fine here."

"I didn't bring you to a party to leave you standing in a corner. Haven't you done that enough?"

"I…"

"You're here with me. Where I go, so do you," he said.

I was grateful for that comment. I didn't want to stand in a corner of a room full of strangers on my own, but I didn't want him to think he had to babysit me either.

We walked towards the bar, stopped and chatted. While he spoke to the men, I spoke to their partners. All were very pleasant, and I loved the Southern accent of many.

"Mackenzie Miller!"

I felt him tense before a man interrupted our conversation. He walked over with a lovely elderly woman and her younger companion.

"Daniel." That time, he didn't introduce me.

"And who is this delightful creature?"

I tried not to laugh at his corny words. I held out my hand.

"Lauren Perry, and you are?"

"He didn't tell you who I am? Really, Mackenzie. Daniel Collinsworth, the birthday girl's brother, and archenemy of your friend, Mack."

Mackenzie bristled beside me. "Archenemy, huh? How dull to only have that accolade to boast about. Do you do anything else, Mr. Collinsworth, anything of note?"

"Your girl has a smart tongue, how refreshing," he said, leeringly.

"Fuck off, Daniel," Mackenzie said, surprising me.

Daniel laughed, having achieved his objective in annoying Mackenzie, and walked away.

"Such a douche," the elderly woman said to me. I laughed at her choice of words.

"And my son, unfortunately. Mackenzie, you have my permission to punch him in the nose, but after the party, please," she added.

Mackenzie laughed and kissed her on both cheeks. "Ma'am, it would be my pleasure to knock your son on his ass, it's long overdue. But I wouldn't spoil a party over him."

She patted his cheek, perhaps it was a Southern thing as her daughter had done the same, then asked her escort to show her to her table.

"I love her, so regal. Who is the man with her?" I said.

"Latest boyfriend, I think. No, I shudder to think."

"So, want to tell me about the *douche* whose own mother gives you permission to punch him?"

He turned to face me. "He stole my wife."

I stared at him, unable to utter a word. He stared back at me, not in challenge though, there was a pleading in his eyes to not ask for more information. For a moment we were silent.

"Our table is being seated," he said, finally.

I followed him, still stunned at his confession. When I'd Googled him there had been no mention of a marriage, but then I hadn't really looked beyond confirmation of a South Carolina upbringing and his college photos.

A waitress showed me to my seat. I had Mackenzie to one side and the mother's 'boyfriend' to the other. Mrs. Collinsworth sat regally in her chair next to him. I breathed a sigh of relief that Daniel wasn't on our table. Gabriella placed her hand on my shoulder as she walked to her seat, beside her mother. She leaned down to whisper in my ear.

"I just heard what happened, steer clear of Daniel, for Mackenzie's sake, please?"

"Trust me, I have no intention of getting within five feet of him."

"Mackenzie is very protective and volatile. I'd hate to have my party end in a fistfight."

"It won't, certainly not because of me." I smiled up at her.

When she walked off, I turned to see Mackenzie staring at me.

"What was that all about?" he asked.

"Girl talk."

Wine was poured and I chatted to the 'boyfriend,' whose name I discovered was Paul. He was very charming, regaled the table with funny stories and kept us all entertained. I could see why Mrs. Collinsworth liked to have him around, although there had to be at least a thirty year age gap.

Small plates of seared duck breast in a balsamic sauce were placed in front of us, artisan bread rolls were offered from a basket, and more wine was poured. I opted to alternate, one glass of wine and one glass of water.

I was spoken to and treated as if I was one of the family. Mrs. Collinsworth grilled me on British etiquette and asked what royals I'd had the pleasure of meeting. She told me she was on a visit, specifically for her daughter's birthday party and expected Mackenzie to take her on a tour around London. I got the impression no one said no to Mrs. Collinsworth. She reminded me of a character from *Gone With The Wind.*

I told her she must do afternoon tea at The Ritz, and it pleased me when she'd asked me to arrange it and join her. She loved my accent and wanted to spend some 'girl' time. As the evening wore on, I had to catch the guilt that bubbled in my stomach. Those people thought I was Mackenzie's partner, and I knew I wasn't.

The table was cleared and Mackenzie stood, holding his hand out to me. I reached for it and we walked to the bar. He asked for two whiskeys, both with ice. The bartender placed two coasters on the bar, then the glasses on top.

"Enjoying yourself?" he asked.

"Very much so."

Other than the night out with Jenny and Sally, it was the most enjoyable evening I'd had in over a year. The band struck up and we turned to watch the sprightly Mrs. Collinsworth be waltzed around the dance floor.

"He's good for her, keeps her young," I said.

"Mmm, he also knows she is worth fucking millions."

"As long as she has her finances in place, what does that matter? Look at her, look at that smile. You know, it's not always about the money. Sometimes it's about the company and having fun."

He took a sip of his whiskey. "I'll respectfully disagree with you there."

"You may have gotten burned, Mackenzie, but it doesn't mean everyone else is out to do the same."

I regretted the words as they left my mouth. His face hardened, and for a moment, I'd lost him. I used the excuse of picking up my drink, so I didn't have to face his stare.

"Dance with me," he said, throwing me completely.

He took hold of my hand and led me to the dance floor. I didn't do classical dancing; I had no idea about the dance other people were doing. I just followed his lead, laughing as I stumbled around. He dropped the hold and pulled me close, opting for the safer option of swaying gently. We dance for a couple more songs before heading back to the bar.

Once again we were stopped en route. But when I saw Daniel approaching, a little unsteady on his feet, I pulled gently on Mackenzie's arm to continue to the bar and out of the way.

"I need the ladies," I said. He nodded as he ordered another round of drinks.

I made my way out of the ballroom and along the corridor. I'd locked myself in a cubicle just as I heard the door open and two women walk in.

"Did you see who Mackenzie brought?" one said.

"She's staff, works for his new company," the other said.

"Really? Fucking her way to the top then, I guess."

I held my breath as bile rose to my throat at their words. I was about to stand and flush, alerting them to the fact they were not alone when I heard a cubicle door open.

I recognised the voice immediately. "Ladies, keep your trash talk out of my party. It doesn't matter who she is, or where she works, she is here as his guest. It's not like either of you haven't had the pleasure of Mackenzie now, is it?" I saw feet scuttle to the main door.

I let out a sob as I opened the cubicle door.

"Aw, sweetie, you heard that, huh?"

I nodded as I leaned on the sink and looked at my reflection. A tear rolled down my cheek.

"Here, you wipe that pretty face and take no notice. Jealous bitches, that's all."

"Does he *fuck* all this staff?" I whispered.

"No, those two were a mistake, a long time ago. Why they are still around is beyond me. In fact, I don't think they will be for very long."

"You can't ask him to fire them," I said.

"Lauren, I do the hiring and firing, and I just don't like them. They are easily replaced. Do you like him?" she asked.

"We're just having fun right now," I said, not knowing what the correct term for our *arrangement* was.

"Then continue to do so. So what if you work for one of the many companies he owns? Does it affect how you do your job?"

"No, not at all."

"Then there is no problem, for now," she said gently.

It wasn't a veiled threat, more a caution, and I believed she meant it in the kindest way. Perhaps she was telling me to be careful.

I was interrupted from answering by the door being pushed open and Mackenzie striding in.

"You really shouldn't be in here," I said, as I wiped my eyes.

"Usual?" he said to Gabriella. She nodded.

"Deal with them as you wish," he said.

"How did you know?" I asked.

"They are complaining about receiving a tongue lashing from Gabriella, I guessed."

"I'll leave you two to it," she said, and then left.

"Come on," he said, taking my hand.

We walked back into the bar and straight to Mrs. Collinsworth.

"We're calling it a night. I wanted to let you know, I'll be in touch in a couple of days in case we miss you in the morning," Mackenzie said.

"That would be wonderful. Good night to you, Lauren," she said.

Without a goodbye to anyone else, we left the room. Mackenzie didn't speak while we crossed the foyer and headed to the lift. I saw him glance at his watch, I also watched as he nodded to a suited man, standing by reception.

We rode the lift in silence, and as it ascended floor-by-floor, so he changed, again. The wicked smirk had returned, as had the glint in his eyes. His body tensed and his stare became intense.

"I have a surprise for you," he whispered, as he opened the suite door.

I walked in expecting to find the surprise. There was nothing obvious.

"Bedroom," he said.

Again, I expected to see something, flowers maybe, but it was as we'd left it, other than the bed had been turned down. I stood in the middle of the room and watched him walk towards me. He passed and opened the closet, reaching into his overnight bag. Whatever he had retrieved, he held it in a closed fist. He turned me so I was facing the full-length mirror.

"So I can see your face," he whispered over my shoulder.

I felt my heartbeat increase. He raised his hand and I noticed black material. He slipped an eye mask over my head, covering my eyes. He unclipped the neck of my dress and it slid from my body. I stepped out of it and heard him push it away, with his foot I guessed.

"I'm asking you to trust me," he whispered. I nodded my head. That was my biggest mistake.

Chapter Nine

I knew Mackenzie was standing behind me, he held my wrists to my hips. The sound of the suite door opening and then softly closing had me on alert, but it was a minute later when I felt a fingertip, or more importantly, a nail trail down my chest. I opened my mouth to speak and found soft lips on mine. I tried to raise my arms, I wanted to pull the blindfold from my eyes, but he held me still.

I tried to speak, but when I did, a smooth tongue swiped across mine. I twisted my body, wanting to break free.

"Shush, relax," he whispered in my ear.

My heart hammered in my chest; it sped further when I felt those fingers gently strum over one breast. As much as I wanted to kick out, to fight, I was paralysed into submission. My body immediately fucking betrayed me. My skin goosebumped at her touch, and I knew that it was a woman by the feel of her lips, by her touch. My nipples pebbled, painfully hard. My body started to shake.

"Just feel," he whispered.

As much as I didn't want to, my tongue responded. Her kiss was so very different to a man's, it was delicate, tantalising, teasing. She rolled my nipple around in her fingers, increasing the pressure. She stepped into me, and I could feel a naked body. I could feel pert breasts and erect nipples. Mackenzie stepped closer as well. I could feel his erection against my back. I was sandwiched between them. I guess he'd done that to stop me from stepping back or turning around. I was trapped.

He still had my hands held tight to my hips and his restraint, her kiss, had my stomach knotting.

He kissed the side of my neck; he trailed his tongue from my shoulder to my ear as she slid her hands up to my shoulders, then gently down my sides, ghosting the sides of my breasts. My body shuddered at her soft touch.

"Remember, you can always say no," he whispered. I didn't reply.

I tried to stop the moan but it was released before I realised. It was as if my brain was one step behind my body's reaction. My clitoris throbbed.

109

"Good girl," he whispered.

She stopped kissing me and I found myself missing her mouth. Her lips travelled down my throat, and I leaned my head back on Mackenzie's chest. I could hear his breaths; I could feel his heart beat rapidly against my back.

She gently licked, nipped at my skin until she took a nipple in her mouth. The texture of her mouth was different, her technique was different; she knew how to pleasure me. She knew the exact pressure to apply when she gently bit down; she knew the pace to flick her tongue over the hardened bud.

'Oh, God," I whispered, struggling to catch my breath.

I was totally in the zone. I wasn't in a bedroom in a hotel, I wasn't a woman who had been cheated on; I wasn't someone who worked hard with no play. I was a wanton woman, whose flesh was been brought to burning point by another woman's tongue. I was a woman, who had all train of reasonable thought stolen by another woman's lips. I was a woman, who had lost all desire to fight against the touch of another woman. I gave in, completely allowing her to take over my body and my mind. I relaxed and felt the tension drain from my shoulders. I also felt the pressure of Mackenzie's hands lessen on my wrists.

He threaded his fingers in mine.

I missed her mouth on my nipple when she pulled away to give the same attention to the other. While she did, she lowered her hands some more, stopping at the top of my panties.

She kissed down my stomach as she lowered them. I lifted one foot, then the other, and they were removed. I could feel her face close to my pussy, I could feel her breath, and even before she'd touched me, I moaned out loud.

She ran her hands along the inside of my legs, but stopped halfway up my thighs. She applied the gentlest of pressure and I parted my legs.

"You have no idea how fucking beautiful this looks," Mackenzie whispered.

He begun to gently grind his cock into my lower back, at the same time she kissed the inside of my thigh, trailing her tongue slowly upwards. My legs began to shake and I tightened my grip on Mackenzie's hands. If she went where I was imagining, wanting her to go, I wasn't sure my legs would hold me up.

"Don't let me fall," I whispered.

"You'll fall, baby, just not in the way you think. But I'll catch you," he replied.

His hot breath on my neck had the same effect as her tongue on my thigh. She trailed further up and over my hip, across my lower stomach and then down the other side. When she pulled away, I felt coldness on my wet skin. By the way her hands slid back up my sides, I knew she had stood up. When her soft lips found mine, I made no attempt to stop her that time. I opened my mouth, I let in her tongue and I kissed her back, fiercely. When she moaned, I nearly fell apart. Her moan was absorbed by my mouth and travelled to the pit of my stomach. That sound alone took me to the brink of an orgasm.

"Step back," I heard Mackenzie say.

"No!" I said, surprising myself.

He chuckled as he let go of my hands and placed one arm under my knees. He lifted me, laying me gently on the bed. For a moment I lay on my own. I made no attempt to take off the blindfold, I had no doubt at some point I would though.

I heard the scrape of a chair as it was brought close and the rustle of discarded clothes. I licked my dry lips, as I understood.

I felt the gentle dip of the bed and she lay beside me. Her fingers trailed down my body and I parted my legs. She twirled them around my pubic hair before leaning over and kissing me again. That time I wrapped one hand in her hair. It was silky and straight. As she inserted two fingers inside me, I fell apart. My body jerked off the bed. I parted my legs as far as I could and slid one hand down my stomach, pushing my fingers inside me to join hers.

"Fuck," I heard Mackenzie hiss.

I cried out. I writhed as my orgasm rolled over me. Her mouth was on my nipple again and her body partially covered mine. I tightened my hand in her hair as our fingers fucked me through an intense orgasm. My legs shook, my stomach knotted, my skin felt on fire as wave after wave of heat travelled over me.

"Lick her cunt," I heard him say, there was desperation in his voice.

When her head moved down my stomach, I pulled off the eye mask. She looked up at me with a smile. She was exquisite. Red hair framed a pale face with a smattering of freckles across her nose. I couldn't take my eyes from her as she lowered her head, slid her body down the bed and knelt between my legs, all the while her fingers still worked inside me. I pulled mine free as her tongue lapped at my cum. I raised my hand to mouth, turned my head to Mackenzie and sucked the juices from my fingers.

He was naked; one hand was wrapped around his cock, pumping furiously. The other gripped the arm of the chair he'd sat in and that he had pulled close to the bed. I could see every tendon, every muscle tensed.

I wanted to close my eyes, I wanted to absorb the sensation of her soft tongue on my clitoris, but I wanted to see him watching us.

His eyes were dark, his pupils dilated with lust. He bit down on his lower lip and as I cried out, he moaned. His chest heaved as he breathed heavily and sweat had beaded on his forehead.

The sight of him enhanced what she was doing to me. She held my hips but I tilted my pelvis, giving her better access to me. She darted her tongue inside, although not able to reach those areas he could, she curled her tongue, the tip dragging down inside me. I gripped the bedding, pulling the sheet towards me as I screamed out in pure pleasure.

My head spun as I came again. I could feel the wetness drip from me. I could smell my arousal. At the same time, I heard Mackenzie cry out, as if through gritted teeth. I watched as milky fluid spurted from his cock and coated his hand. He'd thrown his head back; the knuckles on the hand that gripped the arm of the chair, were white. He bucked off it slightly as he pumped his cum over himself. It was a beautiful sight.

I reached out for his hand and he opened his eyes at my touch. I pulled it towards my mouth and licked the cum from his fingers. His hand shook slightly as he inserted two fingers inside my mouth. While she sucked my pussy, I sucked his fingers.

She crawled up my body, inserted her tongue in my mouth, and we both licked his fingers. He groaned, and I moaned, as she lay on me. The feel of her soft skin on mine inflamed me further. The texture of her nipples against my breasts made me needy for them. I pulled Mackenzie's fingers from my mouth, and I placed one hand on the back of her head, one on her hip, I rolled us over. While I lowered my head to taste her skin, to circle my tongue around her nipple, I felt Mackenzie climb on the bed beside us.

He trailed a finger down my back, already slick with sweat. He parted my backside and there was no need for lubricant, my cum had seeped to the place he gently pressed his finger against. I raised myself to my knees; I wanted him to finger my arse, while I sucked on her nipple. I wanted to be pleasured by him, while I pleasured her.

I didn't know, nor cared, whether her moan was genuine, but her puckered nipples and hot skin were enough to have me believe it might be. I licked down her stomach, pausing at her navel. She shuffled up the bed, I moved slightly up while Mackenzie rearranged himself to kneel behind me. It was all so fluid; there was no awkwardness in repositioning ourselves. He fingered my arse and I licked her clitoris. Her scent, her taste, blew my mind. She was sweet yet with a slight metallic tang. The texture against my tongue as I inserted it inside her was like nothing I'd experienced before. Hot spongy flesh demanded my tongue delve deeper. She raised her hips, giving me a better angle.

I felt Mackenzie's mouth on my lower back; he'd sunk his teeth into my skin, licking his bite afterwards.

I raised my head slightly, angling it towards him. "Fuck me," I said.

He didn't question, nor waste time retrieving a condom. Within seconds he was inside me, and the fullness of him, the scrape of his ridged cock against my walls after the softness of her tongue, had me spiralling. I licked, I sucked and she moaned. I watched her raise her hands above her head and grip the headboard. Her head rolled back slightly, and her delicate mouth opened as she gasped.

Something clicked inside me; I lost control and all sense of responsibility. I didn't care what I did; I wanted it all. I wanted him, and I wanted her. I wanted to be fucked every way he could, and I wanted to fuck him.

I raised my head and shifted my body forwards; he had no choice to pull out of me.

"Lie down," I said. For the first time in my life I was taking control, I was calling the shots, demanding and taking.

He slid down the bed and I looked over to her. "I think we need to fuck him," I said.

I had no idea where the words had come from, and I didn't recognise the husky voice that had produced them.

The conspiratorial smile between us made me tingle. We were two women, who knew what they wanted, and were about to take it. I slid my legs across his waist, and I watched as she crawled down the bed and slid across his face.

"Lauren…" he said.

"Relax, just feel. I want to watch you fuck her with your tongue."

This wasn't me; someone had taken over my body, my mind. Years of mindless, boring sex had me behaving like an animal, like a slut, and I loved every second of it.

The sound he made as he licked her, the sounds she produced when he did caused my core to tighten further. I lowered myself gently onto his cock. I closed my eyes and listened. Flesh collided with flesh; the scent of sex filled the room, and the sounds of moans reverberated through me. I rode him hard. I felt her lips on mine, as he licked her. While I rode him, we shared a gentle and tender kiss. The contradiction of that wasn't lost on me.

When I'd come again, he tried to lift me off him by raising his hips, but I wanted his cum inside me. I wanted to raise my body from his and feel it run down my thighs. He cried out my name as his body shuddered and his stomach tensed. He pumped his cum inside me, his cock pulsing as he did. I felt every single minute movement.

She raised herself from his face. He'd slumped back on the bed, trying to get his breathing under control. His chin glistened. She placed her hand on the side of my face and mouthed two words.

"Thank you."

She climbed from the bed, pulled a robe from the floor, and wrapped herself in it. She left us alone.

The silence was interrupted by his growl, a sound that had the hairs on my neck stand on end. He sat up, he reached for me, grabbing my shoulder and pushing me sideways until I fell. He positioned himself above me, and he fucked me again. I couldn't even begin to think where he'd gotten the energy from, how he was able to produce another hard-on after so many orgasms, but he had. My legs trembled and all strength left me. He raised one of my legs and wrapped it around his waist; he repeated his action with the other. I couldn't do it myself. While he pumped his cock inside me, the cum from his previous orgasm slid down to my arse.

Our bodies were slick with sweat. My hair had stuck to my forehead. He fucked me hard as if punishing me. He held my hands above my head, not caring that he hurt my wrists. There was not a shred of emotion, of tenderness, on his face. He was devoid of all feeling as he gave me what *he* needed. He'd lost control earlier; he was taking it back.

I think I passed out from the orgasm that tore me apart. I know I screamed; I heard him scream out, too. I know I cried, sobbed even. I felt tears run down my face and when he kissed me, I felt the wetness of his own tears on his cheeks.

We'd gone beyond the game; we'd crossed so far over the boundary there was no way back.

****

I had no concept of time, other than I heard birds chirping outside the window, and dawn was breaking when I woke. Mackenzie was asleep beside me and the bedclothes were a tangled mess beneath us. I looked at him and let more tears roll down my cheeks. I felt guilt that I had enjoyed every second of being fucked by another woman, shame that I had fucked her back. I felt embarrassed that I'd wanted him so desperately I'd done whatever he had instigated.

I gently rolled from the bed and padded to the bathroom. I closed the door behind me. I didn't want the sound of a shower running to disturb him; instead I filled the sink and washed her, him, and me from my body. I dressed as quietly as I could, threw my dress and shoes in my overnight bag. I left the suit carrier, deeming it too bulky to carry myself.

Then I ran.

I left the hotel, not caring that my hair wasn't brushed and in knots. It was too early for other guests to be up and about. I wanted to kiss the doorman for having a taxi arrive so quickly, and I was taken to the nearest train station, where I waited. I think I was in shock, my body moved on autopilot as I climbed aboard the carriage. I curled into a corner seat for the one and a half hour journey to London Victoria.

I tried to stop the shaking. I closed my eyes against the memories and the tears that threatened to fall. I was so cold and without a coat. A half-hour into the journey, I heard my phone ring. I ignored it and it went to voice mail. It immediately rang again, then again. I heard the beep of text messages. I pulled it from my bag and switched it to silent. Mackenzie had rung me three times; he continued to ring as I held the phone in my hand. I read his texts.

Lauren, where are you?

Call me, please. I'm fucking worried.

Where the fuck are you? I can't leave until I know you're safe.

Tell me where you are. I'll come get you.

Answer your fucking phone, damn it!

My fingers shook as I finally replied.

I'm on my way home. I'm safe. I can't explain, please leave me alone, just for now.

He replied.

I'm sorry, Lauren, I can't do that. If you don't text me to say you arrived home safely, I'll kick your fucking door down.

I covered my mouth to hold in the sob.

I'll text.

I didn't receive another message from him.

I closed my eyes, hoping for some sleep, anything to stop the images flooding my mind. I could still smell her, and me, on my skin.

I felt sick to my stomach. I needed a drink; I needed to eat to quell the nausea. The first thing I did when the train arrived in Victoria Station was to buy a disgusting bagel from a fast-food burger outlet. I drank down a full fat Coke, something I never drank normally, without taking a breath. My hands shook as I guzzled down the food. I must have looked like a drug addict coming down from a high. It hit me like a kick to the stomach and I doubled over. That was exactly what was happening.

I was coming down from such an intense high; it may well have been cocaine rushing through my veins instead of the unbridled passion I'd experienced.

Mackenzie Miller should have been a class A drug. He was as addictive, as powerful, and as damaging.

When my body returned to some form of normality, I headed out to one of the waiting taxis. Other than to give my address; I didn't speak. I didn't answer any of the questions thrown at me. As we pulled up at my apartment block, and I fumbled inside my purse for money, the driver looked in his rearview mirror again.

"Are you all right?" he asked.

I looked at him and caught sight of myself in his mirror. My eyes were red with the tears I'd shed. I placed the money on the tray in the glass panel that divided us.

"No," I said, and then climbed out.

The first thing I did was to run a bath. I hadn't used the bath in a long time. When it was filled with warm water, I lowered myself in.

A burn raged between my thighs and my back stung from his bite. I didn't want to entertain the idea I could have caught something.

She had to be an escort. I wouldn't hold that against her, but the thought that he even knew where and how to find one disturbed me. She hadn't spoken at all, and he hadn't used her name. Did that mean he didn't know her? If so, how did he know she was clean? I shuddered at the thought.

I had no idea what to do; I'd make a point of calling my doctor in the morning. But could I sit there and explain I'd had sex with him, and her, at the same time, and ask what the health implications of that were?

Then another thought hit me. We hadn't used protection and I wasn't on the pill. Yet another round of tears rolled down my sore cheeks.

The idea that I could have gotten pregnant horrified me. It wasn't the getting pregnant part that upset me, but carrying a child outside a relationship, trying to go it alone, terrified me. My life was a mess, my divorce was going to be traumatic, and I did not need the stress of becoming a single mother added to that.

I knew I was overthinking everything, but my brain wouldn't let up. I was scared, but I couldn't get past the fact that I had loved the experience.

Mackenzie Miller had fulfilled my fantasies; that was the game, it's what he did. But in doing so he'd left me feeling empty and lonelier that I ever had. I'd been a fucking fool thinking I could play along.

I lowered my head to my hands and sobbed. I cried harder than I had when Scott had betrayed me. In one way, it felt worse. I'd opened myself up to the pain and disgust I felt inside.

I climbed from the bath and wrapped a towel around me. I picked up my phone and my heart froze when I saw the last text he'd sent.

I'm on my way. You didn't text.

'Oh, God," I said as I replied.

I'm home. I took a bath. Please, I need to think, I need to be alone. If I have to beg, Mackenzie, I will. Let me be, please.

Jesus, Lauren. I just... I don't know what to say. He replied.

Don't say anything. Just let me be. I'm saying no, just for today.

He didn't reply again. I made tea, as if that would cure me, and carried it to the bedroom. I climbed under the duvet and drank. Despite my bath, it took a while before my body stopped shivering. I sank down into the pillows and slept.

Chapter Ten

I slept through the day and most of the way through the night. When I woke, my body ached. I climbed from the bed and took a shower, scrubbing my skin until it was red and sore.

I didn't want to go into work, but we had a meeting scheduled at eleven. Jerry was making an announcement, and I believed it to be his decision to sell out. I'd resign immediately, regardless of whether Jerry sold his remaining shares or not.

I decided to see if I could find a sexual health clinic locally. I needed the morning after pill, although it was technically the morning after the morning. I wasn't sure what I'd do if they told me it was too late. I waited until eight o'clock and made a couple of phone calls. I then texted Jerry to tell him I had a doctor's appointment but would be there for the meeting.

Are you ill? He'd asked.

Girl stuff. From experience those two words tended to end any further questioning.

I also texted Jenny to let her know I'd be late.

****

I took a taxi to the clinic, not being familiar with the address. I was thankful that there wasn't a neon sign flashing *'sluts welcome.'* I mentally slapped myself for that thought. I had to take a ticket and wait for my number to be called. I sat beside a gum-chewing girl, wearing grubby clothes and with filthy nails.

"What you here for?" she asked, blowing a bubble once she'd spoken.

"Same as you, probably," I replied.

She laughed, hacking up her lungs at the same time.

She looked me up and down, and I wasn't sure she was admiring my suit. "I doubt that, love."

I wanted to shuffle up a couple of seats but was too scared to offend her if I did. I read the signs on the walls, terrifying myself further by learning of all the diseases I could have caught.

When it was my turn, I rushed through the doors to an examination room.

"Hi, take a seat," the nurse said. "Right, let's get some details from you."

She wanted the usual, name, address, date of birth, known illnesses and doctor's details. She then asked me what I was attending for.

I swallowed the lump that had formed in my throat and knew tears had welled in my eyes. She placed her hand on my arm.

"You can tell me, there isn't anything I haven't already heard," she said.

"I, err, I need the morning after pill, except the unprotected sex was Saturday night, or it could have been early hours on Sunday morning, I'm not sure."

"You're not sure? Can you explain that?" I saw concern flash over her face.

"Oh, it was consensual, don't worry, it just…it just went on over a period of time."

"Okay, so we can offer you Levonelle, it's effective up to seventy-two hours after unprotected sex. I need to warn you of some side effects. You may experience headaches, queasiness, dizziness, experience tender breasts, or abdominal pain. If you vomit, you have to return for another dose."

I nodded as she handed me a tablet and a small plastic cup of water. I was expecting a prescription. "Now, birth control?" she said.

"I don't need to worry about that, this was a one off, trust me. I won't be…"

She handed me a tissue as the tears fell. "I'd still like you to consider some form of birth control. Just take this leaflet and have a read through."

"There's something else. I don't know how to say this." I took a deep breath. "There was another person involved, I think she may have been an escort. I'm worried about being *clean*." I'd blurted the sentence out.

"Are you experiencing any unusual symptoms, discharge, itchiness, bleeding?"

"No."

"Do you know where the escort came from? Were they picked up from the street, for example?"

"No, we were in a hotel and I think it was all pre-arranged. There was a man in a suit; I didn't connect it until now. He might have been her pimp."

"A man in a suit probably isn't a pimp, more her security."

"She was clean, as in washed and…you know what I mean?"

"I do. Now, Lauren, we can do screening, but it's a little early to tell. I would recommend the first thing you do is to speak to your partner. I can book an appointment for you, it's a simple blood and urine test, and the results can be sent directly to you."

I nodded my head. "I'd like the screening."

"I'll book an appointment for a week's time. If you experience anything on this list, you call." She handed me another leaflet and a small card with a new appointment.

I left quickly, avoiding eye contact with anyone, and hailed a taxi.

****

"Are you okay? Jerry said you had a doctor's appointment," Jenny asked as I walked through to my office.

"He has a big mouth. Just girl stuff," I said.

"Okay, they called the meeting early, I did text you. They're starting in a few minutes."

"Oh, I had my phone on silent, did they say why?"

"No, but there is a stunning woman with Jerry right now."

I frowned. *Gabriella?* I thought.

"Okay, I'll dump my bags and head on up."

The boardroom was on the same floor as Jerry's office. Not because he had the space but he was too lazy to walk anywhere else. I was the last to walk into the boardroom. The other heads of department were already seated and Gabriella was standing with Jerry. Both smiled over at me. I took a seat.

"Guys, you know Mackenzie bought into the business. Well, he has made me an offer I can't refuse," he chuckled. "Get it? He looks Italian doesn't he?" No one laughed with him.

"Anyway, I've decided to accept this offer and sell out."

A murmur went round the office. Jerry was bombarded with questions. He held up his hands for silence.

"I'd like to introduce Gabriella Collinsworth. She pretty much runs all Mackenzie's operations in the U.K. She'll explain how this is going to work."

I watched her take command of the room. She was confident; she stood tall and made eye contact with every person in that room. She lingered a little longer on me.

"Thank you, Jerry. First I'd like to congratulate you guys. You've helped to build a thriving business. I know this may have come as a surprise, and I'd like to assure you this business will be left in good hands."

"What about our jobs?" Scott had interrupted her.

"You are?"

"Scott Perry, Head of Development. I'd like to know how secure our jobs are."

"Mr. Perry. This business will merge with another of a similar nature. Whilst we try to ensure all members of staff retain their positions, I can't guarantee you that will be the case for everyone. However..." She held up her hand to stop the immediately chatter.

"However, if we have a duplication of positions, in the first instance we offer relocation and retraining. We don't walk in and put people out of jobs, if we can help it."

"Who will run this new company?" Scott asked, disdain in his voice.

"We have CEOs running the day-to-day stuff, but I oversee all U.K. operations, Mr. Perry."

"So no Mackenzie then?"

"Mr. Miller has many businesses to oversee, both here and abroad. As I said, I run all U.K. operations. I have alongside me a dedicated team of chief executives."

"So you'll appoint someone to take over from Jerry?"

"Yes, that person will report directly to me."

"And who will that be?"

"That isn't a decision to be announced yet."

She then cut off the rest of Scott's questions and informed us of the company we would be merging with. She handed out a brochure; although it was a company I wasn't aware of, the brochure certainly made them look impressive.

"Are there any questions?" she asked.

I raised my hand. "Lauren," she said.

"I'd just like to welcome you. I'm thrilled to be on board at this exciting time."

"Arse licker," I heard whispered loud enough to prompt a chuckle. I slunk back in my seat.

"Thank you, that was kind of you. I'll be meeting with each of you individually, over a period of time. Mr. Miller has already formed an opinion on where he sees each of your positions within the new group. You'll be notified of any changes the minute they happen."

Chairs scraped against the wooden floor, and with grumbles, the guys left.

"Lauren, do you think I could have a moment?" Gabriella asked.

"I'll leave you to it," Jerry said, leaving and closing the door behind him.

Gabriella perched on the edge of the table. "I'll come straight to the point."

I held my breath, waiting for the tongue-lashing I thought I'd receive.

"I want you as CEO, as does Mackenzie."

I wasn't expecting that, at all. "I…I don't understand."

"We believe in placing as many capable women in positions they deserve. We both feel you have the potential to do the job."

"But if we're merging, isn't there already a CEO?"

"Yes, someone wanting to leave. But he's willing to hang on a while and assist you."

"Have you spoken to Mackenzie about this?"

"Of course."

"When?"

"We've been speaking for weeks about it. He's had to fly to one of our projects in Scotland last night, otherwise he'd be here himself."

"I think you should reconfirm that with him."

"Did you guys have a falling out?"

"Yes."

"I can assure you, Lauren, when Mackenzie makes a business decision, he doesn't let personal issues interfere with that. I have no doubt he hasn't changed his mind."

"I'd just like you double check. I was going to tender my notice today."

"Can I persuade you to wait?"

"I don't know. I guess he's told you. I'm going through a divorce; it's going to get nasty. For that reason alone, I'm not sure I'm your best candidate. I don't have the respect of my colleagues, and I most certainly won't once they know what I've done."

"Oh, Lauren." She sighed. "No one needs to know anything. And you know what? You Brits really have an uptight attitude towards relationships sometimes." She smiled as she spoke.

"It's hard enough being a woman in a position of authority in this country. We don't get treated the same, nor paid the same."

"It's the same worldwide, Lauren, and it's one thing Mackenzie is dedicated to eradicating within his organisation. I won't accept your resignation today, not until you've had a chance to work out whatever happened between you two, and not before you've had a taste of what's being offered. Give me a couple of months, at least. If you still wish to resign, then so be it."

"He's very much into empowering women, isn't he?" I said, not for one minute meaning within his businesses.

"After what his wife did to him, yes."

I looked at her. "And I guess you won't tell me, will you?"

"No. It's his story to tell. Ask him."

I smiled at her. I very much doubted, other than at work, I'd see him again to be able to ask.

"Oh, and don't forget, you promised my overbearing mother that you'd take her to The Ritz. She will hold you to that," she said then laughed.

"I love your mother."

"Until she's your mother."

We laughed as she collected her mug and we left the boardroom. She headed for Jerry's office and I took the opposite direction to the stairs.

"Sucking up, huh?" I heard as I entered the stairwell.

"Yeah, something like that," I said, not wanting to give Scott a dignified answer.

"I sent the divorces papers back. Sandra and I want to get married as soon as possible, so if you could rush it along."

"That's great news, Scott. I'm thrilled for you."

Inside I died just a little more.

"Yeah, we have such a great time together, we should have done this years ago."

"You should have. So what exciting things did you do this weekend?"

"Shopped for new furniture, I don't want anything from the apartment. Did you manage to get out at all?"

"I did, I spent an amazing weekend, down on the Sussex Coast. Wasn't looking at furniture though." I leaned a little closer to him. "I was having the best sex I've ever had, so yeah, you should have left a long time ago. I can't believe what I've been missing out on."

I carried on walking down the stairs. I wouldn't cry. I held my shoulders high and my back straight.

"Bitch," he said and I laughed.

I returned to my office, collected my bags and left, telling Jenny that I had a meeting I'd totally forgotten about, to attend. She didn't look up from her computer but waved anyway.

I took a taxi straight home.

I sat at my kitchen table and twisted my phone in my hands. I had to ask. I sent a text.

I know you're in Scotland right now, but I have to ask this. Was she clean?

It was a half-hour before a reply came.

Are you fucking kidding me? Do you think I'd subject you to anything I hadn't checked out first? Of course she was clean, I even paid for the fucking tests. I'm going to call in a half-hour, okay?

No, I can't talk right now. I'm about to go into a meeting. I just needed to ask, I lied.

I switched off my phone, just in case, and then cried again. I grabbed a tissue from my bag and wiped my eyes, took a couple of headache tablets to stave off the raging one I could feel coming on, and stripped out of my clothes. In just my underwear, I climbed back into bed. It wasn't that I needed sleep; I just wanted the comfort and warmth of the duvet to hold me.

****

I must have slept because I was jolted awake by a banging on my front door. I lay still; pretending I wasn't in, and hoping whoever it was would go away. I sure needed to speak to someone about how easy it seemed to be to get through the main block door.

The banging persisted. Eventually I heard Jerry call out. I climbed from the bed and dragged on jeans and a t-shirt.

"Jesus, you look like shit," he said when I'd opened the apartment door.

"Thank you," I replied, opening it wide to allow him in.

"What's wrong, Lauren?"

"I feel like I look. Maybe I have a bug coming, I'll be back in tomorrow, and I'll catch up on anything I missed today."

"I'm not worried about work, I'm concerned about you."

"Honestly, I have a ton of shit to deal with, Scott and the divorce. I guess it's just got me down today. I'm fine."

He stared at me, not convinced. "Coffee?" I asked.

He took a seat at the kitchen table while I put the kettle on. I made two cups then joined him. I told him what I'd received from the solicitors, about the division of assets, and what Scott had said that morning.

"I guarantee he isn't rushing to get married, he's just trying to hurt you."

"I know that, and he succeeded. And stupidly I told him a load of shit that I bet he'll spread all around the office."

"What did you tell him?"

"That I'd spent the weekend having wonderful sex."

"Did you?"

I looked at him. "You did!" he said.

"Don't for one minute think I'm going to tell you anything. Anyway, if I divide up my assets, because you can fucking bet all of a sudden he doesn't have any, I don't know if I can afford to stay here."

"So move. It's all a bit…sterile," he said.

"That may well be, but it's *my* sterile. It was my money that fucking bought this."

"You must be able to argue that?"

"No, because he paid bills, contributed, and what's mine is half his."

"I know he has a pension, I see his payslip," he said.

"But how can you divide up a pension, something neither of us gets for another thirty years?"

"I don't know, ask your solicitor."

"I've emailed her. I just want it all over and done with, to be honest. I'm going to call an estate agent tomorrow and get it valued, then see where to go from there. Maybe it is time for a change."

"That offer of joining me on a holiday is still open," he said.

"I'd love to, but you know I can't. I have to get down and see Mum at some point soon. And my boss isn't overly generous with holiday leave," I said with a wink.

"Since I'm not about to be the boss anymore, you never know what the terms of the new one will be."

"Are you happy about selling out?"

"I was, now I'm not so sure, but I signed the contract so I don't think there's any backing out. I can't turn down the money, it would be a risk to continue for another ten years, so I have to make myself happy."

"I think you did the right thing."

"I guess it's time for changes all round," he said.

I smiled and sipped on my coffee. "I told Mackenzie part of the deal was that he had to keep you employed," Jerry said.

"I wish you hadn't done that."

I wanted to fucking thank Jerry, in a not so nice way. Did that mean I was only offered the position of CEO so a deal could be struck? That thought just about topped off my day.

"There were a few people I said I was concerned about, I wanted to make sure you all had jobs after I left. Anyway, I'll be off. You know where I'll be if you need me."

I walked him to the apartment door. "Oh, how did you get through the main door?" I asked.

"Key code thingy is broken, the door's open. Although, last time I came here, I just pressed a button, thinking it was your number, said, 'it's me' and they opened the door."

"Great. I'll get on to someone tomorrow. So much for security."

Jerry left and I washed up the two cups. I made myself a snack, not having much appetite and fired up my laptop. I opened my emails to check on what I'd missed. My fingers hovered over one from Mackenzie sent the previous day.

You know what infuriates me? You ignoring me. I've tried calling. I've texted. Your phone is switched off. I gave you an opportunity to experience something you said you wanted. And I fucking hate having to explain myself in an email. I do face-to-face, Lauren. If we have a problem, we sit and talk about it. I can't begin to understand what's going on because you're not talking. I'm not going to apologise for that night, it was one of the best I've ever had. The ball is in your court now. You know where I am.

Mackenzie

The first emotion I experienced was anger. I bristled at his words. But then I reread. I hadn't explained why I'd run because I wasn't sure how. He'd left it open for me to contact him, but I guessed he'd also made it clear he wasn't chasing after me. I didn't want him to either. He was a man ten years older than me, a very worldly man, I imagined. I thought I was mature enough, but maybe my life had been more sheltered than I believed. I scrolled through the internal email contact list, hoping I'd see the addition of Gabriella. When I did I sent her a message.

Sorry for the message, but I wondered if you could let me know when Mackenzie is back?

She replied from her phone.

He arrived home this afternoon; I've just left him. He took an earlier flight, cancelled his last meeting. Are you okay?

I replied just letting her know I thought I'd caught a bug but everything was okay otherwise.

I rushed from the room and dragged a brush through my hair. I grabbed a jacket and my handbag then left the apartment. I flagged down a taxi and then froze when I was asked where I wanted to go.

"Oh, fuck, address! It's a gated community on Hampstead Heath."

"You want to check?"

"No, I can call when we get closer."

I checked my watch, although only six o'clock I wondered if he'd be busy with dinner. Nearly an hour later the taxi crawled along the boundary road to the heath.

"There," I said.

"That's not the gated community, that's further up," the driver said.

"No, that's it." I opened my purse and took out some notes.

"You want me to wait? What if no one's in?"

He had a good point. "If you can."

I climbed from the taxi and walked to the intercom. I pressed the call button and held my breath. At first there was no answer, but as I was about to walk back to the taxi, I heard his voice.

"Hello?"

"It's Lauren," I said.

He didn't reply but a few seconds later the gates started to swing open. I raised my hand to the driver, who pulled away. My heart beat frantically in my chest as I walked up the drive, more so when I saw him standing at the open front door. His brown hair was tousled; his white shirt was crumpled, as if he had just climbed from bed.

"Hi," I said, as I walked up the steps to the front door.

He took a step aside and allowed me in. He didn't speak as he led the way to the kitchen.

"Coffee?" he asked.

"That would be nice."

He gestured with his hand to a stool at the breakfast bar, and I watched as he ran the other through his hair.

"I was sleeping, sorry," he said.

"I should have called first, I can always come back another time."

"You're here now, no point leaving just to come back."

At first I couldn't put my finger on his tone of voice. It was only when he turned to me that I saw sadness in his face. I wouldn't presume that was because of me though. He placed the two small cups on the bar and sat on the stool next to me. He stared and I took a deep breath.

"I thought I was mature enough to play the game with you. I guess I'm not. I understand now. I've led quite a sheltered life. What I *want,* as opposed to what I'm capable of dealing with, appears to be two very different things."

At first he didn't speak. I distracted myself from his stare by raising my cup to my lips.

"Bullshit," he said, quietly.

"Bullshit?" I stood from my stool. "You blew my fucking mind, Mackenzie. I loved every second of that weekend, and then I got disgusted with myself for doing so. I got scared, I was confused." My voice rose in frustration. "I felt on such a high, and then I crashed, my whole body fucking crashed. I did things so out of my comfort zone, so fucking far out of the stratosphere for me; I can't comprehend how or why, I did it. For a while I didn't recognise myself, do you have any idea how much of a mind fuck that is?"

"And now we have the truth. Sit your fucking ass back down and listen to me."

I stood still.

"I said, sit down." His voice was low, controlled. I sat.

"You asked me not to let you fall. I told you that you would, but not in the way you thought. You did not give me the opportunity to stand you back up, you ran instead. You proved your lack of trust in me."

"I…" I hadn't thought of it that way.

"You did a beautiful thing. Not for me, not for her, but for yourself. Didn't you prove to yourself how courageous you are? Didn't you prove to yourself how sensual and sexy you are? She wanted you; I wanted you. You made her come; you made me come. You, Lauren, you."

I didn't respond, I couldn't.

"There was nothing disgusting about what we did; we were three consenting adults. And before you say you didn't know it was coming, you could have said no. You didn't. You were supposed to experience the high; you were supposed to crash after. I was there to fucking catch you." His voice had risen. "I was there to kiss away the tears I knew would follow. But you didn't allow that. Yes, you are immature, Lauren. You have led a sheltered life. But you have a choice. Grow up and live life, or stay exactly where you are." He finished in a more gentle tone.

"So you did something that you expected me to cry over?"

"I expected embarrassment, I expected guilt, I didn't expect you to run and then ignore me."

"So if you *expected* those things, why do it?"

"Because I could have helped you through that. I could have shown you there was nothing to be embarrassed about, nothing to feel guilty for."

He shuffled his stool closer, until his knees touched mine. I bowed my head.

"How did you feel?"

"Aroused, beyond anything I've felt before," I said quietly.

"More."

"Alive."

"More, Lauren," he whispered.

133

"My skin felt on fire, my heart beat so fast. It was exciting, like a rollercoaster, scary but exhilarating at the same time."

"Do you feel aroused now, thinking about it? And don't lie to me, I can smell you."

I swallowed hard. "Yes."

"Would you do it again?"

Finally, I looked at him. "Yes."

"Then tell me, what is wrong with that?"

"Nothing," I whispered.

He stood from his stool and positioned himself between my thighs. He held my head in his hands and he kissed me. He kissed me so fiercely he stole my breath and scrambled my mind.

When he broke away, I gasped for air.

"You do not run from me, Lauren, ever. I will not chase you," he said, as he rested his forehead against mine. It was all I could do to nod.

"Are you hungry?" he asked.

"No."

"Then I need to sleep a little. I haven't slept much since Saturday night."

I slid from my stool and picked up my bag. "I'll get a taxi home," I said.

"No, you won't, you'll sleep with me."

He took my hand and led me from the room. We walked back to the hallway and up the stairs to his bedroom. He had a large bed, and it was clear from the crumpled bedding, he'd been sleeping on top. He pulled off his shirt but left his jeans on. I kicked off my shoes and waited. He climbed onto his bed and patted the space beside him. As I joined him, he wrapped me in his arms.

"Don't ever fucking run from me again," he whispered.

****

I didn't sleep as such, just dozed. It felt good to be wrapped in his arms, to have my head nestled in the crook of his neck. I could feel his heartbeat under the hand I'd placed on his chest. It beat at a far steadier rhythm than mine. I didn't want my mind to go where it clearly was. For a moment we felt like a couple.

I had no idea what we had, and I wasn't sure I wanted a relationship, certainly not until I'd sorted out the issues with Scott. Having a fuck buddy just wasn't in my makeup either. In one way, I envied the women that could just have sex and not attach emotion to it. Or maybe, like me, they were trying to convince themselves they could.

Didn't all women want to be taken out to dinner? Hold hands with someone? To just sleep, curled up against a warm body?

Didn't all women want to share their lives with someone they could come home to, from work, and discuss their day with?

Had I been ten years younger, maybe I could have done the sex without strings thing. But my biological clock was ticking, and although a baby wasn't something I wanted right then, I missed a stable relationship.

I sighed.

"What was that for?" I heard.

"What?"

"The sigh." He turned his head to face me and opened his eyes.

"Just thinking."

"About what?"

"I don't have to tell you every thought that runs through my mind, do I?"

"No, but you never know if it's something I can help with."

"I don't think you can with this."

He pulled his arm from underneath me. "I'll grab a shower and then cook us something to eat," he said.

"I can do that," I said.

"The shower, or the cooking?" he said as he unbuttoned his jeans.

135

"Both."

"Then why are you still dressed?"

"You didn't ask me to undress," I said, pulling my t-shirt over my head.

"If you want to fuck me, or have me fuck you, Lauren, instigate it. Don't wait to be *commanded* to do something. I might be an asshole sometimes, but I didn't just fall out of one of your novels," he said, laughing.

He strode naked to the shower.

"Shame," I whispered and then smiled.

I stepped out of my jeans and underwear and joined him. Soapsuds ran down his body as he pushed his hands through his hair, rinsing it. He reached out for my hand and pulled me close to him. He squirted gel in his palms and ran them over my body, deliberately missing the parts I would have liked him to touch. He then turned me away from him and washed my hair, massaging my scalp as he did. His fingers ran through my hair, gently untangling it.

"I want to do something," I said and turned back to face him.

"Do whatever you want, Lauren," he replied.

I held his hips as I lowered to my knees. I kept my gaze on his face and watched the smile form on his lips. With just one lick of my tongue, his cock was hard. I wasn't sure exactly when it had occurred to me, but I'd never pleasured him.

I licked up his shaft, flattening my tongue against him until I reached the tip. With one hand, I guided him into my mouth. I sucked while running my hand up and down the length of him. He fisted his hands into my hair, and as I lowered my head, taking more of him into my mouth, he gripped harder.

I sucked his cock and rolled his balls in the palm of my hand. I wasn't an expert at blowjobs, but I was certainly giving my best. I was rewarded with a moan and a painful pull of my hair. For every moan he released, I sucked harder.

He started to rotate his hips, gently at first. He pulled my head back, just slightly, before driving into me. He fucked my mouth like he'd fucked my pussy. My eyes watered as his cock hit the back of my throat. I breathed in deep, to relax. I palmed his balls again and felt them tighten. At the same time, he pulled hard on my hair.

"Lauren," he said, almost like a growl.

I held my position. I'd never had a man come in my mouth before, but I wanted to do that for him, for me. I felt his cock twitch, pulse, and his hot milky fluid shot down my throat. I swallowed as quickly as I could. When he'd finished, I released him gently, keeping my tongue against the underside of him, and licked him clean. I ran my tongue over the tip of his cock once he'd pulled free of my mouth.

"That was on my list," I quietly said.

He smiled. "Then I'm pleased we checked that one off."

He reached down for my shoulders and helped me stand; my lower legs were numb. I raised my face to the showerhead and opened my mouth, allowing it to fill with water, and then swallowed again.

The water stopped running, he hadn't turned a dial or pressed a button.

"Timer," he said as he stepped out.

He grabbed two towels, wrapped one around his waist and the other around me. For a moment, he stared at me without speaking. I got the impression he wanted to say something but held back.

"What?" I asked as I dried myself.

"Nothing." He smiled at me as he walked to his bedroom.

I followed him and that awkward after-sex moment, which should have followed long before then, occurred. I watched him dress and had no option but to pull on my own dirty ones. I towel dried my hair and scrunched it into a bun.

"Would you like something to eat?" he asked.

"I think I ought to be heading home."

"I'll drive you, but you're welcome to stay for dinner."

He'd spoken as if I was just a casual visitor, not someone who just sucked his cock and swallowed his cum. I was confused.

"No dinner, it's fine. I can get a taxi if you have a number."

"I'll drive, it's no problem."

There was a little part of me disappointed, were we back to the game? I wasn't sure if I wanted to play anymore.

****

We drove back to my apartment in near silence. When we did talk it felt forced and unnatural.

"Did you speak to Gabriella?" he asked when he pulled into the car park.

"I did. I told her I intended to resign. She asked me to think about it."

"Why would you want to resign?"

What could I say? *Because of us?* I wasn't sure there was an *us*. I said the first thing that came into my head.

"I don't have that much respect from my colleagues, I think if I was in a position above them, I'd have even less. That won't be good for your business."

As I spoke the words I realised they were true.

"Then earn their respect," he said, turning in his seat towards me.

"Sorry? I haven't done anything to deserve their lack of." I was a little astounded that he could say that.

"I don't suppose you have. But quitting, just because a few people don't like you, plays straight into their hands. You can earn their respect, and it will be begrudgingly, by taking that position and showing them just how capable you are."

"What if I fail?"

"If you think you will, you will. You can be scared of challenges your whole life, or you can face your fears and rise above them."

"Is this another lesson? Another part of the game?" I said, adding a chuckle.

"I've told you before, I don't play games. I'm deadly serious in everything I do. Now, think about what you want from life, Lauren. Like I said earlier, instigate it. If you don't know what you want, how can you achieve anything?"

"So the ball's in my court again?" I wasn't sure if the conversation had switched from a job offer to sex.

"Yep. It's time for you to man up. I thought I was doing something wonderful for you over the weekend, turns out, I wasn't."

He leaned a little towards me and reached out with his hand to cup my chin.

"The next *lesson* as you call it, will be entirely up to you."

So the game was still on? The man was giving me a headache with all the switches in personality and the cryptic messages.

I opened my car door, not waiting for him to do it. I struggled out and then leaned on the roof to look back in.

"Thank you for the ride home, Mackenzie. I'll think on that offer, both of them."

I walked away. He didn't leave immediately. I took a sneaky peek over my shoulder as I walked through the door to the lifts. He held a mobile to his ear but hadn't looked my way.

"Fuck you," I whispered as I called the lift.

I'd prove to him that I was man enough for a challenge. I'd never shied away from a difficult task before but running a business?

When I got to my apartment I opened my laptop and sent a message to Gabriella, asking her if she'd give me more details on what the position entailed.

I then sent a text.

My next *lesson* – I want to watch someone having sex.

I stifled the giggle that threatened to leave my lips. I held the phone in my hand and waited for his reply. It didn't come.

"Bollocks," I said, as I rose and decided I needed something to eat.

As I sat with a glass of wine and a sandwich I thought on the text I'd sent. What Mackenzie was offering was addictive. He was giving me the opportunity to experience all those things I'd read about and been turned on by. But, like the previous weekend, it was all well and good in fiction. I swallowed down the panic.

No harm could come from watching another couple, right? I thought.

The problem was, I'd already experienced the *ultimate*. I'd discovered what it was like to be with another woman. I wasn't sure where I could go from there. What if fulfilling my fantasies was all that was on offer from Mackenzie? How did we behave when it was all done? What I didn't want to do was get so addicted to the high, the excitement, that it became impossible to have a normal relationship after. Somehow, though, I suspected I was already on that slippery slope.

****

It was mid-afternoon the following day when I heard back from Mackenzie.

Friday 8pm. I'll collect you. Wear loose clothing.

My hands shook as I read his text, a bubble of excitement formed in my stomach, and a grin spread across my face. I wanted to text back. I wanted to know more, but then I wanted the element of surprise as well. I sat back in my chair and wondered who I'd be watching. My grin slipped a little when a thought struck me. It wouldn't be him with another woman, would it?

I had no claim on him, but the thought of seeing him fuck someone else filled me with dread. I swallowed down the pang of jealousy.

I was quickly brought back to the present by a knock on my door.

"Do you have a minute?" Gabriella asked.

I wasn't even aware she was in the building.

"Of course, come on in. Can I get you a coffee?"

She shook her head. "Would I be a terrible snob if I said I can't stomach that instant?"

I laughed. "No, I can send Jenny out for one."

I popped my head around the door and asked Jenny to head to the nearest coffee shop.

"Thank you for reconsidering that offer. I thought it might be nice to meet with Alex, informally, this week. I wondered what your plans were."

"I'm free, except Friday evening."

"I know he's available for lunch tomorrow. I just want you to sit down with him and chat. He's excited to meet you."

"You already told him about me?"

"I told him you were a possible candidate," she said with a smile.

"My reservations come, not because I don't think I can grasp what's required, but more to do with letting you down if I can't cut it."

"You wouldn't have been considered, Lauren, if we didn't believe you could. You should have a little more faith in yourself."

"And the fact Jerry said he wanted to ensure I still had a job," I said.

"Whenever we take over a company there are always members of staff the owner wants to ensure stays. The deal would not have been done had we not agreed with his demands, however, we wouldn't deal if we didn't agree." She laughed when she'd finished her sentence.

"He is rather demanding, isn't he?"

"I really like him, and I know Mackenzie wants to keep a relationship with him."

"I have to say, I was surprised Jerry took on a partner, let alone sold out. This has been his life for so many years."

"I guess the offer was just too good not to accept. At the end of the day, one man can only take a business so far. And the prudent thing is to always bail out on a high offer, while still at the top of the game."

Jenny returned with two takeout containers from Costa.

"I got black, I didn't know what you wanted," she said as she placed them on the desk.

"Thank you, black is perfect for me," Gabriella said.

"I'm honoured that you have such belief in me," I said.

"You know, sometimes it's great to take yourself out of your comfort zone, try new things."

I blinked a couple of times. *Were we still talking about the job?* I thought.

"That's what I'm doing."

We chatted a little more about the companies she controlled, and then she surprised me.

"I started off the same as you, Lauren. The man I was desperately in love with had been killed in a car crash, and for a long while I was totally lost. Mackenzie took me under his wing and look at me now."

How had Mackenzie taken you under his wing? I wanted to ask.

Was that what he was doing to me? I shook the thought from my mind; I wasn't going there.

"Well, I need to get across London in less than ten minutes," she said, and then laughed.

She stood, we said goodbye and then she left.

I liked Gabriella, she was honest, clearly a good businesswoman, and someone I'd aspire to. But I was curious as to how she'd gotten to her position. I mentally slapped myself, wasn't that very thought the same as I received? Didn't it piss me off?

It was one of the things that I hated the most. My experience was that women didn't often support their female colleagues, especially if one was rising up the ranks. I made a vow never to be that woman. I vowed to be like Gabriella.

I thought back on what Mackenzie had said, about giving respect. Maybe, because I was so isolated, because I was on guard all the time, I did come across aloof. I didn't support my female colleagues; perhaps I was just getting back what they perceived I gave.

I carried on with my day, making a point to take a moment to say goodnight to my team as they left for the evening.

Chapter Eleven

I took a taxi to the restaurant where I was meeting Gabriella and Alex, because I wasn't sure on where it was. I was nervous. I stood outside the door, trying hard not to wipe my sweaty palms on my trousers. I took a deep breath and entered. I was met by the maître d' and asked if I had a booking.

"I'm meeting Gabriella Collinsworth," I said.

"Ah, we are expecting you, please, follow me."

I was led through the restaurant to a table set in an alcove. Gabriella stood, and as she did I saw Alex. I was expecting an elderly gentleman, considering she'd told me he wanted to leave. I guess I'd translated that as retire. I wasn't expecting the man, who stood to greet me, to be not much older than Mackenzie. Nor was I expecting him to be as charming. He took my hand and raised it to his lips. He planted a gentle kiss to the back of my hand.

"Lauren, it's good to finally meet you," he said, in a very upper class English accent.

"You too, thank you for taking the time to meet with me."

He pulled a chair out for me to sit. Before I'd gotten myself comfortable, a waiter was beside me with iced water, pouring a glass.

"Would you prefer wine?" Alex asked.

"No, water is fine for me, thank you." Not that I would normally drink wine during a 'work' meeting, but I noticed both Gabriella and Alex had soft drinks only.

A waiter placed menus on the table that we ignored initially.

"So, Lauren, tell me a little about yourself," Alex asked.

I guessed the 'interview' had started. I gave details of my work life, the companies I'd worked for while at college, and what I did. He would occasionally interrupt to ask me to expand on something I'd said.

We paused so the hovering waiter could take orders.

"Now tell me about you," Alex said.

On that, I was stumped.

"Erm, I'm currently going through a divorce, but I can assure you that doesn't affect the quality of my work," I said.

Gabriella placed her hand on my arm.

"You've no need to justify that," she said. Once again, I was reminded how kind she was.

I thought for a moment. I had no hobbies; I had nothing to talk about. I bought myself some time by taking a sip of my drink.

"I've spent the past ten years immersing myself in my job, Alex. I was on board from day one. I made it a priority to give my all to Jerry while he was building up the business."

"And now?"

"And now, I guess, I'm up for a new challenge."

"And you can balance home life with work life?" he asked. I thought it an odd question at first.

"Yes, I believe I can."

"We don't want someone who works all the hours and burns out. We're looking for someone to be with us long term, Lauren. It's important that you have a home life, free time," he said.

I simply nodded. I didn't feel burned out.

"People that have a varied home life, we find, produce the best work. As an organisation, we think it's important to socialise, to bond over a bottle of wine or our annual BBQ."

It all sounded very 'American' but then, I guessed it was.

"Tell me a little about what would be expected of me," I said, diverting the conversation away from me.

Alex spent a little time detailing what he did before our conversation was halted with the arrival of our lunch. I'd chosen a seafood salad but wasn't expecting the large portion that was placed in front of me.

While we ate, we engaged in small talk. Gabriella regaled us of stories from her hometown, and I was once again transported back to those days in *Gone With The Wind*. We laughed at some of the antics of her mother. It seemed, as lunch progressed, that Gabriella and Alex were more than just work colleagues. She would tell a story of something funny that had happened and Alex was often featured in that. Either they socialised a lot, or there was a relationship there.

Once our meal was eaten and plates cleared, Alex ordered coffee.

"So, do we have you on board?" he asked.

"I passed the interview then?" I replied with a smile.

"I think we will make a great team until you're ready to take over," he said.

"Can I ask; why do you want to leave?"

"Because I've been given an opportunity abroad that I'd like to pursue."

I didn't press any further; although Gabriella hadn't lost any of her composure, I did notice the very slight frown that had developed on her forehead.

"Ladies, I have to leave you. Please, stay, enjoy your coffee," Alex said.

Alex stood and buttoned up his suit jacket. He was a very attractive man; his dark hair was gently peppered with flecks of grey at his temples. He held himself upright with an air of dignity, breeding, but without being condescending about it. Unlike Mackenzie, who oozed power, Alex came across as calm and serene, but when he smiled there was a twinkle in his eye, a little mischief there.

Gabriella and I stood; he shook my hand and gave a slight bow of his head. I watched him then place a hand on Gabriella's shoulder and kiss her cheek. There was something intimate in that gesture.

After we'd taken our seats, there was a moment of silence, as if Gabriella wanted to compose herself.

"So," she said, turning towards me. "Do you think you'd work well with Alex?"

"I do, he's very charming. I suspect he's going to be a great loss to you."

"He is, and he will be." She took a sip of her water, and I noticed the very slight shake to her hand.

"What happens now?" I asked, wanting to divert her attention away from Alex.

"I'll have some contracts drawn up, we're a month or so away from merging, so plenty of time for you to go through that. There will be a loss of some staff members. Sadly, that can't be helped. We have an overlap, especially in our development section, and the better person for the job isn't Scott."

"I understand," I said, but inside my stomach knotted. If he lost his job, he'd want the sale of the apartment completed quicker.

"You seem a little sad about that."

"Not *sad*, it's complicated. At the end of the day, Gabriella, if he isn't up to the job, then he isn't."

"Complicated in what way? Although you don't have to tell me anything that's personal, of course."

I sighed. It might be good to actually talk to someone about it.

"He wants half the equity in our apartment, half my savings and pensions. It was my money that bought the apartment, so I'm a little gutted about that, bearing in mind it was him that had an affair. If he's out of work, he'll push for that to be concluded quicker, I imagine."

"As I said, we are a couple of months away yet. He'll be offered a leaving package, he won't walk out without a dollar in his pocket."

"He's just not a nice person. He already thinks I'm sucking up."

"Sucking up?"

"Getting cosy with the new boss to secure my position," I said, with a laugh.

"Ah, I had so many images flood my mind then." She gave me a wink.

I was grateful I'd already swallowed the sip of water I'd just taken. I think I would have spat it over the table otherwise.

"Do you have a lawyer? We have a few, maybe you could chat with one."

"I do, Gabriella, and he's entitled to half. I'm just a little worried that I'll need to move out of London, for financial reasons, once it's all dealt with."

"Not that I should say this yet, but you will be on a higher pay grade than you are now. If you want my advice, get it all over with as quickly as possible. Don't drag it out. Then you can move on, have a fresh start."

"Yeah, I think I will. You sound like you're speaking from experience," I said, and then thought I shouldn't have. It was a little personal.

"Not me, I've never married. But..." She pursed her lips as if thinking on whether to continue or not. "Our mutual friend has been hauled over the coals, as you Brits call it, for a long time."

Has been, not was. Did that mean he was still being 'hauled over the coals'?

"We don't, sort of, talk about personal things," I said.

"No, he's very closed off. He was deeply hurt by her betrayal."

Gabriella laid her napkin on the table and made to stand. Our conversation was clearly over. I stood and we walked to the entrance of the restaurant.

"It was great to chat to you, and Alex, of course," I said.

"It's nice to make a new friend. It gets a little lonely sometimes, being so far away from home," she said, surprising me a little.

"Well, if you ever want to meet for dinner, or drinks, just give me a call."

She smiled. "I will, thank you. I'll be in touch about those contracts."

Although she'd placed her hand on my arm, there was no hug goodbye. She smiled and then walked in the opposite direction. In that last half hour, I'd noticed the sadness. I hailed a taxi and headed back to work.

I sat in my office, not working, and just thinking about her, Alex, the job, my life, for ages. Things had progressed so fast, I hadn't taken the time to sit back and really decide if I was going in the right direction or not. I'd always planned. I'd always known where I was going to be in a year's time, and for the first time ever, I had no idea what was going to happen the following day.

Part of that was Mackenzie, most of that was me. Maybe this was an early mid-life crisis, or the result of a traumatic break-up. Wasn't it usual to go *off the rails* for a while? I wanted to go with it, to just experience being free of any commitment. Perhaps I'd put a time limit on myself. I'd enjoy Mackenzie, and all he offered, for another couple of months and when I started my new job, I'd rein myself in, become Miss Sensible again.

****

For the next couple of days, I noticed the change in atmosphere at work. It felt like people were winding down a little. Everyone was on edge, not sure what the future held. I guessed they didn't want to put in any effort, in case they lost their jobs. I did the total opposite. Someone would either be replacing me, or my work given to another team. I wanted all loose ends tied up; I wanted everything in order so someone could literally walk in and pick up where I'd left off. I even reorganised all my filing, archiving the old and preparing files for new projects. I was back to some late nights.

I hadn't heard from Mackenzie and I didn't expect to. I understood what it was between us. It was nothing more than two people getting together for some fun. We didn't date; we didn't talk much either. Being the woman that I was, someone used to a relationship, it felt strange. I was lonely, especially at night. I pushed all thoughts of any kind of a relationship with Mackenzie to the back of my mind. Whatever had happened between him and his wife must have affected him greatly, and he was hardly in the country at that moment.

Chapter Twelve

I'd taken a shower and giggled as I *prepared* myself. I was nervous, as if I was about to embark on a first date. I'd shaved every stray hair from my body, pampered, manicured, and painted my toenails. I stood naked, in front of my wardrobe. He'd told me to wear loose clothing, I hadn't thought about that at the time. I wondered why. I selected a shirt and a pair of loose fitting trousers, not sure if they constituted his version of *loose* or not.

I constantly checked my watch as I blow dried my hair and applied my makeup. The closer it got to eight o'clock, the more nervous I became. It felt a little late to be going out to dinner. I wondered where he would take me.

I was dressed and standing in the kitchen, sipping on a glass of wine, when the intercom buzzed. I saw him in the TV screen and released the door. I checked my teeth for lipstick, or red wine stains, in the hallway mirror before opening the door.

He was dressed casually but smart in a white shirt and dark jeans. He smiled as he exited the lift. He placed his hands on my shoulders and leaned down to kiss my cheek, as one would greet a friend.

"Hi," he said.

"Hello. I was just having a glass of wine, if you'd like one."

"No time. Are you ready?"

"I am." I walked into the kitchen and collected my handbag. "Do I need a jacket?" I asked.

"No."

As I shut the apartment door, he threaded his fingers through mine. I like that he'd held my hand, it was a comfort and helped quell the nerves.

"Where are we going?" I asked, as I climbed into his car.

"Surrey," he said, closing my door.

"Surrey?" I asked, when he'd reappeared at the driver's side.

"Yes." He clearly wasn't giving much away.

"So, how did you get on with Alex?" he asked, as we pulled out of the car park and into the traffic.

I told him about our lunch, and how I felt I could work well with him. I also watched his body stiffen a little when I'd said I thought he was a very charming man.

"He was impressed with your work ethic, what you've done in the past. I think you'll work well together," he said.

"How long will I have before he leaves?"

"That depends on when he thinks you're ready to take over."

"You don't have a say then?"

"I know everything that goes on. I can veto anything I want, but I trust my team to make the right decisions."

"Do you meet with them all frequently?" I asked, because he seemed to be out of the country a lot.

"Weekly, either face-to-face or by Skype."

He had entered the motorway and headed away from London. A thought occurred to me.

"Where exactly is your office?"

"I have two, one at home and another, as I've already told you, in Canary Wharf. Not far from your apartment block. I'll take you there," he said and smiled over. "I've been coming back and forth to the U.K. for about ten years now, but only moved here three or so ago."

"Do you miss home?"

"Sometimes, for sure. I don't miss LA, pretentious place, but I miss my family."

"Do you have brothers, sisters?" I really didn't know that much about him when I'd thought about it.

"No, only child."

"You don't give much away, do you?" I said, and then laughed.

He looked over to me. "I answered your question, Lauren."

"I know, I was kidding." I wasn't, but I didn't want to start the evening off on a sour note.

He sighed, took one hand off the steering wheel and clasped it around mine.

"I'm a little stressed lately, I have some personal shit going on. I don't want to bore you with it all. Let's just concentrate on having some fun, we both need it right now."

I smiled at him. I didn't want to, I wanted to ask if that was all I meant to him, *a little fun*. But then, hadn't I decided that's all I wanted as well? When I wasn't with him I could rationalise it all, but the minute I saw him, smelled his aftershave, or heard his voice, I was in knots. My stomach was somersaulting and my mind clouded by his presence.

"How about some music?" I said. I didn't want to spend the rest of the journey in silence; he obviously wasn't in a talkative mood.

****

We drove through a pair of large, ornate iron gates; the headlights illuminated a long gravel drive with lawns to either side. In front was a manor house, very old, imposing yet beautiful at the same time.

"Wow, what is this place?" I asked, as we pulled to a halt in a circular drive. I could see a man standing on the steps beside the front door.

He turned off the engine and shifted slightly in his seat. "Are you ready to play?"

"Play?"

"Are you ready to fulfil the fantasy you asked for?"

I swallowed hard, all of a sudden the air in the car had changed, it became dense, electrified.

"I'm nervous," I said.

"Nervous is good, but one rule, Lauren. You do not run. If you don't like what you see, you speak out and we leave."

"You're scaring me a little," I said, with a nervous chuckle.

"Nothing to be scared of. I'll be with you all the time. I just don't want a repeat of that weekend. You fucking scared me, and I don't like being scared."

I stared at him; *I'd scared him*? Before I could respond, he'd opened his car door. At that point, the man beside the front door of the house walked forward. Mackenzie walked around the car, ignoring him, and opened my door. He held out his hand to help me. Once he'd closed the door, he then handed the man, who had stood silently, his keys and his mobile phone.

"Do you have a phone?" Mackenzie asked me.

I nodded. "Can I have it?" he asked.

I took it from my bag and handed it over. I watched as he gave it to the man, who nodded before getting into Mackenzie's car and driving off.

"And that was...?"

"Valet parking, Lauren. No phones or cameras are allowed inside."

"Why?"

At first he looked at me as if he couldn't believe I'd asked the question, then he smiled that wicked smile. His pupils had dilated, his voice lowered a little.

"You'll see."

He took hold of my hand and we walked up the stone steps to a large, oak front door. Before we'd reached it, it was opened by a stunning blonde woman, dressed formally in a trouser suit with her hair pulled tight in a bun.

"Good evening, Mr. Miller, Miss Perry. May I escort you to the bar?"

I wanted to ask Mackenzie how she knew our names, but I was struck dumb by the opulence of the hallway we had entered. A grand oak staircase dominated the vast area and a chandelier lit the room. Wood panelling covered the lower half of the walls and the light blue paper above it, shimmered. If I touched it, I imagined it would be silk. My heels clipped across a marble floor as I followed our host.

We were shown into a room with sofas, a roaring fire at one end and a large oak bar at the other. It reminded me of a gentlemen's drinking club. There were couples and small groups already seated or standing at the bar. Each smiled or offered a greeting as we passed.

"Mr. Miller, we have your whiskey. Miss Perry, what may I get for you?" the woman asked as she stood beside us.

The barman had placed a small cut crystal glass on the bar and was pouring Mackenzie a drink.

"I'd like a wine, red, please," I said, trying hard not to stammer and show my nerves.

"Perhaps you'd like to see a wine list?" She smiled as she spoke, putting me at ease.

"Thank you."

She handed me a menu and I was thankful to hold something to stop my hands from shaking.

"I'll leave you to make a decision, please let Hendrick know what you'd like."

I watched her walk away and chat to some of the guests before leaving the room.

"You've obviously been here before," I said.

"Yes."

"And what exactly is it here?"

He took a sip of his drink before answering. "A club, a very exclusive, members only, club. Have you decided?"

I looked at him. "On a wine," he said.

"Oh, I don't mind, you choose." I handed him the menu as I perched myself on a stool.

"You won't leave me, will you?" I asked, quietly.

"Of course not," he said, and then ran the back of his hand gently down my cheek. My stomach flipped at his touch.

He ordered me a glass of wine while I scanned the room. Like the hallway, the walls were panelled with wood halfway, large paintings in ornate frames were hung on every wall. Above the open fire was a large mirror, its glass tinted with age. Red tapestry curtains hung from floor to ceiling windows and two chandeliers gave a warm glow over the room.

"Shall we sit?" I asked, indicating to a sofa opposite another and separated by a low table.

"No, we're not here to *mingle*," he said with a smirk.

"Mingle?" Then it dawned on me. My eyes widened with shock.

Before I could speak, he'd placed one of his fingers over my lips. "Shush," he said.

I quickly took a large sip of my wine, then another. I tried my hardest not to make eye contact, but I was curious about the occupants of the room. They were very well dressed, the women expertly made up. The men were either in suits or smart casual dress. People chatted and laughed, as if on a regular night out. I watched as one couple left the bar and sat on the sofa I'd been looking at. I then watched another couple introduce themselves and join them for drinks.

"So, if you sit on the sofa it means you want to *mingle?*" I whispered.

Mackenzie laughed, "Yes. If you sit at the bar, or take one of those chairs over there, then you're not looking to *mingle*."

I followed his gaze to a small collection of chairs, in pairs, at one end of the room.

"Shit," I whispered.

More couples came into the room, each time escorted by the blonde woman and each time, they had drinks waiting for them. I appeared to be the only one asked what my preference was, obviously the newbie.

Despite what I thought the house was; there was a nice atmosphere. The low hum of voices, the tinkle of laughter, and the crackling of logs on the fire reminded me of a country manor hotel.

"Relax," he said, running his fingers across the back of my hand.

"I'm trying to. I have to say, this is a gorgeous house."

"Victorian. It still contains a lot of the original features."

"You know the house well, then?"

He didn't answer. He'd already told me he'd been there before, but I was curious to know how many times. I wasn't sure how comfortable I felt about that. I pushed it to the back of my mind; reminding myself again, there was no relationship.

It seemed as if the people in the room had some kind of internal timer. All at once, they started to rise and either as a couple or in the groups they'd formed they left the room.

When only two couples were left in the bar, Mackenzie took my hand in his.

"Come," he said.

I slid from my stool and let him lead me back to the door. My mouth was dry, I hoped from the red wine and not fear. Excitement started to build inside and my stomach flipped.

"Mr. Miller," I heard. The blonde woman was standing to one side at the base of the staircase. "The Clarence Room," she said, and then handed him a key.

It was an old-fashioned brass key with a purple rope and tasselled fob.

"Thank you, Veronica," he replied. I wasn't sure I liked him knowing her name.

The width of the staircase would have allowed four abreast to climb and still have room to spare. We kept to one side, and I was grateful to be near the handrail. I used it to steady myself the closer to the top we became. The staircase separated, fanning to the left and right. Mackenzie edged me to the left.

Deep carpeting covered a wide hallway floor, and I suspected it was to control noise level. I guessed it wasn't so nice for the occupants to hear people traipsing up and down. The corridor had rooms on either side. Each one with an identical dark oak door, and each one with a nameplate.

Mackenzie paused before The Clarence Room. He inserted the key and before he turned the lock, he looked at me. He didn't need to speak; I'd already nodded.

I heard a click as an old lock disengaged, he pushed the door open and stood to the side to let me enter.

The room housed a large bed with oversized pillows, a white cotton and perfectly pressed bottom sheet. A comforter was folded across the bottom. In a corner were two, leather, high-backed armchairs; the brass studs that decorated them were polished so they shone. Against one wall was an ornate sideboard and against the wall opposite the bed, heavy curtains that were pulled.

"Drink?" Mackenzie asked, as he strode to the sideboard. His brand of whiskey and a bottle of the red wine I'd drunk, were sitting on top of it.

I shook my head. "Water though, if there is any," I said.

He opened one door, which contained a mini fridge, and retrieved a bottle of water. He poured some in a glass, added ice from a bucket, and walked back to where I stood in the middle of the room.

He waited until I'd taken a couple of sips of the water before taking the glass from my hand and placing it back on the sideboard.

He placed his hands on my shoulders and gently turned me to face the curtains. He stood directly behind and encouraged me to take a couple of steps closer.

"Don't move," he whispered in my ear.

My heart rate had accelerated and my palms were sweaty. I took in a deep breath as he stepped to one side and pulled on a rope. As the curtains parted, I took in a gasp of air.

The curtains had concealed a window, a window into the next-door bedroom.

"Oh my God," I whispered.

"They can't hear nor see you. One-way glass. You'll see and hear them only," he said.

"But they know we're here?"

"Yes, the minute I pulled those drapes a small light turned on, letting them know they have guests."

"Guests?"

"Guests."

I fell silent as Mackenzie walked and stood behind me again. His placed his hands over mine, holding them to my hips.

"Don't speak, just watch."

Their room was decorated in a similar fashion, except for one thing. Instead of a bed, there was a fucking, great, wooden X in the middle of the room; to one side, a low brown leather…I wasn't sure what it was. A sofa without a back and arms? A chaise?

"I…" Before I could speak, Mackenzie had raised one hand and placed his fingers over my lips.

I watched a tall, athletic blond man circle a petite redhead, who stood side on and close to the mirror. He came to stand in front of her. He placed his fingers under her chin and tilted her head, so her gaze met his. I saw them smile at each other. I wasn't sure why, but that smile pleased me.

Mackenzie's fingers left my lips, leaving a tingling in their wake, and he placed his hand back over mine.

The man looked directly at the mirror, and although Mackenzie had said he couldn't see us, it sure felt like he was staring straight at me. I wanted to step to one side, to hide, but Mackenzie held me still.

The man reached forward and he slowly undid the buttons of his partner's blouse. At the same time, I felt Mackenzie's hands run up my sides and copy him. He popped each button open in time with the man in the opposite room, then slid my shirt from my shoulders.

The woman wore a skirt; I wore trousers, but we both had them removed at the same time. I stepped out of my trousers, as she stepped out of the skirt that had pooled around her feet.

Mackenzie unclipped my bra from where he stood behind me, and slid the straps down my arms. The man reached around his partner. I felt my hair being swept away from my neck and lips at the base. As Mackenzie kissed the length of my back, the man did the same to her chest, then stomach. I felt fingers hook under the waistband of my panties, either side of my hips. As he continued to lower, he pulled them down. He tapped one ankle and I raised it, he then did the same to the other. All the while, I watched the man do the same to her.

That was where the synchronised stripping ending.

Mackenzie stood and placed his hands on my hips, pulling me back against him, he held me there.

I bit down on my lower lip to stop the gasp as I watched the man run his tongue up the length of his partner's inside leg. She parted them slightly. He held her hips, while his mouth hovered over her pussy.

I saw him extend his tongue and lick, I watched her grip his head and close her eyes. Her mouth parted slightly. He licked again, a long slow lick that had my stomach clench.

My clitoris throbbed with a need for Mackenzie to do the same. The more the man licked her; the more her hands tightened in his hair. I could see her fingers flex, her head fall back slightly, and her mouth open. Then I heard her; a low moan left her lips. That sound had goosebumps chase the heat that flowed over my skin.

My nipples hardened and my heart rate accelerated a little more as I watched him stand. His tongue circled one of her nipples before his mouth closed around it and he sucked. I saw his cheeks hollow a little as he did. She cried out again. My body started to gently shake, and Mackenzie held me tighter against him.

I watched as he pulled back his lips, exposing his teeth a little, which clamped down on her. He moved to her side, reaching around and down with his hand. When his fingers trailed through her pubic hair and plunged inside her, I moaned out loud. I'd never seen anything as erotic. He would pull his fingers most of the way out. I could see

159

the slickness of her juices on them. If we'd been in the same room, I'm sure I would have been able to smell her arousal. He fucked her with his fingers, and I watched in utter fascination.

"Touch me," I whispered.

I felt Mackenzie's mouth at the side of my neck; his hot breath ghosted my skin.

"No. When I touch you, I want your cunt soaked," he said.

I wanted to tell him it was. I wanted to show him the wetness that coated the inside of my thighs. As his tongue trailed up my neck, I wanted to close my eyes and absorb his touch, but I didn't want to miss one second of what was happening in front of me.

His fist tightened in my hair as he pulled my head to one side. He raked his teeth down my skin and across my shoulder. A shudder ran through me.

The woman's moans began to get louder, closer together. I watched her ball her fist at her side, and I saw her stomach quiver. Her head was thrown back, and as he fingerfucked her harder, faster, she screamed out as she came.

"Oh, God," I whispered.

Her legs shook as he withdrew his fingers, and I gasped as a string of her cum kept them connected for a little longer.

He raised his fingers to her lips and she opened her mouth, sucking and licking. I clamped my thighs together, trying to gain some relief from the heat, from the throbbing, between them.

"No you don't" Mackenzie said, he kicked at the inside of my ankles to encourage me to part my legs again.

"Please," I whispered.

I heard as well as felt his chuckle against my skin. "Fucking torture, isn't it?"

"Yes."

He slid his hand around my waist, his fingers stopping just shy of where I wanted them. I placed my hand over his, pushing it further down. When his fingertips brushed over my clitoris, my stomach trembled as the muscles went into spasms. Heat coursed over my body, and I could feel my chest and neck flush.

While Mackenzie gently teased me, the man led his woman to the cross. He turned her so she faced it, and then raised one arm and secured her by the wrist to one point on the cross. He did the same to her other. He ran his hands down her sides, over her waist, and then down one leg. He secured her ankle, repeating the process with the other. He was slow and deliberate with his movements. When she was spreadeagled, he stepped away.

I could hear her pant; a soft moan escaped her lips as he walked away. He opened the door of their sideboard, and when he turned, he held a leather bound stick, strings of soft leather fell from one end.

"What is that?" I whispered, trying to regulate my own breathing.

"A flogger."

The man trailed it down her back; the sensation had clearly excited her. I heard her gasp. I watched him raise his arm; I heard the swish as he brought it through the air and then the crack as leather hit skin. The sound seemed magnified in our room and I startled. She cried out, but it was a cry of pure pleasure. He did it again, and then again.

"More," she said.

He brought the flogger down against her arse. I could see her skin begin to pink. He gave short sharp flicks, until his final one, the one that had her orgasm again, was against her pussy.

Mackenzie pushed his fingers inside me, although not able to reach as deep as I wanted, it was enough. I came instantly. I mirrored her cries.

I wasn't sure how long we'd been standing there, watching. I know my legs had begun to ache as I stood naked in my high heels. But no matter how my body felt, I could not take my eyes away from the spectacle in front of me. Everything they did was controlled, precise, practiced. Every touch of his elicited a response, whether that was a moan, a scream, or a tensing of her body.

There was something beautiful in what they did.

He unfastened her wrists and ankles and led her to the brown leather chaise. He supported her as she lowered and lay on her back. Her legs dangled off the sides, and I had full view of her glistening pussy.

I heard the sound of a zipper being lowered and at first wasn't sure if it was his or Mackenzie's. That was until I saw his jeans fall to the floor and felt Mackenzie's. Both men had removed their clothes at the same time.

I felt the void as Mackenzie stepped back and away from me. I wanted to look over my shoulder, but I didn't want to miss anything. I heard the scrape of furniture as a low footstool was placed in front of me.

"Take off your shoes," he whispered.

I slid my feet from my shoes as I watched the man wrap his hand around his cock.

"Stand and place your hands on the glass. Bend over," Mackenzie said.

I took a small step up and placed my palms against the cool glass. I heard the sound of a foil packet being torn open. Every sense seemed heightened; I could smell the latex, the lubricant.

The man was standing between his partner's legs, at the edge of the chaise. He ran his hand up and down his cock before pushing inside her.

Mackenzie did the same, taking me by surprise. He fucked me from behind, while I watched. I saw the man's cock, coated with her juices, pull out until just his tip was inside her, then plunge back in, over and over again in slow strokes. As he sped up, her moans became more frequent.

I struggled to keep my hands on the mirror. As my arousal escalated, my palms sweated a little.

"You're so fucking hot, so wet," Mackenzie whispered.

The sound of skin hitting skin, moaning and gasps of pleasure echoed around the room, theirs and ours.

I couldn't hold on any longer, I pushed my arse back towards him, needing more as my orgasm rolled over me. I screamed out and lowered my head, wanting to rest my forehead on the cool glass. Mackenzie wrapped his hand in my hair, pulling, forcing my head back up. While my body shook, my stomach clenched as he fucked me harder through it.

I heard a growl that rumbled from Mackenzie's chest before leaving his mouth. His fingers dug into my hips as he gave in to his release.

Shortly after I saw the man do the same.

I felt my hands slip down the glass as my arms shook. Mackenzie pulled out of me, and I was able to sit down on my heels and rest my hands on my knees. I couldn't get my breath, my chest felt tight, and my throat was dry.

If I thought my body was done, I was wrong. I heard the click of a door opening. I raised my head to see a dark haired man enter their room. He was naked.

"What…?"

My question was cut off when Mackenzie placed his hands under my arms and encouraged me to stand again. I wasn't sure if my legs would comply.

"Step down," he whispered.

He kicked the footstool away.

While I watched, the woman sat, still with her legs astride the chaise. The second man stepped forward, massaging his cock as he did. He placed his hand behind her head, pushing her face towards it. She opened her mouth and extended her tongue to lick from his balls to the tip, before sucking him in.

While she sucked his cock, the blond man walked behind her. He took her wrists and bound them behind her back.

I heard Mackenzie drag one of the chairs to where I stood. I felt the cool leather against the back of my legs.

"Sit," he said.

As I did, Mackenzie placed his hands under my knees and drew them up, placing my legs over the arms. I was totally exposed to him. He knelt before me.

"When you've seen enough, you tell me," he whispered.

I nodded my head.

The first man knelt behind the woman. He leaned forward, sliding his hands through the second man's hair and drawing his head towards him. Their kiss was deep, eliciting a moan from one.

I felt Mackenzie's breath on my swollen clitoris; he blew very gently as if cooling me down. His breath alone couldn't extinguish the fire that raged between my thighs. Watching the two men kiss, observing as they changed positions, and their mouths parted just enough for me to see their tongues, was about the most erotic thing I'd seen that evening.

There was unbridled passion in their kiss. It wasn't two strangers and my perception that the first pair was a couple, changed. The men were the couple. There was familiarity in what they were doing.

The dark haired man pulled his cock from her mouth; it was coated in her saliva. While the blond stood, with his legs on either side of the chaise, she was encouraged to lie down. They continued their kiss, while he stepped slightly towards his partner. My eyes grew wide as I saw her lick his balls, then suck one into her mouth.

I felt Mackenzie's tongue gently flick my clitoris, and I gripped the arms of the chair as static flowed over my body. Every nerve felt charged. The blood rushing through my body heated my skin. I moaned as his lips closed around my sensitive bud, and he sucked it into his mouth.

The dark haired man broke the kiss first. He smiled as he stepped back, leaving his friend still standing over the woman. When his friend moved away, he reached for the woman's hips and gently flipped her over. He held her head, turning it to the side, so she was facing me. He brushed her hair from her face, gently tucking it behind her ear. The blond man had stepped out of view.

Mackenzie sat back on his heels and then stood. He held out his hand, wanting me to stand. I slid my legs from the arms of the chair, and as I stood, he turned the chair side on to the mirror.

Without a word, he placed his hand between my shoulder blades, bending me over the arms. He ran his fingers down my back, and I shivered as he paused half way down the crack of my backside.

"Relax," he whispered.

I took a deep breath as the tip of his finger teased, pushing in very gently, and then slowly pulling out, back in a little further. The fluttering in my stomach intensified, my clitoris throbbed harder with each insertion. The more I relaxed, the more I loved what he was doing.

The dark haired man pulled the woman up by her hips, so she knelt on the chaise. He stood directly behind her. I watched as he ran his hand down her back, over her backside, and I wondered if he was going to the do same as Mackenzie.

The blond man returned, and I saw him hand over a small container, the contents of which were squirted onto her and over his cock. I watched him run the tip over her backside before gently pushing into her. He leaned over her as he fucked her arse.

But it was the sight of the blond man, as he did the same to his partner, which threw me over the edge. As Mackenzie fingered my arse, he pushed his cock inside me. And I watched one man fuck another, while the first fucked the woman.

I screamed out. I gripped the arm of the chair so hard, my nails dug into the leather. The sounds of skin on skin, of moans and cries of pleasure coming from the other room echoed around my head, competing with the white noise. My arousal was off the scale, every nerve ending screamed: my fingers, toes, even my scalp tingled as static coursed over my skin. My nipples ached with their hardness.

My stomach clenched at the sound of Mackenzie, growling out my name. He pulled his finger from my arse. I wanted to tell him not to. One hand held my hips, his nails digging in and breaking my skin; the other wrapped in my hair and pulled my head up. He fucked me harder than he ever had.

Tears ran down my cheeks. I felt so light-headed as I came, I could no longer hold myself up; my legs shook. I was thankful when I heard Mackenzie shout out as he came himself.

Then I passed out.

I wasn't sure how long I'd been asleep. My eyelids felt puffy and sticky when I tried to open them. More tears ran down my cheeks.

"Shush, baby," I heard. I felt emotionally drained.

Mackenzie was dressed and sitting on the bed beside me. I glanced quickly towards the window thankful to see the curtains closed.

"It's okay," he said.

At first I couldn't speak. I lay on my side, still naked, with Mackenzie stroking my hair.

"Can you talk to me?" he whispered.

I nodded my head.

"Why did that turn me on so much? What's wrong with me?" I said, unable to stop the hitch in my voice. I was so confused.

I tried, but failed, to stop the images of what I'd witnessed flooding my mind.

"There's nothing wrong with you, Lauren. You're exploring your boundaries, finding yourself right now."

"I don't know that I like what I find though."

"Then you don't need to explore anymore."

"But that's the point. Watching them aroused me, beyond belief. I'm so confused," I whispered, not making eye contact.

"Look at me," he said. I raised my face.

"How do you feel, truly feel inside? I'm not talking about arousal, I'm talking about you as a person."

I sighed and licked my lips. "Alive. I don't feel dull, uninteresting."

"Then you are halfway to finding out who you are, what you want, and what you like."

"And then what?"

That was the million-dollar question. What happened when I'd found myself? What happened to Mackenzie and me?

He didn't answer; I guessed I didn't expect him to.

I was thankful for the small bathroom attached to the bedroom. Like a hotel it had a selection of towels and Bulgari toiletries. I took a quick shower, careful not to wet my hair and redressed.

"So, what do we do now?" I said, as I sat on the bed beside him while he tied his shoelaces.

"We can get a drink, or we can go home?"

"Do people stay here, overnight?"

"They can, though not in these rooms. They have accommodation in the grounds."

"Have you stayed here?"

"Yes."

"What did...? No, don't answer that. I don't think I want to know."

"I will answer any question you want, if I think you can handle that answer. I'm not sure you can right now. It's a conversation for another day."

He stood and held out his hand.

"One thing, you, and the blond man...was that rehearsed?"

"I don't know what you mean."

"Removing clothes at the same time."

He chuckled a little. "No, I imagine I was a split second behind him. I think us men tend to only have one routine and we stick to it. It's why I asked for loose clothing, they're easier, and quicker, to get off."

I stood and allowed him to lead me to the bedroom door.

"What if we bump into them?"

"They don't know *who* was in the room. Would you like me to poke my head around the door and check they're not leaving?"

"Please."

He looked at me. "I was kidding. If we happen to leave at the exact same time, thank them for a wonderful evening."

****

I remembered getting into the car, and then I was shaken awake and found we'd arrived at my apartment block.

"What time is it?" I asked.

"Three."

"Fuck!"

"At least you don't have to get up early," he said.

He'd parked the car near the door to the lifts. He climbed out and walked around to my side. Once again, he helped as I joined him. We took the lift to my floor and I opened the door to my apartment. I expected him to walk in behind me but he hadn't.

"I need to get home," he said gently.

"Oh, okay." I wasn't sure what to say really.

He took a step over the threshold and placed his hands either side of my head.

"You were stunning tonight," he whispered.

"I'd like you to stay."

"I wish I could. I have a very early Skype meeting. In fact, in about an hour and a half."

We stood in silence for a moment and he just stared at me. I felt the spark between us; I thought I saw it in his eyes, but I was too scared to say anything.

"I can smell myself on your hands," I whispered.

He leaned forward until his mouth was near my ear.

"And that's why I didn't shower. I want to smell you for as long as possible."

He gave me a gentle kiss and then he was gone.

Chapter Thirteen

I didn't go straight to bed. I sat for ages with a cup of tea at the kitchen table and watched the sun begin to rise instead.

I thought on what Mackenzie had said, *I was finding myself.* I was discovering what aroused me, what I had been missing out on after spending years of being with one man: a man who had no sense of adventure.

I just needed to decide if the person I was discovering was someone I liked. I certainly enjoyed the experience, although I was left confused. I guessed I was conditioned to not want that, to find it disgusting or perverted even. I'd read the sexy novels, thankful I had a Kindle, so others couldn't see what I was reading. I'd even gone to the extreme of changing the cover on a hardback once. I'd been jealous of the female characters, as irrational as that was. Experiencing it, in real life, was exciting and terrifying, shameful and uplifting, I wanted to stop; yet I wanted to continue.

I'd never seen two men have sex though, and it was that, which aroused me more.

I sent a text.

BDSM, what do you know about it?

Mackenzie's reply was almost immediate, and then I remembered he'd be in his online meeting.

Why?

Because that's next on my list.

I turned off the phone, not expecting a reply and headed to the bedroom. I stripped off my clothes and naked, climbed under the covers. I slept until mid-afternoon.

****

The first thing I did when I woke was to turn on my phone. Mackenzie had replied.

BDSM – Google it, then decide. You did *not* witness BDSM, just a small part of it.

I did as he asked. I opened the laptop and Googled. Pages and pages of information came up. Some, the extreme elements such as being led around on all fours by a dog lead, did nothing for me. Others, like the St. Andrew's cross, the flogger, the spanking bench even, produced that bubble of excitement I was getting addicted to.

I closed down the tabs and thought. *Exactly what was it I wanted?*

I didn't want to be a submissive, I didn't want to be collared and have to call Mackenzie 'Master' or some other shit. But I did want the restraint; I wanted to feel those leather cuffs against my skin and be held in one position. I wanted to feel the painful pleasure, and the heat my skin would produce after the sting of being flogged. I wanted Mackenzie to take complete control of my body, of my mind, and of my soul.

I will not fall for him, I reminded myself.

I was under no illusion it would hurt. I was also confident I could handle it. I kept an image of the pleasure on the woman's face in my head, as I texted back.

Okay, maybe not full-blown BDSM, but what I saw is what I want. Not the men, the flogger and cross.

That time he didn't reply and I smiled. The game was on.

****

My stomach grumbled, reminding me I hadn't eaten yet. I decided to take a walk to the local deli and stock up the fridge. I grabbed my keys and debit card then headed out. It was a sunny afternoon and the usual tourist activity was in flow on the riverbank. I smiled as I walked and it surprised me to receive smiles in return. If only those people knew what I was thinking about. I laughed out loud.

The deli was a place where I could spend hours. Although small, it housed an array of foods, wine, coffees, and artisan products. It also reminded me that I'd never collected my coffee from Mackenzie. I purchased more. When my basket was full and I'd paid, I took a slow stroll back to the apartment.

I opened the French doors onto the small balcony and allowed the breeze to waft through. I prepared something to eat and took that, and my Kindle, outside.

I tried to read but thoughts of the club ran through my mind. More importantly, thoughts of what Mackenzie had done at the club. I wanted to ask him. He'd said if he thought I could handle the answers he'd tell me. Could I?

What could he tell me that I wouldn't want to hear? He'd fucked other women? That I could handle. He'd been the one holding the flogger? My stomach tightened at that thought. Threesomes? We'd sort of already done that.

At the thought of the woman, my stomach tightened further.

As the sun started to lower, a chill crept over me. I took my plate and Kindle back inside. Once I'd poured myself a glass of wine, I settled on the sofa to watch some crap Saturday night TV. Like the Kindle, not much kept my interest for more than a few minutes. I flicked from channel to channel, watching a few minutes before becoming bored.

I grabbed my laptop and brought up a search engine. I typed in 'sex clubs.' I decided I'd like to find out what else was on offer at Mackenzie's members only manor house. I found plenty of sex clubs, some which had me howling with laughter, others that had me want to wash my eyes with bleach. I found nothing on the one in Surrey.

What I did see among the listings were sites advertising sex toys.

I'd never used one, I'd pretended of course. On the very rare occasion I'd had a girls' night out and B.O.B was the topic of conversation, you'd think I owned *Ann Summers*. I scanned through one site, fascinated by some of the objects on sale.

I choked as I came across a glow in the dark clone-a-willy, a vibrator moulding kit. For an extra few pounds I could add a lovely drawstring bag to carry it around it. I passed on the pussy pump but paused over a mini G-spot vibrator.

I rose to collect the debit card I'd left on the kitchen counter and placed the item in my virtual basket.

After my second glass of wine, I found myself debating between a six-inch dildo and an eight-inch. It wasn't like I'd ever measured myself inside before. I opted to play safe and placed a six-inch Rabbit in my virtual basket.

I added lube, not that I generally needed that with Mackenzie, and vibrating bullet eggs. As I was about to head to the checkout, I spotted something that had me wide-eyed: a clitoral and G-spot stimulator controlled by a smart phone. I deleted the mini G-spot and added the We-Vibe instead. I checked out.

By the time I'd gotten halfway through the third glass of wine, I was crying with laughter. *A smart phone controlled vibrator!* I was so in the dark where all things sex was concerned.

I closed the laptop, and as it's glow was extinguished, I realised I hadn't turned on the apartment lights. The TV flickered creating some light; I muted it and just sat.

In that moment, with thoughts running through my head that I didn't want and too much wine in my system, I felt lonelier than I ever had.

I was doing things I'd never considered before. I felt alive only when I was doing them, but I couldn't determine if that was because it was Mackenzie I was with or not.

The thought of not being with him, or not exploring my sexual side, horrified me. But I pushed that niggle, that had started to gain a louder voice, from my mind.

What I was doing wasn't healthy for my mind. What was I getting addicted to? Mackenzie or the experiences? And what happened when it all came to a halt?

In the past month, I'd had sex with a woman. Mackenzie had fucked me to the point of passing out, and I'd been overly aroused, if there was such a thing, by watching two men together.

I wasn't sure where I could go from there.

Chapter Fourteen

I guessed I'd been crying during the night, although I didn't remember, it was only because my pillow was damp and my eyes puffy again. I glanced at my watch to see it was past nine o'clock. Even though it was a Sunday, and I had no reason to get up early, it was still later than I'd normally rise.

My body ached, perhaps it was Friday night catching up on me; maybe it was because I felt wrung out. I cringed when I remembered I'd drank too much, chuckled at the thought of my online purchases and was thankful that when I moved, my head wasn't spinning.

I took a shower and dressed, walking around the empty apartment with only the noise of my feet on wooden floors for company. For the first time, I didn't want to be there.

I sat with a cup of tea and pulled my divorce papers from my briefcase. It was time to finalise everything. I wanted Scott out of my life and before he realised he was going to lose his job. I signed the division of assets; he could have his half, deservedly or not. I would send the documents off first thing the following morning, and instruct the solicitor to proceed as quickly as possible.

I then had to make a decision about Mackenzie.

I read through the text messages we'd exchanged. I still wanted to experience what I'd asked for but maybe that should be last one. I just wanted one more night with him and then I'd walk away. I'd give up the game.

I didn't think, for one minute, Mackenzie was capable of any kind of relationship. He had neither the time nor had he shown any inclination that was what he wanted. I got it though; I understood what he was doing. The game was a way of empowering me, of allowing me to prove to myself that I was worthy, I was interesting, I was sensual, sexual, whatever words I wanted to use.

In one way he'd achieved what he'd set out to do. But in doing so, he'd forced me to take a hard look at my life and the changes I needed to make. I wasn't convinced I'd find another man like him.

I needed to get out of the apartment; it felt claustrophobic. I picked up my phone and dialled.

"Hey," Jerry said when he'd answered.

"Hi, what are you doing today?" I asked.

"I was going into work, why? Want to do something?"

"I do. I can't sit here all day."

"Okay, how about I pick you up in an hour?"

"Sounds great, thank you."

"See you then."

Was that fair? I knew how Jerry felt, but he was my friend, my only friend. I needed company that day.

I put on some makeup while I waited, brushed and tied my hair in a high ponytail, and hunted the apartment for clean socks.

I was downstairs and waiting in the car park when Jerry's car pulled in. I opened the rear door and slid in beside him. He smiled as he leaned forwards to give me a hug.

"Lonely, huh?" he said.

"No, I wanted to spend some time with my friend," I lied.

"Lonely or not, I'll take whatever," he said, then sat back with a laugh.

We pulled out into the traffic.

"So what shall we do?" I asked.

"I fancy a nice lunch, then a walk somewhere."

"Okay, where?"

"Me and Mackenzie went to a nice pub the other day, not far from where he lives."

My stomach clenched at Mackenzie's name. Jerry leaned forwards and asked Steve, his driver, to take him to the place he'd been. Thankfully, Steve knew where to go.

"I'm sure there are some nicer places closer," I said.

"Probably are but you'll like it, it's a gastro pub. And how do you know he doesn't live just around the corner?"

He turned to me and smirked.

"I just assumed he didn't live in Canary Wharf," I replied, hoping my cheeks hadn't flamed. "So, made any plans for your retirement?"

I wanted to divert the conversation away from Mackenzie, but I wasn't sure Jerry was fooled. He paused before he answered. He told me he'd booked that holiday to the Caribbean, and then when he returned, he'd think on what new projects he wanted to get involved in. We chatted as we drove, but the closer we got to Hampstead Heath, the more agitated I became.

The gastro pub sat on a corner of two streets. Steve pulled the car alongside the curb and we climbed out. I followed Jerry in through the door and kept my gaze on him as he threaded his way through people to the bar. He asked for a table and ordered a bottle of wine at the same time.

I scanned the room. It was a wonderful old building, one side a dining room and the other, the bar with sofas.

"There's a wait for the table, do you want to sit?" Jerry said.

"Of course."

He picked up the bottle of red and the two glasses and we headed to the only available sofa.

"What's up, Lauren," Jerry said as he poured the wine.

"Nothing, why do ask?"

"You don't seem your usual self."

"I'm fine, just a little stressed, and I needed some company today. I should have rung the estate agent but I keep putting it off. Although I signed the division of assets form this morning. Scott can have what he's demanding, I just want closure now."

"Better to do that before he sees what your new salary is likely to be."

"I don't know what my new salary is going to be. I wonder if I could ask Gabriella to delay my appointment until the divorce is done."

"How long does it take to get divorced?"

"It's straightforward. He hasn't contested the reasons so I'm hoping a couple more months. It's been about six months already."

"Don't you have to do the two-year wait thing?"

"No, because I cited his adultery and he didn't fight that."

I took a sip of my wine.

"I'm glad you're getting rid of him. He's nothing but a waste of space."

I sighed. "Yeah, and I wasted nearly fifteen years on him."

Jerry raised his glass to mine. "Well, here's to our exciting new futures."

It was as I started to take another sip that I saw Mackenzie. My glass hovered near my mouth when he walked in. My jaw dropped when I saw his companion.

A tall blonde, immaculately dressed woman accompanied him. He placed his hand on her back as they threaded their way through the throng of people to the bar.

"Mack…" I placed my hand on Jerry's arm to halt his words.

He turned to me, his brow furrowed.

"He has company, he might not want to be disturbed," I said.

However, Mackenzie had heard. He looked over, following the sound of his name.

Jerry stood and I had no choice but to follow as he walked over. If I'd stayed put, Jerry would have had a hundred questions as to why I'd been so rude, I was sure of that.

"Jerry, Lauren," Mackenzie said, as he shook Jerry's hand.

"Lauren was lonely so I thought I'd introduce her to your pub," Jerry said. I cringed, not wanting Mackenzie to know that.

"You'll love the food here," he said, looking at me.

Until that point he hadn't introduced his companion, she stood just to his side with a smile on her face. I watched her place her hand on his arm.

"Introduce us," she said. She had an American Southern accent, the same as Gabriella.

"I'm sorry. Jerry, Lauren, this is Addison. Addison, Jerry owned a company I've just acquired and Lauren is to transfer as CEO."

She reached out to take my hand; she had a firm handshake.

"It's a pleasure to meet you," she said to us both.

"We just booked a table, do you want to join us?" Jerry said. I could have kicked him.

Addison wore a cream trouser suit and high heels that had her tower over me. Her makeup was perfect, her nails manicured. In my jeans and shirt, with Converse on my feet, I felt completely dull beside her.

"That would be wonderful," she said. "Shall we?" she asked Mackenzie. He nodded.

"Let me change the table," Jerry said. He left me standing there as he went back to the bar.

"Erm, we have a bottle of wine, if you'd like some," I said. Wanting to shrink from her gaze.

"Thank you, it's kind of you to ask us to join you," she said.

"I'm sure Jerry and Lauren would prefer to spend their lunch time on their own," Mackenzie said.

"No way, it's cool," Jerry said, as he returned carrying two more glasses. "Table changed, just got to wait another ten minutes."

I turned and walked back to the sofa we'd left our drinks at, wanting to curse that the one opposite was then vacant.

Jerry and I sat one side; Mackenzie and Addison took the opposite one.

"Are you here on holiday?" Jerry asked, as he poured more wine.

"Sort of. It's a beautiful country, Mackenzie has been showing me around."

Jerry peppered her with questions and I kept my gaze low as I sipped my wine. I listened as she explained that she'd recently taken a tour around Europe, detailing museums and art houses she'd visited in Milan and Paris.

"Have you been to Milan?" she asked. It was the pause that alerted me to the fact she'd addressed me.

"I haven't, I hear it's a stunning place."

She detailed her holiday, laughing as she recalled memories. Jerry asked her a question but I'd tuned out. That was until she answered one.

"Mackenzie and I honeymooned in Europe," she said.

I froze; I think I even blinked rapidly.

"Oh, so you're married?" Jerry said.

She was interrupted from answering by the waitress approaching to tell us our table was ready. I wanted to kick the fucking waitress as well. I wanted the answer as to whether they were divorced or not. Gabriella had told me her brother had seduced Mackenzie's wife. But I had no idea if that caused a divorce or even how long ago that was.

They didn't live together; I'd been to his house, twice. There had been no evidence of her there. But then he was back and forth to the U.S. constantly. Did he live with her when he was back home?

We stood and I allowed Mackenzie and Addison to walk ahead. Jerry lowered his head to mine.

"She's a stunner," he whispered. I pinched him hard on the arm.

I trailed behind and was thankful Addison had taken the seat beside Mackenzie and not opposite. I let Jerry sit first, which meant I was left facing Addison.

"So you work with Jerry, Lauren?"

"I did, until he sold out, of course."

"And now what?"

"Now I transfer to one of Mackenzie's companies. It's all a little in the planning stages right now," I said.

"How exciting for you."

I didn't think she was being condescending, and I hated the fact that she was actually a pleasant person. I didn't want to like her, but I did. She was friendly, talkative, and interesting.

I certainly didn't want to see her place her hand on Mackenzie's arm, to defer to him when menus were placed on the table and she asked him to choose for her. I didn't want to see her smile up at him. My stomach lurched when he smiled back.

"I wanted to see as much of the U.K. as I could while I was here. Mackenzie has offered to show me around London, but where else should I visit?" she asked me.

"If you have enough time, the South West is wonderful. My mum lives in Cornwall and it's one of my favourite places," I said, once I'd placed my order.

"I'd love to see some of Scotland, too." She looked over to Mackenzie. "Maybe we can do that?"

Before he answered, I excused myself. I didn't need the ladies, just not to hear his reply.

I sat in a cubicle for a few moments. I couldn't imagine Scott and I being so civilised. I began to wonder what had caused her to have an affair. Or had she? I only knew what Gabriella had said. *Daniel had stolen Mackenzie's wife.* I had no idea what that actually meant, or even if Addison and Daniel were still together.

Did Mackenzie still love her? Was that why he was *showing her around London*? I wasn't jealous, or at least I didn't think I was, I just needed to know where I stood in that relationship. Maybe I didn't *stand* anywhere.

When I thought I'd spent enough time away, I returned to hear her laugh at something Jerry had said.

"I'd love to spend a little more time with you guys," she said, as I sat. "You are a funny guy, Jerry."

There was no opportunity to answer as the waitress placed our meals on the table.

Jerry and Addison chatted through lunch, Mackenzie joined in when required, and I stayed mostly quiet. I'd lost my appetite and pushed most of my food around my plate. When I finally laid my cutlery down, having given up on eating, I noticed the others had finished their meals.

Another bottle of wine was ordered, and as much as I wanted to drown myself in alcohol, I opted for water.

"How long are you in town, Addison?" Jerry asked.

"I'm not sure, I guess that depends on Mackenzie," she replied.

I kicked Jerry on the ankle before he could ask any more. He frowned at me, in a not so subtle way.

"Sorry, getting comfortable," I said, with a smile.

"We're off to the theatre later, I've been dying to see a show," she said.

"What are you seeing?" I asked.

"*Les Misérables*, Mackenzie was able to secure a box for us. I'm so excited."

"I've seen it, many times. It's a wonderful show. I'm sure you're going to enjoy it."

"We saw it on Broadway, some time ago, but seeing a show in London just has to be done. I'd also like to see some Shakespeare, maybe at the open-air theatre in Regent's Park."

"I'd wait for some nicer weather for that," I said.

A pot of coffee and four small cups were placed on the table. Mackenzie poured. He slid one over to Jerry and Addison picked hers up. Mackenzie handed me a cup and as my fingers brushed his, I felt a spark of static. I wouldn't look at him though. I could feel his stare, but I mumbled my thanks and raised the cup to my lips.

I willed the time to speed up and was thankful when I saw Mackenzie glance at his watch.

"We need to get going," he said, as he waved at a passing waitress to gain her attention.

"Isn't it a little early?" Addison replied.

"I have to shower and change. I have a call to make as well," he said.

181

The waitress placed the bill on the table and both Jerry and Mackenzie reached for it.

"I'll get this," Jerry said. "Lauren and I are not in a rush to leave just yet."

We stood to say goodbye. I held out my hand and Mackenzie took it. "Mr. Miller," I said.

Addison ignored my outstretched hand and pulled me into a hug instead.

"It was great to meet you, Lauren. Hopefully we can do this again, soon," she said.

I smiled instead of giving a reply. I slumped back into my seat as they left.

"I didn't know he was married," Jerry said.

"I think they're separated, or maybe divorced."

"How do you know that?"

"Gabriella said."

"Sure doesn't look like it was an acrimonious split."

"No, doesn't, does it?"

I picked up a clean glass and filled it with wine. I handed the bottle to Jerry, who topped up his own.

For a moment we were silent. I kept my eyes down, looking at the table.

"Lauren," Jerry said. I raised my gaze slowly to his.

"Aw fuck, babe. It's him, isn't it? The mystery man."

I let a tear roll down my cheek.

"You cannot say a word, Jerry. You need to promise me that."

"I won't but, Jesus, Lauren! And there was me wittering on about their marriage. Are they married or what?"

"I don't know. They're separated or divorced, like I said."

"He hasn't told you?"

"We're not dating, Jerry. Just…spending some time together."

'You are on dangerous ground here."

"I know."

He took a sip of his wine and for a while he wouldn't meet my gaze. He looked hurt. I placed my hand on his arm.

"You're my friend, Jerry, probably my only friend. I wouldn't risk that friendship for anything," I said.

"I know, but sure doesn't feel good to know you're *spending time* with him." He gave me a sad smile.

"I've fucked up, haven't I?" I whispered.

"Not with me. I'll get over it. But I don't want you to get hurt, and I have a feeling you're about to."

"So do I. I got in to whatever it is with open eyes; I'm a big girl. I'll deal with it, and to be honest, it's coming to an end anyway."

"Your choice, or his?"

"My choice."

One more night, and I'll call a halt to it. Hadn't that been my thought?

"Can we skip that walk? I think I'd like to go home," I said. Jerry laid some cash in the leather holder with the bill and we left.

****

Jerry gave me a hug as I was dropped off back at my apartment. I tried not to let the misery overwhelm me as I opened my apartment door.

Why couldn't Addison have been ugly? Or mean? Why did she have to be pretty and nice?

I made tea and sat at the kitchen table. My phone began to ring. I rifled through my handbag to retrieve it. Mackenzie had called me.

"Hi," I said, as I answered the call.

"Hey. I'm sorry about that. I guess that wasn't the best lunch you've had."

"It's okay. I was a little surprised, of course. You have every right to dine with your wife."

"Ex-wife. We're divorced, Lauren."

"Ex-wife then. It's okay; there was no need to call. She seemed a lovely woman."

"Yes, there was. I wanted to make sure you were okay."

"Honestly, I'm fine. You have a lovely evening," I said, forcing my voice to sound cheerful.

"I'll be in the office tomorrow, I want to meet with you."

"Of course, just let me know what time."

He paused and I heard him sigh.

"Mackenzie, I'm not going to kick off about you spending time with your ex-wife. You have every right to spend time with whoever you want. It's not like we have any kind of a relationship."

He didn't answer and I wondered if the call had been cut off. I brought it away from my ear and looked at the screen.

"Are you there?" I asked.

"Tomorrow then, Lauren. Say ten o'clock?" His voice was clipped.

"I'll be there. Thank you for calling," I said.

He said goodbye and I cut off the call. I placed the phone on the table and then cried.

I will not fall for...fuck, I already had. I cried harder.

****

I dressed in a purple shirt, black trousers, and black high-heeled shoes the following morning. I piled my hair on top of my head, letting loose tendrils fall around my face, and I applied my makeup. I wasn't going to let Mackenzie know that I'd spent the night pining for him; or that my stomach ached for his touch.

I concealed the nerves as I walked into my office and bade a good morning to my team. I laughed at the wolf whistle I received from

Jenny. I kept the fake smile on my face until it was nearly ten o'clock.

As I watched the clock, my palms sweated and my stomach knotted. I held my breath as I heard a knock on the door.

"It's open," I called out.

Instead of Mackenzie, Jenny popped her head through the door. I breathed a sigh of relief.

"They're heading to the board room," she said.

"Who?"

"Everyone, it seems. Just got an email."

I hadn't checked my messages but gathered a pad and pen. I walked up the one flight and made my way to the boardroom. Some of my colleagues had congregated outside the boardroom. Sally was handing around mugs of coffee from a tray.

I noticed little glances thrown my way, and the usual whispers followed as I took a mug and thanked Sally.

"Lauren, may I speak with you?" I heard.

Mackenzie was standing at the boardroom door.

"Of course," I said.

He stepped to one side and closed the door behind us, blocking out the chatter from outside.

"I want to announce your appointment today. The merger is going to be a little quicker than we anticipated."

"Oh, I…erm…shit."

"Is there a problem?"

"I wanted to ask Gabriella if she'd delay any announcement until…"

"Until what?"

"Until my divorce. I don't want Scott to know anything about it; he's trying to fleece me as it is. If he loses his job and he knows I'm on a higher pay grade, I'm not sure what he'll do. I suspect he'll delay the divorce, hoping to get more money from me."

"Why didn't you tell me this?"

"Probably for the same reason you never mentioned your wife was here."

"Ex-wife."

"Ex-wife. We haven't spoken about anything personal at all. I'm sorry, it's okay, you go ahead with your announcement, and I'll deal with it."

I hadn't wanted to mention his ex-wife, it was petty, but he'd thrown me off balance a little.

"You have a lawyer, I take it?"

"Of course I have a lawyer. I've just sent her all the paperwork. Listen, I shouldn't have just said what I did. It's okay, I'm fine with it all."

"Will you stop saying, 'it's okay' and 'you're fine.' *It's* not and *you're* not. *Don't* be fine with it."

Don't be fine with it? What on earth did that mean?

"Mackenzie, don't presume to tell me what I am or should be, please. I have a mess to deal with and I will. It won't affect my work."

"I don't give a shit about work, I worry about you," he said.

I glanced over to see Scott looking through the window.

"They're getting restless, wondering what we are talking about. Make the announcement. It's probably best to get it over with now anyway."

He sighed as he looked at me. I planted a fake smile on my face.

"I'm excited about this new opportunity," I said, hoping to bring our mind-set back to work.

"I can't tell what you're thinking, that annoys me," he whispered.

"Back at you with that one," I snapped.

He stared at me. "I'm not here to fight with you," he said.

"I'm not either. I'm just answering your question. You called me in here. I've explained why I was a little hesitant about your announcement. But I'd like you to go ahead with it," I said, hoping I'd made myself clear.

He turned away and beckoned to those staring through the window, to join us. Mackenzie sat at the head of the table. He tapped the place to his left and I sat.

"Thank you for joining us, and I apologise about the impromptu meeting. I would have waited for Gabriella to make this announcement, but she's otherwise engaged. As you know, I intend to merge this company with another of mine, Trymast. Although both companies are involved in media there are areas they, and you, operate in that are differerent. However, there is an overlap. It's that overlap that we have to work on.

"You've had details of Trymast, you can see their offices are in Canary Wharf, and as a company, are much larger. One of our proposals is to move all business and staff to that location."

He paused as he scanned the room. It was the first piece of information anyone had been given about the merger.

"The second announcement I have is that Lauren Perry will be heading Trymast. Our current CEO, Alex Duchovany has other areas of my businesses to concentrate on, and we believe Miss Perry will be a perfect replacement. Not only has she headed the marketing team here but has been with Jerry from day one. There's not much she doesn't know about this business."

A murmur ran around the room. I covered my discomfort but taking a sip of my coffee.

"So that means she'll be our boss?" I heard, recognising the voice immediately.

"Yes, that's exactly what it means. So, you guys have a decision. You can work with us, and I include Miss Perry in the *us*, or you can have a hard think about your future."

I nearly choked on his words. They were rather harsh. But I liked his use of the word 'us.'

"I've met you all individually, so I hope you have a little idea on how I work. I have a team of CEOs that run each of my businesses for me. That allows me to develop the organisation; direct it's growth, without being bogged down in the day-to-day running. My second in command is Gabriella, who you've already met. In my absence, she has complete control."

"How will this work?" Gary, Head of Accounts, asked.

"I will be honest, I will look at each head of section, both here and at Trymast, and the right person will get the job. As Gabriella previously explained, we don't like to let go of valued members, but I cannot guarantee that everyone will keep their jobs. Those that don't will be offered alternative posts should they wish to accept those. Of course, there will be fair remuneration if they choose to leave. Miss Perry will be leaving her post shortly and transfer to Canary Wharf. We have a head of marketing that will take over her team immediately."

He turned to me. "I'll leave you to address your team, perhaps later today?"

"Of course," I replied.

"In the meantime, I hope you'll continue to work to the best of your abilities. I appreciate that there is a little uncertainty at the moment. I'll be here for the rest of today, using Jerry's office, and the door is open should any of you wish to speak with me privately. You'll all receive details of the move shortly; I understand Gabriella has that all in hand. I would also like to thank you for your patience while this merger occurs. If anyone has any questions they'd like to ask, fire away," he said.

No one asked a question initially. I guessed it was because they were still absorbing the information. Mackenzie had repeated some of what Gabriella had already said, so job security wasn't new but the move to Canary Wharf was.

"I live in the opposite direction to Canary Wharf, where we are now is pretty convenient and getting across town is going to cost," Gary said.

"Trymast has a higher salary rate than here. I'm sure what you would lose in additional travel expenses would be adequately covered," Mackenzie answered.

Gary nodded, satisfied with the answer. "If there isn't anything else, then remember, my door is open all day," Mackenzie said, then stood. "Miss Perry, please join me."

We left the boardroom just as the chatter started. Mackenzie didn't pause to listen but strode along the corridor to Jerry's office. Jerry wasn't in and I wondered why. I was under the impression there was a handover period.

"Where's Jerry?" I asked.

"He and I have a little project we may work on, he's over at Trymast," he said as he closed his door.

"I thought you had an open door policy."

"I do, once we have concluded our meeting. Sit, please," he said.

He took the chair that I was used to seeing Jerry in, but he commanded the space much more.

"How awkward will your remaining time here be?" he asked, throwing me a little.

"No more than usual, I hope."

"You are free to move over to Trymast as soon as you want, but I'd like for you to be there by the end of next week. That gives you two weeks to finish up any existing projects. Is that feasible?"

"I've already started to do that. I've reorganised everything so it's easy to find, and I've started a document to detail where I am on any given project."

"Then maybe we can cut it down by a week?"

"I think so. So next Monday you want me in Canary Wharf?"

He blinked a few times in rapid succession. "Yes, next Monday I want you in Canary Wharf."

I wasn't entirely sure we were talking about the same thing.

"How was your show?" I asked, wanting to change the subject.

189

"Boring. I didn't enjoy the company."

"The company? As in the actors or…"

"My ex-wife, Lauren. I don't enjoy her company. You may have fallen for her nice guy act but underneath…Let's just say, her and Scott would make a great pair. Now, enough about them. I wish for a private meeting with you this evening. We have things to discuss."

"Things?"

"You put in a request, Miss Perry, remember? Unlike your previous requests, this one involves some discussion."

"I…I'm not sure now," I said.

"You're not sure about what you requested?"

I saw him hold himself rigid. Was he worried about my reply?

One more night.

"I'll be sure after a discussion," I said.

He had tried to conceal his sigh of relief; he hadn't been successful.

"Then we'll talk about it later," his face softened a little. The businessman was gone, just for a split second. "We'll go for dinner, after work."

"I'm not talking about that, in public!"

He raised his eyebrows. "Trust me."

I nodded and stood. Before I turned to walk away I sighed.

"Can I ask one thing from you?" I said.

"Yes."

"I have some questions that I want you to answer. Can we do that later as well?"

"I'm sure you have many questions. I'm surprised you're able to wait until this evening."

"They can wait," I said. "Do you want me to leave this door open?" I placed my hand on the handle.

"Might as well, since they fell for that bull," he laughed; it was a sound that had my heart race.

I shook my head and left his office. I held my head high as I walked through the gap my colleagues had created. It was like the parting of the Red Sea.

****

I pulled my team together, and it upset me to think, although I knew their names, I didn't really know much else. How I conducted myself had to change. I had to be more approachable, more open, and dare I say it, friendlier.

"I have an announcement. I'm leaving you ladies. Well, I've been promoted, and as you know, we're merging with a company called Trymast. I'll be heading over there from next week. There is someone who will be replacing me, I'll make sure you all get introduced as soon as possible."

"That's great news, Lauren," Jenny said. She appeared to be the only one enthusiastic about my new appointment.

The four ladies in the team seemed indifferent. There was no 'congratulations' from them, just a shrug of shoulders before they left to continue their work.

"What happens to us?" Jenny asked.

"From what I know, Trymast will do their best to absorb everyone into their company. It might not be in the same post, but they don't let people go in the first instance. And we will be moving to their Canary Wharf offices."

She nodded and smiled. "I'm excited about it. Any hot guys over there?"

I laughed, "I have no idea, but I'll let you know next week."

She left to fetch some coffees and, for a moment, I felt a little lost. I'd made sure all my work was up-to-date, my diary cleared, and new projects put on hold. I was both excited and terrified at the same time.

"Did you sign the papers?" I heard. I looked up.

Without any form of greeting, Scott walked into my office.

"Yes," I said, assuming he meant the division of assets.

"Good, because I want it all done and dusted as soon as possible."

He was acting as if he was the wounded party.

"So do I, Scott."

"I bet you do." He took a seat.

"And that means?"

"Well, you're on the up, aren't you? Guess you need shot of me quick as."

I raised my eyebrows. "I needed shot of you, the minute you betrayed me."

"We've been over that." He fell silent for a little while. "I miss you," he said, taking me completely by surprise.

"I'm sure your wife-to-be would be pleased to hear that."

He didn't respond, but I watched as he ran his hand through his hair.

"Do I still have a job? I mean, what with you becoming my *boss* and all." He hadn't even tried to hide the bitterness in his voice.

"In all the years you have worked here, a far shorter time than I have, I should add, have you ever seen me act unprofessional in any way? Unlike you, Scott, I kept my mouth shut, my head down, despite my utter humiliation, and got on with my job. You fucked up and revelled in that with your schoolboy colleagues." My voice had started to rise. I took a deep breath.

"You verbally abuse me, you disrespect me at every opportunity. You can't handle a female *boss*, but all that aside. *If* you are the best man for the job, then you'll keep it. Providing you grow the fuck up."

It was the first time I'd ever voiced my opinion and it felt fucking wonderful.

He sat open mouthed for a moment. "You've changed," he said.

"You've noticed. Absolutely I have. And hopefully I'll continue to change. You see; I gave fifteen years of my life to you. You threw that all away for a fuck across a boardroom table." I shook my head and laughed.

"I was..." I held up my hand to halt his excuses.

"You were bored, you were having a mid-life crisis, I worked too hard, and I didn't pay you enough attention. I've heard it all, Scott."

I saw movement from the corner of my eye. Mackenzie stood leaning against the doorframe. He'd arrived so silently, Scott hadn't noticed.

"I think it's time you left my office," I said.

"Too important to talk to me now, are you? I can make things difficult for you, you know that? I want what's mine, or maybe I'll hang out a little longer and see what else I can get. I'm fucking glad I left you. Want to know something? You don't compare to Sandra, you were like a dead fish in bed."

He stood and turned, then froze. No one spoke as he walked towards the door. Mackenzie reached out his arm, placed his hand on the opposite doorframe, blocking Scott's exit.

"If I ever hear you speak to her that way again, I'll put you on your fucking ass." His voice was so low, so aggressive; it sent a shiver up my spine.

"I..." Scott couldn't form the words.

Mackenzie lowered his arm and Scott scuttled away.

Jenny walked towards the office carrying two takeout containers of coffee, as was our new afternoon ritual. Mackenzie took them both and kicked the office door closed. I could hear her outside.

"That was mine," she said.

He placed one cup on the desk and sat opposite me. I sighed.

"What will be your first job as CEO?" he asked, taking a sip of the coffee then wincing. "What is this shit?"

I laughed. "Caramel Latte. My first job?"

"The first thing you do. I'd like to think it would be sacking that fucking douche."

"I'd never be that unprofessional, Mr. Miller."

He laughed, "Jenny!"

She poked her head around the door. He held out the coffee.

"Here, I think this is yours."

"Can you I get you another?" she asked.

"No, Miss Perry and I are leaving now. Thank you anyway."

She stepped in and took the coffee.

"Oh, good job with the arsehole," she said, then laughed.

I guessed the whole office had heard our exchange.

"Come on," Mackenzie said, then stood.

"I thought you had your open door session?"

He raised one eyebrow at me. "No one wanted to play."

My stomach lurched, in a good way.

I followed Mackenzie out of the office, he hailed a taxi and gave his home address.

"I feel like playing hooky," he said.

"I'm not sure my new boss will be pleased if I do that," I replied.

"I think your boss will be just fine. Call it a meeting."

He settled back into his seat, and I wondered if this was our question and answer session brought forward.

We pulled up outside his house, and he paid the taxi as I climbed out. He keyed in a code and the gates swung open.

"2207," he said.

"Sorry?"

"The gate code, if you arrive unexpectedly, it's 2207."

"You're telling me your gate code?" I wasn't sure if that was significant or not.

"I'm not going to leave you standing outside, I might be in the shower or something."

"Is Addison here?"

He stopped and turned to me, we were halfway up the drive.

"No, of course not. She's staying in a hotel. Why would she be here?"

"I just thought…"

"You think too much."

"Are you going to show her the sights?"

"Like fuck am I."

"Why is she here?"

"Do you think we can get inside? Then I'll tell you."

He took my hand and we continued to walk to the front door.

I was seated at the breakfast bar and Mackenzie made us coffee. He had a built in stainless steel machine, the kind I'd see in a coffee shop. When he'd made two, he took a seat beside me.

"I met Addison when we were in high school. There was a small crowd of us: her, Gabriella, Damien, Daniel, and me, we were best friends. Addison and I dated, on and off. I started working in my father's business and quickly learned that it was in trouble. Addison's family came forward with a proposal to save his business. Her father invested in ailing businesses. What I didn't know was there were conditions. Two conditions. One, I was to marry his daughter. The other, which I didn't find out until after the wedding, he was to strip my father's business, put everyone out of work, sell off the plant, and make a shitload of money along the way."

"You married her to save your father's business?"

"I was in love with her. Saving my father's business was just the icing on the proverbial cake."

"How long after did he shut your father's company down?"

"It was a year or so. I knew the company wasn't viable, but it was the way he did it. He walked in one day, laid off all the staff without a care about them or their families. He sold off every piece of equipment, then the factory. All I could do was sit by and watch. I saw grown men cry, not knowing how they would feed their children. I watched my father suffer cardiac arrest because of the stress.

"But I was tied to him. By marrying his daughter, he thought he owned me. He provided the house we lived in, the cars we drove. I got bitter because there was fuck all I could do in the beginning. I had to work for him and stuck it out for five years. Then I told him to shove his job. I'd make it on my own. I'd saved a little money and I got lucky. I invested that in a bar, turned the business around, and sold it for a profit. I did that again, and again."

"What happened to you and Addison?"

"We stayed together for another couple of years. She came home one day and told me she was pregnant. I packed a bag and left."

"You left her!"

"I can't father children, Lauren. There is one thing I will not tolerate, and that's betrayal. I loved her; I struggled doing something I didn't want to do, for her. I stayed quiet and put up with her controlling father, only for her."

He paused, taking a sip of his coffee.

"You want to know why Addison plays the nice girl? Because now, I own her father. I own all his businesses."

"How?"

"Over a period of years, I bought them all, and he didn't have a fucking clue who owned the company he was selling out to."

I wasn't sure what to say at first. "I'm sorry you can't father a child, I bet that hurts."

"It did, although I came to terms with that a long time ago. It's why I never settled down again. I didn't want to fall in love with someone and not be able to have the ultimate gift, my own child."

I could see the pain in his face. I placed my hand on his arm.

"That was all a long time ago, don't feel sorry for me. I knew I couldn't have children after a car accident. I ignored it, hoping maybe medical advancement would help me. I should have told Addison, I didn't. At some point it would have come out, after years of trying, I guessed we would have visited a doctor."

"What happened when you left her?"

"Her father threatened to ruin me, he tried real hard and nearly did. She begged for forgiveness, and when she lost her child, she blamed me."

"She blamed you?"

"Yes, the stress she'd been put under. But then it came to light, the father of her child, who wanted nothing more to do with her, was her cousin, Daniel."

"Her…"

"Yes, her cousin. So, the Addison you met? Don't be fooled by her for one minute. She's a money-grabbing whore, who'll do whatever she needs to do to get what she wants. She's jealous of everyone, which is why I tried not to acknowledge you at lunch. Not because I didn't want to, but because I wanted to shield you from her poison."

"But you seemed so friendly together."

"Yes, I know what her father is up to if I string her along a little. I throw her a bone and she gives me information. It's how it's worked since we divorced, ten years ago now. She wants a rich man, and when she's bored and without one, she tells me that she loves me. I don't fall for it."

"How often do you see her?"

"Once or twice a year, this is the first time she's been to the U.K. though. Sometimes it's hard to avoid her. Vivienne, Gabriella's mother, and her aunt, likes to torment her, so she's occasionally invited to family events," he said with a laugh.

"What is your relationship with Gabriella?"

He smiled before he answered. I heard him take a deep breath and exhale slowly. "She loved me, she didn't tell me that in the beginning, but she was there for me when Addison and I split. She was there all the way through the worst times of my life, when I wanted to end it all. She was the one who picked me up and dusted me off. We're great friends, Lauren. She's someone who will always be in my life."

"Loved?"

"Yeah, she's in love with Alex and his move is causing her pain."

"Why is he leaving?"

"Because I want him to run my U.S. operations, so I don't have to spend so much time abroad. Of all the people on my team, he's the one I trust the most. I want her to go with him. She doesn't want to leave me."

"I thought you liked flying back and forth."

"I did, I do, but there's something wanting me to stay put for a while. Most of my businesses are back home, Lauren. I need someone there on a permanent basis."

The fact he'd said *something* led me to assume he meant the merger or perhaps another larger business deal.

"I'm glad you told me all that. Thank you."

He stood to refresh our coffee cups. "So, you have questions," he said.

"They don't seem so important now," I said.

"All questions are important. What is it you want to ask me?"

I sat and looked at him for a moment.

"How often do you visit your club?"

He smiled, "I was waiting for that one. Not as frequently as you imagine, maybe once a month. I haven't had time to form a relationship, Lauren. And as I said, not being able to father a child has always stopped me. But I still have needs."

"Have you…since we…"

"No. That was the first time. I wanted you to experience something in a safe environment."

"Why are you doing this?"

"This?"

"What we do, why?"

"Because I want to, because you want to. I want you to love yourself again, to explore and discover who you really are."

"The Facilitator, huh?"

"No, just Mackenzie Miller. A man who wants to be alongside you while you explore."

"What if I don't like what I'm discovering?"

"Such as?"

"Friday. What if there's a part of me that says I should not have enjoyed that as much as I did?"

"Then it's that part of your brain you need to work on. I don't *enjoy* watching two men; I get nothing from that. I *enjoyed* watching your reaction to it. There is nothing wrong in what you, we, did."

"I guess I've just not been around that level of, I don't know what the word is, sex, maybe?"

"Which is why it fascinates you, isn't it? Which is why you get so aroused by it."

His voice had lowered, that gravelly tone was back. My hand shook slightly as I held my coffee cup.

"I'm scared, Mackenzie. How far do I go? Where do I stop? What happens when those experiences aren't enough?"

"Then you find someone who's able to give you what you want on a regular basis," he whispered, as he pulled his stool closer to me.

I blinked back the tear that had formed in my eye. He'd made it clear there would be no relationship between us and my heart broke a little. In light of what I knew, the age difference, and despite trying to convince myself otherwise, I was in love with him.

"Now, BDSM," he said.

"I don't want that, I couldn't be submissive, call you Master, and all that," I said.

He laughed. "There are so many elements to what you call BDSM, Lauren. You can explore part or all of it."

"I liked what I saw, the cross thing," I whispered, trying to quell the embarrassment.

"You like restraint, you'd like for me to control your body, when you come, how hard you come?"

"Yes."

"Then we have to discuss this. I need to know how far I can push you."

"I don't know. Have you done that?"

"Flogging?"

I nodded. "Yes, and much more," he said.

"Do you enjoy it?"

"I don't enjoy hurting people, that doesn't turn me on. I don't get a kick out of whipping a bare ass. I get my kick out of the reaction. It's an intense experience, Lauren."

"Who have you done that to?"

"Do you really want to know?"

"Yes."

"Veronica."

I wasn't expecting that, although I wasn't sure who I was expecting him to name.

"From the club?"

"From *my* club," he smirked, and I watched as he slowly swiped his tongue over his lower lip.

"Your...?"

"I invest in lots of businesses, Lauren. She came to me with a proposition, a way to save her ancestral home. Although, I suspect the ancestors would be turning in their graves if they knew what went on. I liked her idea and ran with it."

"I'd like to go there again, to know what goes on."

"You're curious, aren't you? I like that about you. You're not afraid, although you're scared to learn more. That makes you very brave."

"I'm not sure about brave."

He looked at his watch and picked up his phone. I watched as he sent a text.

"Come on," he said.

"Where?"

"No time like the present, is there?"

"Whoa, I'm not going to…"

"You're not going to do anything, other than be shown around and have someone explain exactly what goes on. I want you to know about my businesses, Lauren, all of them. I have plans for you."

****

Veronica met us at the front door, like before. Mackenzie left his car in the driveway, and unlike before, there was no valet to park it. He pocketed his keys and we walked up the stone steps.

"Mr. Miller, Miss Perry. It's a pleasure to see you again." She opened the door and we walked in. "Would you care for a drink?" she asked.

"Coffee would be good. We're not here for pleasure today, I don't think," he said with a chuckle.

She laughed, smiled over at me, and asked us to follow her to her office. We entered a vast room, immaculate, with a large carved desk in the middle of bay windows.

"Please, take a seat," she said, gesturing towards a collection of sofas at one end. She made a call, requesting coffee.

"Lauren would like to know a little more about the house, its origins and what it has to offer," Mackenzie said. The formality of using our surnames had been dropped.

"Of course, I'd be delighted to show you around. Let me tell you about it first. It was my childhood home, handed down through my father's side for generations. It dates back to my great-great-grandfather, who was given the house for services to the queen.

"My family couldn't afford its upkeep and put it up for sale. I couldn't bear to lose it. I've lived here all my life and with no older sibling, the house should have been passed to me. I knew Mackenzie, he'd had dealings with my father, so I approached him for help."

"Why did you decide to offer it as a club?" I asked.

"There were none around at that time, none as exclusive and high end, I should say. There are plenty of clubs, especially in London, but I wanted something different. A hotel that offered the facilities I enjoyed."

There was a knock on the door and a young woman holding a tray opened it. She placed the tray on the small coffee table, and Veronica poured the coffees.

"We decided to make it a members-only club. They pay an annual fee and in return are allowed to use the facilities. We have cottages in the grounds, a mini spa, and indoor pool. And then we have the function rooms. We hold events, parties for like-minded people. A member can hire the whole venue if they wish, we've even had a wedding."

"So it's run like a regular hotel?"

"Yes, but for people who wish to experience what we offer. We don't take outside bookings, can you imagine the shock a little old couple would get if they stumbled into one of our playrooms?"

I laughed at the thought.

"You said you wanted a facility for people who enjoyed what you do?"

"I did. I'm very much into the BDSM scene, Lauren. It's a lifestyle that I've practiced for many years."

"Do you have a master? Or is that too personal a question?"

She chuckled, "Sometimes, although I don't use that word. I also like to dominate. It's very liberating to give control to someone else. Likewise, it's very empowering to take control."

I sipped on my coffee, thinking how surreal the whole conversation was. A month ago, I couldn't have imagined sitting there discussing a stranger's sexual habits.

"I'm interested in learning more, Veronica. I don't think BDSM is for me, but there are elements I've researched that I'd like to participate in. But I don't know exactly what, or how far I'm willing to go." I thought there was no point in not being honest.

"Then you are in good hands with Mackenzie," she said, smiling over at him.

"Veronica taught me all I know," he said.

Veronica raised her eyebrows at him. "She knows," he said.

"Okay, then yes, I taught Mackenzie to give me what I needed. He was a reluctant student. He's not comfortable with inflicting pain, but we found a balance that suited us both."

"I'm not sure about the pain part," I said.

"There are levels, Lauren. As I said, I'm hard-core, that's not for everyone. You will find a very enjoyable balance. If it's something you wish to explore, then Mackenzie is absolutely the right person to start that journey with."

She placed her cup on the table. "Shall we do the tour?"

"Are there people here now?" I asked as I stood.

"Yes, although only a few."

"Will they mind us walking around?"

"Of course not, the guests we have at the moment would love nothing more than to have you watch," she said, with a laugh.

She led us from the office and we crossed the hall to the bar I'd visited before.

"As you know, this is the bar area, it's where our guests can relax if they choose to. We have strict rules; the area towards the back is for couples only who do not wish to engage in swinging. If you wanted to meet up with another couple, or more, you'd opt to sit on the sofas, that's a clear invitation that you'd like company."

"Do you have singles visiting?"

"Yes, we have single members. All our guests are vetted prior to admission into the club. We ask for personal details, marital status, and even financial data. We don't allow admission to anyone under the age of thirty, as we want mature adults only. Our annual fee ensures we rule out those seeking a quick thrill."

"Can I ask what that is?"

"Thirty thousand pounds per year."

"Wow!"

"It's higher than it needs to be, but ensures we attract the right members," Mackenzie said.

"For that, remember, they get use of the cottages, the spa, whenever they want. So if someone wanted a weekend away, every weekend of the year, it represents value for money."

We walked back out of the bar and into the hallway.

"Along the corridor we have a restaurant, there are industrial kitchens in the basement. Over on that side: we have the library, my office, of course, and security. There are no sexual activities allowed on this floor. I have a private wing where I live, that's accessed through that door." She indicated with her head.

"Security?"

"A safety feature. We need to know we have someone on hand should, and it's only ever happened once, a patron take things a little too far. In each bedroom there is a camera and a panic button. There are some that like to engage in role-play, and on that one occasion, it got out of hand. My guys will step in and stop whatever activity is going on if they feel it's getting out of control. There are microphones in all rooms, if we hear a safe word being used, we will check to see activities have ceased."

"How do you know their safe word?"

"The women are given one, discretely, upon registration. It's the same word for everyone. That one word will activate our security system."

"Do the guests know there is a camera?" My mind was immediately taken back to what could be on film when I was there.

"Yes, when they join they are given an information pack. They are also assured that the camera is not routinely connected to any form of backup system; no copies are made. Nothing is watched unless a trigger is activated, the panic button, for example. Only then will it record, and that's to ensure there is documented evidence should police or lawyers become involved."

"Has that ever happened?"

"Not to date."

We climbed the stairs to a long hallway. "There are ten rooms on this floor, five more on the floor above."

As we walked towards one, I noticed a very small discrete light above the doorframe was lit.

"That means this room is occupied, I take it?"

"Yes, when our guests arrive, they are given the key to the room they booked. Although that room can't be accessed unless you have a key, it has been known for a member to forget to completely shut their door."

We walked to one end of the hallway. Veronica explained what each room contained, some were just bedrooms but the guests could request a range of equipment or toys to be available for them. One room was set out like an office, and another was a massage room. One held the cross that I'd seen and next to it, the viewing room that I'd been in.

She opened the door to a vacant room. In the centre was the largest bed I'd ever seen.

"This is a groups room, obviously. The TV has a selection of DVD's pre-programmed in."

"I guess that won't include *Toy Story*," I said, with a chuckle.

"You'd be surprised at some requests," she said with a wink.

The next room was very clinical; instead of the plush carpet it had a rubber floor that extending part way up the walls.

"Now this room is fun. It's our 'messy' room. You can do what you like in here, food play, naked painting, mud wresting; you name it." Both her and Mackenzie laughed.

I was a little dumbstruck.

Finally we reached the last door along the corridor. Veronica paused before opening it. "We have guests, please remember that, and try not to react to what you see."

She slowly opened the door. It was the largest room on the floor and housed what I could only describe as a torture chamber. There were three women trussed up in various ways and two men. One was hooded, bare-chested and in jeans, another wore a suit. He smiled over to me, as if it was the most natural thing in the world to walk in just as he was about to bring a bamboo cane down on a woman's arse.

We shuffled to one side, and I cursed as my back hit a wall of chains, causing them to rattle.

I stared at the women. One was chained between two poles, her arms and legs outstretched and she was naked. Another was tied so intricately with light coloured rope and was on her knees. It must have taken hours to tie her arms and legs that way.

The third, the one who got the cane, had a blindfold over her eyes, a ball in her mouth, and she was lying across a bench in the centre of the room.

"There's no bed?" I whispered.

"No, this room isn't for fucking. They may, or may not, do that during aftercare, but always in another room." Veronica whispered. The word 'fucking' seemed so alien coming from a woman with such an upper class accent.

I watched the hooded man. He was very well built, muscular. He hadn't looked over and was stroking the head of the woman trussed up and kneeling at his feet. It seemed such a tender thing for him to do. A pang of disappointment hit me when Veronica turned to walk back out the door. Our visit had been too short, and I had to remind myself we were interrupting playtime.

We climbed another staircase hidden behind a wooden panel to the attic. One room was a smaller version of the *dungeon*, another was a room with one wall and the ceiling mirrored, two further bedrooms, and the last, another group room.

"All the rooms are soundproofed. I would have liked to have kept the group rooms on this floor, but as you can imagine, with the age of this building, it was a case of make do within the existing structure."

We made our way back downstairs. "Perhaps you'd like to show Lauren the cottages, number seventeen is free," she said.

With a smile, she left us and we walked into the library, a stunning *real* library with floor-to-ceiling shelves, holding what must have amounted to thousands of books. At the rear of that room were French doors that opened to a terrace with tables and chairs. A man sat with a cigar at one, he was reading a newspaper but raised a hand in greeting as we walked through. Mackenzie nodded to him.

"Who was that?" I asked. He looked familiar.

"Member of the House of Lords," he said with a smirk.

"You're kidding me?"

"No, we have many high ranking guests here."

We walked down some steps, and I wanted to take a moment to admire the view. Rolling green fields went on for miles. We took a path and rounded a flint wall to find a row of small single storey cottages. Mackenzie led me to one and opened the door.

We walked straight into a large living room, beautifully decorated in soft pastels and floral accents. It was so very different to the harsh wood and browns of the main house. There was a modern kitchen, a luxurious bathroom with shower and claw-footed roll-top bath. He opened the door to the bedroom, and I fell in love. A four-poster bed sat in the centre of the room, sheer muslin draped from the canopy above. It faced another set of French doors that opened to a smaller patio area.

"It's beautiful," I said, as I walked around the bed. "Just like a holiday home."

"This one is often reserved for the bride or honeymooners even," he said, as he walked behind me. I felt his breath on the back of my neck.

He slid his hands over my shoulders and down my arms. He grabbed my wrists and raised them, clasping my hands around one of the corner poles.

"You see that small hook. I could tie your hands together and then to that," he whispered.

"Why don't you then?" I whispered back.

"I love to see your body crave my touch, I love to hear and smell your arousal."

"I want to spend time here, with you," I said.

"I know you do, and you will. I will give you the weekend experience."

He kissed the side of my neck, just below my ear, sending tingles straight to my core. I heard him unbuckle his belt and the sound of it sliding through the loops of his trousers had my stomach fluttering. He reached up and wrapped it around my wrists, tying it tight before placing the leather over the hook. Then he turned me to face him.

"I could do some terrible things to you," he whispered, as he slowly unbuttoned my shirt.

"I want you to."

He smiled that wicked smirk he had.

He palmed my breasts; his hands ran over the material of my bra. He lowered his head and sucked on one nipple through the lace. While he did, he unbuttoned my trousers. He gently lowered himself to his knees; his lips and tongue trailed a path down my stomach. He lifted one foot and then the other, removing my trousers before running his hands back up the inside of my thighs.

"I like you like this, half undressed and with a wet cunt, waiting for me," he said.

He ran his fingers over my panties, soaking up some of that wetness he so liked. I moaned at his touch. While he kissed my neck, he tore through my panties and pushed two fingers inside me. I cried out.

"Tell me what you want to do here," he said, as he pumped his fingers in and out of me, stroking and teasing.

"I… I want you to restrain me, in that room. I want you to…" I moaned as his fingers found that one spot that had sweat bead on my forehead, a flush creep over my body, and my stomach knot with desire.

"And what do you want me to do to you?"

"Whip me, with the flogger."

"Where?"

"My back, my arse, my…"

"Say it, Lauren," he growled, as his teeth sank into my shoulder.

"My pussy."

"Your soaking cunt, say the words."

"My…" I panted, the vulgarity of his choice of words turned me on even more.

"My soaking cunt," I hissed out between a clenched jaw, as his bites got harder.

"Such a dirty mouth, I love it. That dirty mouth belongs to me, do you understand?" I nodded.

His kiss was fierce and his tongue claimed mine. His fingers fucked me harder, and I arched my back when he inserted a third. I wanted more. I raised one leg, wrapping it around him. I dug the heel of my shoe into the back of his thighs.

He broke our kiss and withdrew his fingers. I wanted to protest, that was until he ripped my panties from my body. He undid his trousers, letting them fall. His cock strained against his tight black shorts. I watched as he placed his hand inside them and stroked himself.

"Fuck me," I said, looking him straight in the eye as I did. I wasn't asking, I was demanding.

He raised his eyebrows. He started to bend down to retrieve something from his trousers.

"No." I said. "I want to feel you inside me."

He grabbed both my thighs and wrapped them around his waist; he held my hips with one hand and guided himself in with the other. He fucked me hard and fast as he held my hips, supporting my weight.

He raked his teeth across my collarbone, my shoulder. He trailed his tongue back up my neck and across my jaw.

I moaned, panted, and cried out. "Come for me, baby," he said. I exploded around him.

He pumped faster until sweat ran down his temple; I caught a bead of it with my tongue. He growled out my name and I felt his cock pulse inside me, his fingers gripped tighter. I could see his biceps strain against the white of his shirt, and a vein bulged in his neck as blood pumped faster throughout his system.

He rested his forehead against mine, while he got his breathing under control. Very gently he pulled out of me, and I lowered my legs to the floor. He opened his eyes and stared at me, and then he laughed.

"You are fucking gorgeous," he said.

His cum ran down my thighs and I loved the feeling of it. It wasn't dirty; it was completely natural; it belonged on my skin.

He unhooked my aching arms and took back his belt. He pulled up his shorts and trousers, and while I stood, a little unsure of what to do, he walked to the bathroom and returned with a box of tissues. I cleaned myself up, buttoned up my shirt and picked up my torn panties from the floor.

"I guess I won't be wearing those," I said, shoving them in my bag. I pulled on my trousers.

"You don't want to clean yourself up?" I asked.

"No, I like the smell of you on me. When I pleasure myself over this memory, I'll have you on my hand." I wasn't sure whether to laugh or not.

"Do you do that a lot?" I tried to keep the surprise from my voice.

"All the time. I only have to think of you and I'm hard. It's a fucking bitch when we're at work."

I smiled; *I turned him on that much!* I wasn't sure whether it was pride or something else that swirled around inside me, but it sure felt good.

We walked back to the main house and he led me to the bar. He ordered two coffees and we sat for a while.

"What happens now?" I asked.

"Here?"

"Yes."

"We'll return on Friday. In the meantime you need to decide exactly what else you want to experience."

A thought ran through my mind, one I was scared to voice. I bit down on my lower lip.

"Tell me," he said, quietly. "What's going through your mind right now?"

I was saved from answering immediately by the appearance of Veronica. She pulled up a stool and a glass of iced water was placed alongside our coffee. I watched her inhale deeply. I hoped I was wrong, but could she smell me on him?

"What do you think of our facilities, Lauren?" she asked.

"I think it's a beautiful place that allows people the freedom to express themselves in a safe environment."

"I think we should use that in our brochure," she said with a laugh.

"What were you going to say?" Mackenzie asked.

"It can wait," I replied.

"Lauren, this is all new to you. Whatever you wish to experience next we need to prepare for. Let Mackenzie know in advance."

"We'll be back Friday, keep the cottage for us, for the weekend," he said.

I took a deep breath. "I'm not sure how well I'll deal with the pain, I don't know what to expect other than what I saw. I…"

I took a sip of my coffee as I composed myself.

"You what?" Mackenzie said, gently.

"Can I watch you?"

He didn't respond immediately and I heard a sharp intake of breath from Veronica.

"Explain," he said.

"Can I watch what you do to Veronica?" My heart hammered in my chest as I spoke.

"I'm not sure that's a good idea, Lauren," she said.

"Why?"

"Can you separate in your mind what he is doing to me is for *my* sexual gratification and not because he wants to fuck me?"

Again that word sounded so strange in her accent.

"Yes, I can. I'm not a jealous person, Veronica. I need to know how hard he's going to hit me, how he *performs*, if that's even the right word."

Mackenzie leaned forward. He placed his hand on my thigh.

"What I *did* to Veronica, will bear no resemblance to what I do to you."

"You can watch anyone, Lauren."

"I need to see it from him. Please don't ask me to explain it; it's just important to me to know how he does it. I know it doesn't make sense, but…"

Mackenzie leaned back on his stool. "I said I'd give you any experience you desired, but this one I need to think about. How you see me with others, Lauren, isn't how I am with you."

"I understand that, and I would expect you to be different. This is all so new to me. I just ask you to think about it, and if it's a no, then fine." I smiled to let him know that if it was no, it really was fine.

He sighed as he picked up his coffee. Once again it felt surreal to be having that conversation in a beautiful environment.

"Thank you for showing me around. Obviously, I've never been somewhere like this before. I meant what I said, it's a beautiful place, I'm so glad you were able to keep it," I said.

"So am I. Now I have work to do, hopefully I'll see you again on Friday," she said. She smiled at Mackenzie and left.

He turned to me, pulling my stool closer so my legs were between his thighs. He ran his fingers down one cheek, across my jaw until his thumb brushed over my lips.

"I wish you'd…" he said.

"You wish what?"

He shook his head. "Nothing."

"You wish I hadn't asked that?"

"No, I wasn't going to say that. Please, leave it."

There was a hint of sadness in his voice. I wondered what I'd done to cause that, if I'd done anything at all.

"I promised you dinner and I'm kind of hungry right now," he said.

His smile had my heart missing a beat. There was no point in chanting my *I will not fall for him* mantra because I had, so it was irrelevant. I decided on a new one. *Don't break my heart*, I thought.

He slid from the stool and held out his hand. His grip was firmer than usual, and we walked out the house and to his car. We drove back to London in near silence.

****

I learned more about Mackenzie over dinner than I had in the whole month I'd been in his company. He told me tales from his childhood, but all the time he spoke he never mentioned his mother, or the accident he'd been involved in. It was over coffee that I decided to ask.

"You don't mention your mother," I said.

He didn't reply immediately. "My mother died, a long time ago."

"I'm sorry to hear that," I said.

"It's okay, she was a wonderful woman. Supported my father in whatever he wanted to do. She got cancer. All I can say is we were thankful it took her quickly. She smiled and laughed right up to the last minute. I was with her when she died."

"How old were you?"

"Seventeen."

"So young still."

"It is what it is, it fucked me up for a long time after. I drank too much, got high on a regular basis and... Anyway, you don't want to hear about that so, now, your turn. Tell me about your family," he said, I guessed to stop me asking more. I wondered if the *drunk too much, got high* had anything to do with the vehicle accident I'd read about.

I told him about my mum, my brother. I'd never known my father, he'd skipped town when I was a baby. I explained that was probably why I was so hung up on having a stable relationship with a man; I didn't want what my mum had for so many years.

"And now? Are you looking for a relationship?" Again there was that rigidity in his body as he waited for my reply.

"I'm enjoying myself right now," I said, hoping that was the answer he wanted.

Whether it was or not, I couldn't tell. He sipped on his coffee his features completely devoid of emotion.

He was a difficult man to read, he kept his body language to a minimum, and there were times when I wasn't sure what he meant when he spoke. I thought I was telling him what he wanted to hear, but like then, there were times when I thought I'd gotten it wrong. I wished he would open up, but I was too scared to ask him to.

The waiter placed our bill on the table, without looking at it he laid his credit card on top. I would have liked to delay the evening a little longer. I wasn't looking forward to returning to my empty apartment.

"I did something the other day," I said, as we stood and walked to the restaurant door.

"What?"

"I bought some *things*."

He shrugged his shoulders. "I think you're going to have to give me a clue."

We walked to where he had parked the car.

"Sex toys," I said. He stopped and looked at me. His smile grew broad.

"Sex toys, huh? What kind?"

"I can't say here, someone might hear."

"And when will these *things* be delivered? I assume you didn't walk into a store and buy them."

"I ordered them on line and tomorrow."

"Then allow me to help you unpack them."

He opened the car door and helped me in. I laughed as he took his place behind the steering wheel.

"What happened to that shy, *worthless, inadequate* woman I met just a month ago?" he said.

There was a pause as he started the car and pulled out on the road.

"You happened," I said, quietly.

Chapter Fifteen

Gabriella appeared at my office door the following day. Although immaculately dressed, as normal, there was something 'off' about her.

"Hi, I wondered if you'd like some lunch then a trip over to Canary Wharf today?" she said.

"I'd love to. I'll be honest; I'm pretty much done here. I'd like to move as soon as possible. Scott is being a total arse."

"I heard about your exchange. He was *encouraged* to tender his resignation, did you know?"

"I didn't, no."

"It's for the best. So, shall we go?"

I rose from my seat and collected my handbag. She had a car waiting on the double yellow lines outside. We slid in the back and she gave an address to the driver.

"I hear you met the delightful Addison," she said.

"I did, although I did think she was delightful at the time. Until Mackenzie told me about them."

"She's a vampire, Lauren, be very careful around her. Don't give her anything she can use to hurt you, she'll bleed you dry. All she's after is money, from whoever she can get it to maintain a lifestyle she believes she deserves."

"Is she still in a relationship with your brother?"

"She picks him up and drops him whenever she wants, when she's bored of her latest conquest, I guess. He's a fool to not be able to see what she does, or maybe he just enjoys her using him. He ran when she fell pregnant, but I think he enjoys spending her money way too much to completely leave her."

"Mackenzie told me a lot about himself yesterday. Your relationship as well."

She smiled at me. "I loved him a long time ago, now I love him like a brother. He's very important to my momma and me. When he lost his own, she stepped in to care for him when his father was too broken to. And talking of my mother, she was most disappointed not to have received your offer of tea at The Ritz, I doubt she'll ever forgive you," she said with a laugh; drawing out the word 'ever.'

"I'll make it up to her, is still here?"

"No, she flew home yesterday."

"What will you do, Gabriella, when Alex leaves?"

"He told you, huh?"

"Yes."

She sighed and for a moment lost her composure. I took hold of one of her hands in mine.

"I'm sorry, I shouldn't have asked that."

"It's okay. I don't have any girlfriends here, so it's nice to talk. Like you, we have a man best friend, and for some reason, women steer clear of us. And as for Alex, I don't know yet."

"They do! Everyone thinks Jerry and I are constantly jumping in and out of bed; I slept my way to the top. Jerry wanted me to walk out of his office one day with my shirt buttons undone and my skirt tucked into my panties," I said, with a laugh.

"Oh, that would have been so funny."

"He wanted to give them something to really gossip about, I think he just wanted to see my underwear."

It felt great to laugh, to gossip, and talk to someone like-minded and on the same level as me. There was no threat, no competition between us.

"I hear you went to the club,' she said with raised eyebrows.

"For a look around," I panicked as I spoke.

She laughed. "Isn't it just the most amazing place? And such fun." She winked and I couldn't stop laughing.

"It certainly is an eye-opener."

We pulled up outside a small bistro near Smithfield. The driver opened the door for us, and we were shown to a table as soon as we entered.

We both ordered a salad and a glass of white wine. And we didn't stop chatting and laughing. Over coffee, the subject of Alex came up again.

"I don't know what to do, Lauren. He wants to marry me and this opportunity for him in the U.S. is an amazing one. I can't stand in his way. But I can't leave Mackenzie either. Well, I didn't think I could."

"You didn't think you could?"

"Now he has you."

"He doesn't *have* me. He's made it quite clear he doesn't want a relationship with me, or anyone."

"Are you sure about that?"

"Has he said anything to you?"

"No, but I know him. Lauren, he's a complex man, half the time he doesn't know what he wants until it's pointed out to him. He withdrew from any serious relationship because of his issues with children, but it's more than that. He's scared of getting hurt. He's set in his ways, he needs a strong and confident woman, who won't take his bullshit, but will allow him to be the man he needs to be."

Was she referring to his activities at the club? I wasn't about to ask.

"Well, it's a moot point, Gabriella. He has made it clear we are just having some fun right now." Or had he? I wasn't sure anymore.

"How do you feel about him?"

I sighed, raised my eyebrows at her and chuckled. She placed her hand over mine.

"I know that sigh, that look, that feeling. Men are just such shits sometimes, aren't they? We love them, they have no idea, or they break our hearts."

I raised my cup of coffee. "Here's to shit men and broken hearts."

"Tell him," she said.

"No. Never. And I beg you, please don't either. I'd have to leave my job, and I don't want to do that."

"I won't, but believe me on one thing, he cares."

"I don't doubt that, but loving me is something different."

I paid the bill, after an argument with Gabriella over it, and we left. We were driven to Canary Wharf and what was to become my new office.

Like all the buildings, it was glass, steel, and ultra modern. We took the lift up to the floors occupied by Trymast. We were greeted with smiles and handshakes. It was a complete opposite atmosphere to what I'd been used to. Gabriella introduced me to everyone as the new CEO, and it took forever to get to Alex's office. Everyone wanted to chat.

Alex was on the phone as we passed by his glass floor-to-ceiling wall. He smiled when he saw us and waved us in.

"Our favourite ladies have just arrived," he said into his phone. "Okay, see you in a minute."

"That was Mackenzie, he's coming down." He rose and without a care, placed an arm around Gabriella's shoulders and kissed her briefly on the lips.

"Mackenzie has the floor above," Gabriella explained.

"Most of the whole floor, greedy sod," Alex said, then laughed. "So, have you been shown around?"

"Briefly, I think I've met way too many people to remember who any of them are. But they all seem so friendly," I said.

"They're a great bunch, not too many troublemakers among them," he said.

Alex waved at a woman hovering by the door. "Can I get you guys anything?" she said, once she'd opened the door.

"Tea?" Alex asked.

We nodded. "Three teas, and his lordship's coffee," he said with a smile.

"Miss Perry, would you like lemon in your tea, or milk?"

"A little milk, thank you," I said.

"Carolyn will be your PA, she's an absolute gem," Alex said.

"He couldn't function without her. I swear, Lauren, some of my presents have been chosen by her," Gabriella said with a wink.

"My darling, I may send her on errands, but I can assure you they are all, mostly, mainly, sometimes, not often, my ideas."

"Mmm, I bet it's closer to the sometimes and not often."

"Lauren, help me out here. I'm a guy, I have no idea what to buy a beautiful woman," Alex said.

"Nope, I'm on Gabriella's side here."

"Being ganged up on, are you?" I heard and felt a hand on my back. Mackenzie had joined us. He kissed my cheek.

"I was just telling the lovely Lauren that I might not always be able to produce the perfect gift for my darling Gabriella," Alex said.

"Fuck! Do we have to do perfect gifts? That'll be me and you in the doghouse then," Mackenzie said.

Gabriella gave me a look akin to *I told you so*. I gently shook my head. He was just playing along.

"Have you been shown around?" Mackenzie asked me.

"I have, briefly. I'll make a point to meet everyone individually next week," I replied.

"Good, then come on up and see my empire, leave these two lovebirds alone for a while."

Playful Mackenzie was a fun person to be around. When he took my hand and led me through the open plan offices, I worried though. I tried to pull my hand away, he held on tighter. He pressed for the lift and we waited in silence. When the doors slid behind us, he turned to face me.

"Yes," he said.

"Yes?"

"I'll do whatever you ask me to, next Friday. But I need your absolute assurance it will not affect how you view me, us."

I blinked rapidly; he'd said *us*. I was desperate to ask whether there was an *us*. I thought on Gabriella's words and decided to wait. I'd watch, see if I could see whatever it was she thought she saw.

"Thank you. You understand why, don't you? I want to do this with you, no one else, but I need to see the expression on your face, how you do it."

"You won't see lust, or desire, Lauren. I did what I did for Veronica because I respected her and there is nothing between us. I have never fucked her."

There were those words again, words to confuse me. Why did he need to assure me there was nothing between them?

Before I could answer, the lift doors slid open to an open plan floor. In the centre was a large table, large enough to seat at least twenty people. To each side, corner offices, which I assumed one to be his. There were two rooms, a bathroom and a small kitchen. In the middle of the two offices was an empty desk. He saw me look over to it.

"My assistant, she's off today. Well, mine and Gabriella's, that's her office over there."

"And I bet you can't live without her?"

He laughed. "I let her think that. She'd kick my ass otherwise."

"So this is where you work?" I said, turning slowing to look at the vast empty space.

"I like open spaces, the only reason I have an office is so I can make private calls or do something naughty while I think of you."

"Yet you have glass walls."

"That turn opaque at the touch of a button. All high tech here, Lauren."

I walked towards the boardroom table. It was highly polished and solid oak by the feel of it.

"I want to fuck you over that," he whispered. I froze as a memory assaulted me.

"I...shit, I'm sorry. I didn't think," he said.

"It's okay, I guess me and boardroom tables will never be best of friends."

"I'll cross that one off my list."

"You have a list? I thought that was only me."

He took my hand and led me to his office. Every wall was glass and the view over London took my breath away. I stepped away from the edge as it made me a little queasy.

"Yes, I have a list," he said.

"What's on it?"

"If I told you it wouldn't be any fun now, would it?"

I turned and smiled at him. He strode towards me, taking my face in his hands, and he kissed me: like he wanted to, like he meant it, like I meant something to him.

I placed my hands around his waist, pulling him closer. I wanted to feel his body against mine. I wanted to feel his erection through his trousers.

He walked me backwards towards his desk, his arm swiped whatever was in the way before he lifted me and placed me on the edge. He stepped between my thighs continuing to kiss me. I felt his heart race; I heard his moan as he gripped my hair.

It was the ping of the lift echoing around the room that startled me. He took a step back.

"Fuck," he said.

By the time the doors had slid open, I was standing; he had adjusted himself to a more comfortable position within his trousers and had picked up the papers from the floor.

An elderly woman walked towards his office.

"Thank fuck, it's Mary. She hasn't got her glasses on, we would have had a few more seconds."

I covered my mouth to contain the laughter as the elderly woman peered through the glass wall.

"Mary, you are supposed to be off today, did you forget?" he said.

"Did I forget? Do you think I'm fucking senile?"

I dropped my hand and laughed out loud.

"Is this Lauren? Introduce me then, don't stand there like an idiot."

"Lauren, my very vocal PA, Mary."

"It's lovely to meet you, dear. I have a list of things I want you to answer, just so I know what you like."

"Okay, I look forward to it," I said.

"She likes me," Mackenzie replied.

"Someone has to, dear, someone has to. Now, I forgot my bleeding glasses. Haven't been able to see a thing all day. I'll grab them then be off. Don't forget, you have an early dinner with that dick from Parliament. Suit's in the wardrobe."

Wide-eyed I stared at Mackenzie.

"I forgot to tell you, Mary is a law unto herself. I've tried to sack her many times for her outspokenness, but she's going out of here in a coffin. Her words, not mine."

"Be nice to have a woman around, Alex is lovely and all, but the sooner he gets his finger out his arse and whisks that Gabriella down the aisle, the better. I can't stand the testosterone in here sometimes. Oh, the tart left a message on my voicemail, not that I know how she got my number. She wanted use of an office, I told her to find a fucking library." She gave me a wink as she walked to her desk.

"The...?" I started to ask.

"Addison. Mary has an irrational dislike of her," he laughed as he spoke.

"I...I don't have words," I said.

"Good, because she's got enough for everyone."

She waved over her shoulder, once she'd retrieved her glasses, and made her way back to the lift.

"Wow," I said, still laughing as she waved again from the lift.

"I inherited her when I took over here. A Londoner all her life, she tells me, cusses constantly. But you know, I couldn't survive without her."

"She's amazing."

"Since the thought of fucking you has now been thoroughly wiped from my mind, thanks to Mary, let's go do another tour."

We arrived downstairs to see Alex and Gabriella about to leave and our cold coffee and tea sat on the desk.

"I just met Mary," I said.

"Isn't she a hoot?" Gabriella said.

"Scares the life out of me," Alex added.

"Are you off?" I asked.

"Just for a meeting, do you need a lift back yet?" Gabriella asked.

"I'll sort that out. You go," Mackenzie said.

We said goodbye and Mackenzie walked me around the floor. He detailed each department on that one, and the one below, that I was yet to visit. There didn't look to be enough space to house all the additional staff and I voiced my concerns.

"We take over another floor next week. It's being fitted out as we speak. You and Alex can decide who moves where."

"So there'll be three floors plus yours here?"

"Yes. I want it all centralised. I have another business in London that I'll move in when we can as well. I hate having to travel around, it makes more sense to have everyone in the same building."

"I ought to be getting back," I said, glancing at my watch. I'd been out of the office for four hours.

"Why? You live around the corner, you might as well go straight home."

"Because, unlike you, I don't play hooky," I said.

"Today you do. Go home. You have a package arriving, don't you?"

I blushed. "I imagine security is scanning it to see what's in it."

He laughed. "Don't open it until I'm there."

"I'm not sure I can wait that long."

"Wait, the anticipation will be worth it."

He walked me to the lifts. "I might have to try them out, see whether I like them or not."

"Then text me a photograph, I'll need something to entertain me through a very boring dinner with the finance minister."

"Yeah, like I'm going to do that!"

"There's a car downstairs, silver Mercedes, he'll take you home."

"I can walk from here."

"We have pool cars, Lauren, at your disposal whenever you want one, day or night. I'll text you over the number to call."

"Thank you, I'll walk today. I think I need some fresh air."

"I'll come down with you," he said when the lift doors slid open.

"Go back to work, it's fine."

"I can kiss you here, in front of all your new colleagues, who are trying their hardest not to stare right now, or I can travel down with you and kiss you in private. Your choice."

I stepped into the lift and pressed the button. "Anticipation, Mackenzie, it will be worth it."

I heard him laugh as the doors closed and I travelled down, alone. I smiled the whole journey back to my apartment block.

There had most definitely been a shift in our dynamics. If I wasn't confused before that day, I most certainly was now. He acted like we had a relationship, and maybe we did, perhaps what we had was his version of one. I made the decision that at some point over the weekend I would ask him outright.

As I walked, I thought. We'd spoken the most over the previous few days, we'd done things a couple would do. Was that because he was more settled in his work? He hadn't mentioned any travel in the near future. With Alex managing his U.S. operations, I guessed he felt a little more relaxed, not itching to jump on a plane.

"Miss Perry, you have a parcel," I heard. As suspected, sitting on the security desk was a brown box, and I wondered whether they actually had a scanner.

"Thank you," I said, as I collected it.

I took the lift up to my floor; while I did I sent Mackenzie a text.

8090 – door code, should you ever arrive unannounced, and I'm in the shower or something.

I chuckled as I repeated the words he'd said to me.

I hope you are in the shower; I'll walk in, naked, and fuck you there. Was his reply.

Is that on your list or mine?

If I told you I wanted to fuck you in every room in my house, I want your scent everywhere, does that make me sound like I have an addiction?

I was at my front door when I read that, I nearly dropped my keys.

It does, I think I should be scared. You appear to be addicted to sex. I replied.

I'm addicted to you.

I'd only just made it over the threshold when those words brought me to a complete halt. *I'm addicted to you.*

My fingers shook as they hovered over the keyboard. I didn't reply, not sure what to say.

I placed the box and my mobile on the kitchen table. I was itching to open it but decided to wait. I had a feeling I wouldn't be opening it alone.

I took a shower, shaved my legs and armpits, washed my hair and piled it on top of my head to dry naturally. I pulled on a pair of pyjamas and made myself a sandwich. I sat looking at the box for ages. I'd left my laptop at work but decided to check my emails and connected via my tablet. I noticed an email from my solicitor.

I opened the email and read. I screwed my forehead, not understanding the words. I read again. My solicitor had received an anonymous letter offering a settlement amount, higher than I would have offered, to Scott, in return for a quick, no complication divorce. The donor also offered to pay all fees. She confirmed an amount of money had been transferred to her account, ready to be sent on to Scott on completion of our divorce.

I replied to her immediately asking if she had any information on who the donor was. I wasn't expecting a reply, but got an automated 'out of office' one. I'd have to wait until the morning. I leaned back in my chair. Had that been from Mackenzie, or Jerry even? It had to be someone with access to fifty thousand pounds, because that's all Scott was entitled to. The email said an amount higher, and then add the fees. How did they know who my solicitor was? Both Mackenzie and Jerry had been to my apartment, could one of them have copied the details? I wasn't sure whether to be angry or relieved. I wasn't taking charity, I didn't need anyone to pay off Scott, but it sure took a weight off my mind with regard to selling my apartment. If I could find out who it was, I'd pay them back.

I closed down my emails, not bothering with the rest, and made myself a cup of tea.

I had settled on the sofa, having put the email to the back of my mind, and was watching a movie when I heard a knock on my apartment door. I smiled as I rose. I opened the door and my smile froze.

Before I could react, a fist hit me on the cheek. I was knocked backwards, landing heavily on my arse.

"You fucking bitch," a very drunk Scott slurred.

He aimed a kick at me, catching my hip as I rolled to one side. I cried out. He reached down and grabbed a handful of my hair. I stretched my arm up to the consul table, using my fingers to find the

227

intercom phone before he dragged me backwards. I grabbed it and pressed the orange call button. I screamed down for security.

I received a punch to my head, I curled as tight as I could and covered my head with my arms. Then he was pulled off me. I kept my arms covering my head, my knees curled into my chest. I heard Scott shouting as he was dragged away, his voice getting distant as the lift door closed. For a few minutes it was quiet but I didn't move.

"Miss Perry," I heard. I peered through a gap between my arms.

One of the security guards was kneeling beside me. "I've called the police," he said. I nodded and then started to sob. "I think I need to call the paramedics too."

"I don't need those," I said, my voice croaky.

"You might not, but I think Mr. Perry will. Your friend has just arrived."

"My friend?"

"Mr. Miller, he's currently kicking the shit out of him."

"Oh, no. Stop him, please."

He rose and talked on his radio. "Dave, stop that bloke from killing Mr. Perry. Tell the police he took a tumble down the stairs or something."

My body ached as I sat up and rested my back against the wall. As much as I tried, I couldn't stop shaking, or the tears that rolled down my cheeks. I brought my knees to my chest and rested my head on them. I closed my eyes and tried to take some deep breaths to ease the pain.

"Out of the way," I heard. Mackenzie had arrived. He crouched down in front of me.

"Baby, look at me, let me see your face." I looked up. "Fucking cunt."

I shook my head. "I'm fine. Just a little shaken, help me up," I said.

He reached under my arms and lifted me to my feet. "Let's get you sitting down," he said.

He placed his arm around my waist and helped me to the kitchen. He pulled out a chair and I sat. He paced and it was then that I saw his balled fists: with broken skin and bleeding.

"The police will be here shortly, you should go wash your hands," I said.

"Fuck my hands, what did he do to you?" He placed his hands on the table and leaned down towards me.

"He punched me, grabbed my hair, and kicked me. I curled up." I began to sob again.

"I'll fucking kill him, Lauren, I swear," he said, as he wrapped me in his arms.

I held onto him and cried harder.

"Police are on their way up," the security guard said. "She's right, go wash your hands, Dave has told them Mr. Perry took a tumble down the stairs."

Mackenzie walked to the kitchen sink and rinsed his hands. He looked around for a towel before drying his hands on his trousers. I heard a knock on the still open apartment door.

"In here," Mackenzie called out. Two policemen walked through to the kitchen.

I gestured to the chairs opposite me and they sat and introduced themselves. Mackenzie leaned against the kitchen counter.

"Lauren, can I call you that?" I nodded. "Can you tell us what happened?" one asked.

I took a deep breath. "I heard a knock at the door, to be honest I thought it was Mackenzie." I looked over to him. "I didn't look through the spy hole, just opened the door, and he punched my face. I fell; he either grabbed my hair then, or kicked me. I can't think straight right now. He tried to drag me but I managed to get the intercom phone. I called security."

"Did he say anything?"

"He called me a fucking bitch but that was all. We're going through a divorce right now. He was drunk, I could smell alcohol."

"Do you think he had any other intent than to punch you?"

I looked at him for a moment before it dawned on me what he was asking.

"No, not at all."

"You said he dragged you."

"He pulled my hair and my body moved on the floor, that's what I call dragging. I doubt he had any idea what he was doing. He'll wake up tomorrow with a stinking hangover and full of remorse."

"Don't defend him, Lauren," Mackenzie said.

"I'm not, just giving the facts."

"I'd like for a paramedic to look at your face," the policeman said.

I shook my head. "I don't think there's a need. There's certainly nothing broken, it's just sore. I'm shaken up more than anything."

"Is there a history of violence?"

"No, he's never done anything like this before. He just quit his job, we worked together, and I guess he felt he had to."

"Okay, he's already admitted to striking you. He'll be taken to the station and charged initially with assault. He also accused Mr. Miller of attacking him."

"He fell down the stairs," the security guard said. "I witnessed that."

"So your colleague said. Mr. Miller, can you shed any light on that?"

"I saw him at the bottom of the stairs, I may have kicked him as I climbed over, I'm not sure. My priority was to get to Lauren."

"But you chose not to use the lift?"

"I guess, when you saw what I did, all I wanted was to get to her. I didn't think of the route. I can run up those stairs quicker than it would take for the lift to descend then ascend again."

"I just want him removed from the premises, and I want to lie down," I said.

"I'm probably going to have some more questions, can I take a contact number?" he asked.

Mackenzie gave him his. "And your relationship is?"

"Friends," I answered before Mackenzie did.

I saw Mackenzie clamp his jaw shut and turn his head away from me.

"More than friends," I added. "We're…"

"It's okay, Lauren, there's no need to explain." The policeman stood, he looked at Mackenzie.

"If he presses charges, Mr. Miller, I'll need to question you. However, in my experience, in these cases, the perpetrator is often easily swayed to not do that. Too much paperwork and all that. However, maybe you're not familiar but taking the law in your own hands is not what we do here."

Mackenzie nodded his head just the once.

The policemen left, security followed them and Mackenzie locked the front door. He returned to the kitchen and pulled the chair up to sit beside me. He wrapped his arms around me, and I leaned into his chest.

"I'm sorry," I said.

"For what? He beat you, don't you be sorry."

"Not for that. I saw how you looked away from me, when I said we were friends."

"It doesn't matter what you said, don't worry about it, okay?"

He placed his fingers under my chin and raised my face. He smiled then placed a gentle kiss to the bruise I could feel on my cheek.

"That makes it all better," I said.

"That's all I want to do, make you better." He sighed. "Somehow I feel a little responsible."

"How?"

"If I hadn't had confronted him, forced him to resign…"

"You didn't talk him into coming here and punching me, so stop that crap. He made that decision."

"What can I do, Lauren?"

"You can make me a cup of tea and maybe sit with me for a while."

"I've never made a cup of tea before."

I laughed, it hurt a little, but he made me laugh. "You've never made a cup of tea?"

"No, never drink it either."

I went to stand. "Sit, it can't be that hard," he said.

I watched him fill the kettle then stare at it until he figured out where the on button was. He opened the cupboard and retrieved two mugs. Despite the tin clearly saying 'Tea' on the front, I had to point it out to him. He placed two tea bags in the mugs, and when the kettle boiled, he poured.

"Do you have milk?" he asked. I nodded.

He pulled the teabags from the mugs with a teaspoon then looked around for a bin. Not finding one, he deposited them in the sink, added milk, and then sat again.

"It looks…lovely," I said, looking at the tea my mum would describe as a cup of gnat's piss.

"I think I overdid the milk," he said.

I took a sip, "I think you did," I chuckled and then winced.

"Let's get some ice on that face," he said and rose to head to the freezer.

He cracked some ice from the tray and wrapped it in a tea towel. He gently held it to my cheek.

"Ouch," I said. The cold stung my skin. "So, how was your dinner?"

He looked at me and shook his head. "Fucking boring. I left early, said I had an important meeting with a box."

"I didn't open it."

"So I see. How about we get you in bed, you must be hurting."

"I ache, but I think that's just the shock. It probably looks worse than it actually is. He never did have a good punch or aim."

"Well, I can guarantee he certainly felt one."

As I stood, I leaned against his chest, wrapping my arms around his waist.

"Thank you, but you know you can't go round beating people up in London. The police don't take too kindly to it, they prefer to do it themselves in a cell, with no witnesses."

Mackenzie picked me up; the action caused me to wince some more as my hip hit his stomach. He walked into the bedroom and placed me on the bed. I shuffled around, dragging the duvet from underneath.

"I'll get your tea, or do you want me to make another cup?"

"It's fine, thank you."

He brought back the one mug. "Sorry, I can't drink that shit."

He walked around to the other side of the bed, pulled off his shirt, kicked off his shoes and undid his trousers. He stepped out of them and climbed onto the bed next to me.

"Come here," he said.

He wrapped one arm under my neck as we snuggled down, and he pulled me to his chest.

"I swear though, Lauren, if he comes anywhere near you again, I will fucking kill him."

"I imagine there will be some sort of restraining order so that he's not allowed. Mackenzie, for all his faults, that was completely out of character. I doubt very much I'll ever see him again."

We fell silent for a little while. I placed my head on his chest and listened to his heartbeat. It made me drowsy. I didn't quite catch what he'd said as I fell into sleep.

I know I cried out in the night, I'd half woken myself as I turned in his arms and landed on my bruised hip. I also heard him soothe me, stroking my hair to lull me back to sleep.

When I finally woke, he was curled into my back with one arm under my neck and across my shoulder, the other on my waist. It felt so good to be spooning with him, to have his breath on the back of my neck. I didn't want to move, but I needed to pee.

I gently untangled myself and made my way to the bathroom. As I was sitting, he walked in.

"I'm peeing," I said.

"So lock the door if you don't want me to see you."

I laughed and threw the toilet roll at him.

"Now that was dumb," he said, unrolling some and handing it to me. As I reached out, he withdrew his hand.

"Please, may I have some toilet roll?"

He gave me the screwed up piece from his hand. I took it and discretely wiped.

I stood beside him at the bathroom mirror. I had a nice purple bruise on my cheek, and when I looked, one on my hip.

"That will cover with a bit of makeup," I said.

"You're not going to work today."

"Mackenzie, I'm fine. It doesn't hurt. Thank you for staying with me, I needed that."

"I don't want you in that office, what if he returns?"

"He won't, he's a fucking coward, and if he does, I'll return the favour," I said, inspecting my face a little closer.

He stepped behind me, wrapped his arms around me and rested his chin on my shoulder. "My heart fucking stopped, Lauren, when I saw him. I didn't even ask why he was on the floor being held down, I just saw red. I knew he'd done something to you."

I reached up and placed my hand on his cheek. He turned his head and kissed my palm.

"You need to promise me one thing, don't do that again. I'd hate it if you ended up in trouble because of me."

"I want you to come and stay with me, just for a day or so. I can work from home."

"No, I have to go into work. I have…"

"You have nothing that you *have* to do, not until next week. I'm cancelling the weekend as well."

I turned in his arms. "Why?"

"Because you have bruises, you're hurt."

"Mackenzie, I have a bruise to my hip and one to my cheek, they don't *hurt*. They'll be gone in a couple of days. I was looking forward to the weekend."

"Then come home with me, let me look after you."

"So it's a trade-off then?" I smiled.

"Yep, I only do negotiations, Lauren."

"I'll stay with you for two nights, you'll be bored of me by then. Then the weekend is on, agreed?"

"I'm not sure I'll be bored with you, although I haven't had a woman in my house for years, so we might have to set out some rules. Two nights and then the weekend is on."

"Deal."

"You drive a hard bargain, Miss Perry," he said.

"I like hard, Mr. Miller."

"I like giving hard."

I reached down and cupped his erection through his shorts. I lowered them so his cock sprang free. I wrapped my hand around it, massaging him slowly. He sighed. He reached for the buttons on my pyjama top.

"No, I don't do enough just for you," I said, as I sank to my knees.

I tried not to wince as he wrapped his hands in my hair; my scalp was sore. I opened my mouth and sucked his cock. His moan of pleasure spurred me on. I sucked harder, deeper, cupping his balls with one hand and rolling them around in my palm. I loved the feel of his silky skin in my mouth; I loved the taste of his precum as he wept onto my tongue.

I held his hips as he gently thrust them; building up speed as his desire grew. I breathed in deep and tried to relax as he fucked my mouth, hitting my throat and causing my eyes to water.

"Fuck, Lauren," he said. "That feels so good."

I dug my fingers into his skin as he groaned, and I sucked harder as I felt his cock twitch, pulse. His balls tightened in my hand, and I dragged my nails down the skin just behind. He cried out as he came. Hot salty fluid hit the back of my throat. I held his cum in my mouth while I gently released him, and then swallowed the rest.

"Shit, I really need to work on my stamina," he said with a laugh.

He could fuck me for hours, and again even after he came, but when my mouth was around his cock, he couldn't hold back. I wasn't complaining; my jaw ached like a bitch.

He helped me stand, and before I was fully upright, his mouth crashed down on mine. He would taste himself on my tongue and I moaned at that thought. No matter what that man did, nice or vulgar, he turned me on.

****

I was showered, dressed, and had packed an overnight bag. As much as I didn't tell Mackenzie, I was excited to be staying over at his house. For once what we were doing felt like a real relationship. I grabbed my Kindle, and it was as I did I remembered the email.

"Something I forgot to tell you. I received an email from my solicitor, someone has deposited an amount of money to pay off Scott."

Mackenzie was tying his shoelaces. He didn't look up. "Someone did what?"

"Someone deposited money in my solicitor's account to pay off Scott, and it's higher than he's actually entitled to. I'm not sure I'm happy about it."

"Did you email and ask who?" he asked.

"Of course, I'll show you the email when we get to yours, which also reminds me, I need my laptop from work."

"I'll have someone fetch it for you. Are you ready?"

I nodded as I grabbed a light jacket. "The box?" he added.

"Huh?"

"The. Box."

"Oh, the box. Can't forget the box," I said, and laughed.

I grabbed it from the kitchen table and held it under my arm as we locked up the apartment.

"Scott doesn't have a key for your apartment, does he?"

"No, he threw that at me when I chucked him out. Although, I'll get the locks changed now, just in case."

"And that front door code needs to change, half the time the door's propped open because it's not working."

"Jerry said that, funnily enough. And talking about Jerry, I think he's ignoring me, he hasn't called or texted in ages."

"I have to meet with him today, do you want me to mention anything?"

"No, no way. He's a little upset with me, I know why. I'll give him a call later. I'm going to miss him when he leaves."

We had arrived at Mackenzie's car. "I don't see why you still can't be friends," he said, as he placed my bag in the boot.

"Do you know how he feels about me?" I asked. Mackenzie nodded as he closed the boot and opened the car door.

"I sort of told him about us, I was a little upset after that lunch," I said.

"What do you mean, *sort of*? What did you say?" he asked, when he climbed into his seat.

"Just that we were having some fun, nothing more."

Again, I saw that clenching of the jaw.

"I didn't want him to think there was anything else, so as not to upset him, initially," I added.

The jaw relaxed and Mackenzie gave a ghost of a smile as we pulled out of the car park.

Gabriella could very well be correct.

"So you told him we were *having some fun,* and he hasn't spoken to you since?"

"Correct."

"Well, we'll have to rectify that, won't we?" He looked at me with a smirk.

"I don't want you to interfere, okay."

"Like I said, I have to meet with him today, he can come to the house."

"I'm not sure I'd…"

"You don't want him to know you're at my house?" We were back to jaw clenching.

"I…"

"What, Lauren?"

"I'm not sure I want him to know about Scott, and if he sees me at your house, he'll ask why I'm there."

"One, why don't you want him to know about Scott? And two, I don't see the problem with him knowing you're staying at my house. Why is this so complicated?"

"I'm embarrassed, Mackenzie."

He slammed the car brakes on so hard that I braced myself waiting for the smash into the back of the car from the one behind. I clenched my eyes closed; nothing came.

"You're embarrassed? What the fuck does that mean? You're ashamed of us?"

The seat belt had tightened and dug into the bruise on my hip, and I winced trying to loosen it.

"No, I'm not fucking ashamed. Why does it have to come around to you or us? I'm embarrassed because I let a fucking man punch me in the face, pull my hair from its roots, and kick me, okay?" My voice had risen to a shout. It competed with the honking traffic. "Sort this fucking seat belt out," I added, wrenching on it.

Mackenzie put the car into gear and pulled into a side road, stopping on the double yellows in front of a traffic warden.

"That's going to get you a ticket," I said.

"I have hundreds of fucking tickets from those assholes," he said as he unclipped my belt.

I sighed at the instant relief, leaned back in my seat and closed my eyes. I angrily brushed a tear away.

"I'm sorry," he said.

"So am I. Can we get to the house, then you question me?" I could see them forming on his lips.

Why the fuck I should feel embarrassed, I had no idea, but I did. I was the hard-nosed career woman, wasn't I? Isn't that what he called me? I was the tough cookie, and yet a pang of nerves had my stomach knotted when we walked out of my apartment, that knot doubled when we walked out of the apartment building. Being nervous to leave my home embarrassed me. Holding my breath until I was safely in the car embarrassed me. Meeting my best friend, knowing I was going to break down and cry as soon as he saw my bruise, embarrassed me. They shouldn't have, but they did.

We drove the rest of the way in silence.

Mackenzie opened the passenger door once we'd pulled onto his drive, and he crouched down beside me.

"I'm sorry. I just…"

I placed my hand on his cheek. "I know it's totally irrational, but I feel embarrassed that somehow I allowed him to do that, I didn't fight back. I should have. I'm not a weak woman, Mackenzie, but he scared me. For the first time in my life, a man scared me. That is what I'm embarrassed about. Not you, not us, not me being here."

"I'm glad you also see that as completely irrational. No matter how tough you think you are, Lauren, you're no match for a drunken man, who took you by surprise. I'll postpone Jerry's visit."

I sighed and smiled at him. "Help me out the car, your fucking stunt driving has killed my hip."

"I wish you wouldn't swear," he mumbled as he helped me.

"Says the man who wants me to say *soaking cunt*," I said, somewhat surprised by his comment.

He laughed. "I wish you wouldn't swear because it turns me on."

"Why?"

"There's Lauren, the professional career woman, the upstanding pillar of community, and then there's Lauren the dirty, devil on her shoulder, sexy as fuck woman. I lo…like them both, of course."

I frowned at him, what was he about to say? *Just say it,* I said, no, shouted, in my head.

I was scared of reading too much into what he was saying, and I blamed Gabriella for putting the thought that he was in love with me into my head. How often had he said he wasn't looking for a relationship? I tried to rack my brain for instances, while he grabbed my bag from the boot of his car.

He opened the door and left my bag at the bottom of the stairs. We walked through to the kitchen.

"I need to get some tea," he said, as he fired up his coffee machine.

"Don't shop just for me," I replied.

"I want to. Now, rules. It might be the traditional thing here in the U.K. that the kitchen is your domain but it isn't. It's mine; all mine. I cook." He smirked at me.

"I'm not going to argue with that. Any more rules? Can I use your toothbrush?"

"Since my mouth has been all over your body, I don't have a problem with you using my toothbrush. Steer clear of my razor though. That might provoke a Mackenzie you haven't seen yet."

"A Mackenzie I haven't seen yet? That sounds interesting."

"Yeah, you might not like that Mackenzie. I cut my face because you blunted my blades? Won't be a pretty sight."

"Yet you have all this scruff," I said, running my hand over his stubble.

"It can come off if you don't like it."

"I like it. Anywhere I'm not allowed to go, in this grand house of yours?"

"You can go wherever you want. I want you to feel at home here, Lauren."

"It would be hard not to feel at home, I love it here."

He smiled at my words. "Good, if you want to rearrange anything, go ahead."

He talked as if I was moving in and not just spending a couple of days.

"Oh, don't touch my cars, massive no on that one."

"I can't drive anyway, maybe you can teach me?"

"To drive my Aston Martins? Are you fucking crazy?" He laughed as he placed two coffees on the breakfast bar. "I'll buy you some beat up Ford, and you can learn in that."

"I was kidding, I don't need to learn to drive."

"Everyone needs to drive, Lauren. Maybe we should organise some lessons."

"I live in London, I'm about to work a five minute walk away from where I live, well, where I live for now. I don't need to drive."

"What do you mean, where you live for now?"

"I'm going to sell the apartment. It's not about the money, I just don't want to live there anymore."

"Because of last night?"

"No, I made that decision a few days ago. Because it's lonely, because it holds memories I'd rather not have."

"You're lonely?"

"Of course I'm lonely. For the first time in my life, I'm on my own, Mackenzie. I haven't gotten used to it yet. I'm sure I will, but I don't want to do it in that apartment."

"Where will you live?" he asked, his voice had lowered a little.

"I don't know; depends what I can afford."

"I'll send a courier to pick up your laptop, is there anything else you need?" he asked, completely changing the subject.

"I'll give Jenny a call, I'll tell her I had a fall or something. Slipped out the shower."

"I'm also going to report what Scott did to Gabriella, she needs to know so she can keep him off the premises. He's supposed to be working his notice but that isn't going to happen now."

"Do you have to?"

"Yes. I won't have that man near my property."

"I hope that doesn't refer to me," I said, with a laugh. He placed his coffee cup down and stood.

"I'd neither insult you that way, nor presume that you were mine. I have to make a call to the police, see what happened."

I watched him walk from the room, holding his body tight. I'd been in his house no more than half an hour and already there was tension.

"We have to have that chat," I whispered to his retreating back.

While he made his call, I decided to explore the house. I picked up my cup and started on the ground floor. The living room was vast, and I wondered if he'd used an interior designer. Two brown leather sofas faced each other in the centre of the room, a large low table sat in the middle. Although comfortable looking, it didn't seem that he used it that often. Cushions were propped on the sofa at precise angles. The room was bright with two large windows looking out to the front.

Another room was set out as a cinema room, a huge TV screen dominated one wall and a less formal sofa faced it. I wasn't sure if it could be called a sofa, it was more like a bed, such was its size.

There was a downstairs cloakroom, and the last door I opened held Mackenzie behind a glass desk. He looked up while still on the phone and smiled at me. He waved me in.

"Yes, she's here now. Okay, hold on," he said.

He handed me his phone. "Gabriella," he said.

"Hi," I said.

"Oh, honey, I'm so sorry to hear what happened. My God, are you okay?"

"I am just a little bruised. Mackenzie is overreacting, but I'm sure glad to get out of the apartment for a day or so."

"What have the police said? Have they charged him?"

"I expect to hear from them today. I gave a statement, and of course, Mackenzie beat him up, so I don't know what will come of that."

She laughed. "Another clue perhaps, to how he feels?"

I turned my back slightly, not sure if he could hear.

"No, instinct. Anyway, I wanted to come into work, I'm perfectly fine..."

She cut me off. "You'll do no such thing. Take the rest of the week off, start afresh on Monday. I'm sending Joanna, your replacement, over to meet your team today. I'd have liked for you to meet her first, but we might as well get it over with. Mackenzie tells me you need some things, how about you email Jenny, and we'll have that couriered to the house?"

"That would be great, thank you. I can't just sit here doing nothing for a couple of days."

"I'll see you at some point, and rest assured, Lauren. Scott will not be welcome here."

"Thank you, I'll pass you back now."

I handed the phone to Mackenzie. "I'm taking a tour, is that okay?" I asked before he spoke.

"Of course it's okay. Let me finish up and I'll show you around."

He placed the phone back to his ear, while he continued I pulled my mobile from my pocket and texted a message to Jenny.

"Gabby, sort out Lauren's things for me and I'll call you later."

He didn't say goodbye, just cut off the call.

"So, what have you seen so far?"

"The huge TV in that room, do you watch it?"

"I spend most of my time in the kitchen or here. Maybe we'll watch a movie later. I called the police before Gabriella. They charged him with assault, he didn't deny it and is out on bail," he said. I nodded.

"So, tour?" he added.

I followed him back to the hallway. "Living room, I don't go in there much, cloakroom, my office, kitchen that way, obviously, and TV room. That door there, takes you to the basement." He walked towards it.

I followed and we descended a flight of stairs and into a gym.

"Wow, do you use all this?" I asked, looking at a range of high tech equipment.

"Yes, every day, usually. I like to keep fit, work out a little frustration. There's a shower room through there," he said indicating to a door.

"You'll have to teach me how to use this," I said.

I stood beside a weight machine with a leather bench underneath. He had running machines, cross trainers, weights, rowing machines, a spin bike, various sized core stability balls, a punch bag hanging in one corner, and in the other, an area of soft mats. To one side was a massage table.

"Do you remember what I told you?" he said, as he stalked towards me.

"When?"

"I said I wanted to fuck you in every room of this house, and I will."

I raised my eyebrows at him, a smile formed on my lips. "I'll make sure to mark my territory, Mackenzie, just in case you decide to bring another woman here when I'm gone."

I heard his sharp intake of breath. "I don't bring women here. You're the first, and last. I like that little jealous streak you have."

"Oh, I'm not jealous, I…."

Was I? I didn't think I was. However, I didn't like the thought of him having another woman at his house.

"I'll also make sure to leave the odd pair of panties around, just in case," I said, with a wink.

He laughed. "If I wasn't so concerned about your hip, I'd start your *marking your territory* right now."

"I'm not that precious," I said.

"You are to me," he whispered. Before I could respond, he took my hand. "Come on, rest of the house."

We walked back up to the ground floor and then up the stairs. Mackenzie grabbed my overnight bag on the way. He took me to his bedroom first, I'd been there before, and he placed the bag on the bed.

"You can shift some stuff around in the closet, make some space."

We then left the room. He showed me three more bedrooms, all beautifully decorated. I paused in one, the dressing table held cosmetics, female cosmetics. I guessed he'd seen me look.

"Gabriella's room, when she stays. Well, I should say, Gabriella and Alex's room. Although I need to shift them a little further down the hallway, they're not the quietest of couples."

I gasped and bit down on my lower lip. "You cannot say that."

He laughed, "It's true."

"Are all Americans so open about their sex lives as you are?"

"No idea. I'm forty years old, Lauren; I don't have time to fuck about. I say and do what I want."

Do you? I wish you did, I thought.

There was a large family bathroom and another shower room. We walked back downstairs and through the kitchen to a set of doors. The garden was laid mainly to lawn but had a large terraced area with sofas. We walked towards a brick building.

"Summer house, or whatever you call them here," he said, as he opened the doors.

"Pool house," I said, as I saw the sparkling expanse of blue water.

"There's an apartment above that, I guess for staff."

"Do you have help?"

"I have someone come in and clean a couple of times a week. Housework isn't my thing."

"No, I can't quite see you being the domestic type. Who does the food shopping?"

"I do. I'm a modern man, Lauren. I don't go to the store, fucking hate that. Do it online, or Kerry does."

"Kerry?"

"The cleaner. Well, she's probably more of a housekeeper since she sorts my laundry as well."

"So other than cook, you don't actually do anything a modern man does?" I teased.

He laughed, "I guess not. But I was halfway to impressing you, wasn't I?"

"You impress me, full stop." I kicked off my shoe and dipped my foot into the water. "Jesus, it's freezing!"

"I don't use it, didn't seem any point in turning it on. I can, if you want, but I suspect it will take a few days to warm up."

"No, don't worry on my account."

"What do you want to do today?" he asked, as we walked back to the house.

"I don't know; you have to work, so maybe I'll read for a while."

"I don't *have* to work, I can take a few hours off."

246

"Then why don't we see what's in *the box*," I said, with mock surprise.

He picked it up from the kitchen counter. "Lead the way," he said.

Chapter Sixteen

Mackenzie placed the box on his bed. He stood to one side and looked at me.

"Open it, show me what you bought," he said.

I tried not to giggle and my hands shook a little as I peeled off the sticky tape. I pulled back the lid and gasped.

"Oh, God. What was I thinking?"

"Show me."

"No, I'm embarrassed."

I turned to face him, keeping the box behind me.

"Embarrassed? Really? After what we've done? I watched you lick another woman's cunt, Lauren. I watched you come in her mouth. There should be nothing in that box that's *embarrassing*," he said, as he took a step towards me.

"I wish you wouldn't use that word."

"What word?" he asked.

"The C word."

"Why?"

"Because."

"Because it turns you on and that also embarrasses you?"

He was so close; I could feel his erection through his trousers.

"Yes. And it shouldn't, it's a horrible word," I said.

"Horrible or not, it elicits the desired response. Trust me, it's not a word I use in my everyday vocabulary. I like being vulgar with you. I like to see your pupils dilate when I say the word. Now, show me what's in the box."

I turned, feeling him press against my back. I lifted out the vibrator, removed it from its packaging, and held it in my hands. It felt silky, real. I ran my hand over it as Mackenzie placed his hands on my waist; he ground himself against my backside as he looked over my shoulder.

"I think we can have a lot of fun with that," he whispered.

I placed it on the bed. The next thing I pulled out was the tube of lubricant.

"Good, always useful," he said.

I showed him the vibrating eggs and he laughed.

Then it was the We-Vibe. It was housed in its own box. I opened that and took out the small black object and an instruction booklet.

"Now that I like. I can control it," he whispered.

"I've never used any of these *things*," I said.

"I'll enjoy initiating you then." He ran his hands up my sides, dragging my t-shirt over my head.

He unclipped my bra and slid it from my shoulders. He then reached around and undid my jeans. I wriggled out of them, pulling my panties down at the same time.

He reached around me for the vibrator and switched it on. I was thankful it had come with batteries already installed. I heard its gentle buzz and felt a tingle as he ran it down my spine.

"I like that," I whispered.

"What do you want to experience, this weekend? It isn't always about pain, Lauren. It's also about sensual touch, having your nerve endings come alive with different sensations. Soft strokes of a feather, vibrations, or the harsh sting of a flogger or paddle."

"All of that," I said.

He ran the vibrator over my backside and I parted my legs slightly.

"One day, I want to fuck your ass," he said.

"Never," I replied, breathlessly as the vibrations shot through me.

He chuckled. "Never say never. It's on my list, so has to be done."

He placed his hand between my shoulder blades and gently pushed my top half to the bed. I swiped the boxes out of the way as I stretched out my arms in front of me. He kicked at my ankles and I parted my legs further.

He ran the vibrator over my clitoris and the vibrations reverberated through me. I gasped. He slid it back and forth, each time causing a moan. I heard a soft chuckle.

"You like that, huh?" he whispered.

"Yes."

Whatever he did to increase the vibrations had me crying out for more. I clawed at the bedding, dragging it towards me.

He eased the tip inside me and I tensed a little. "Relax," he said.

What I hadn't expected was, when he pushed it in further, a small arm hit my clitoris vibrating against it.

"Oh, fuck," I said, as I started to pant.

"Give me that lube," he said. I reached for the tube and passed it behind me.

I felt a cold trickle on my backside and he smeared it down the crack of my arse. I held my breath as he slowly inserted his finger.

"Fuck," I said, again as he pushed down.

My stomach was fluttering, my heart racing. I gripped the bedding harder as he slid both the vibrator and his finger in and out of me.

"I'm going to come," I whispered.

He did it again; he switched the vibrations higher and fucked me through an orgasm. I screamed out his name.

"Now that is a word I like to hear," he said, as he slowly removed his finger.

When he'd pulled the vibrator from me, I could feel a trickle of cum run down my thigh. I tried to stand, he held me down.

"I'm not done with you yet," he said.

He trailed one hand down my back and between my thighs, he inserted two fingers in me, twisting and pumping. I loved the feeling of the vibrator inside; I loved his fingers more.

"I'm going to do something now, Lauren."

Before I could ask what, he brought the flat of his hand down on my arse cheek. For a second I was stunned into silence. I could feel the sting and then heat. My whole body heated up, my clitoris throbbed harder, and that sting seemed to have transferred to my very core; my pussy pulsed and my stomach flipped.

"Jesus," I cried out. "Oh God, again."

He brought his hand down on the other cheek and my legs shook. It hurt but as his fingers fucked me, it was a different hurt. It intensified all my senses. What was already pleasurable became heightened. I could feel every sweep of his fingers, and I could feel every slight movement as he flexed his knuckles. He rubbed his palm over my backside, soothing the sting.

"Again," I whispered.

The third brought me to a shuddering orgasm that had tears roll down my cheeks.

Mackenzie dropped to his knees, and while I came down from something that confused me, he licked and sucked every drop of my cum from me. He ran his tongue up my thigh, over my clitoris, sucking it into his mouth. He dug his fingers into my arse cheeks. My stomach ached, my legs felt heavy. When he'd taken every drop I could give him, he raised his face and very gently kissed my heated cheeks.

He rose, leaning over me and wrapped his arms around my chest; he pulled me up, cupped one arm under my legs and lifted me. He laid me on the bed, face down.

"Stay there," he whispered.

I heard him walk to his bathroom. He returned shortly after, and I felt a cold washcloth placed on my backside. He sat beside me, trailing a finger up and down my back. He removed the washcloth and then I felt a drop of something on each cheek. He gently massaged it in. The sting had gone, but I had no doubt my arse was as red as the cheeks on my face.

He gently rolled me over; I covered my eyes with one arm. He pulled it away.

"Talk to me, Lauren. Tell me how you feel."

"I shouldn't have liked that," I said.

"Why?"

"I..." I looked at him. "I don't know, maybe because it's a form of punishment, and I've done nothing wrong. But...I loved it."

"Good," he said with a smile.

"It felt so wrong, but so..." I struggled to find the words.

"I know," he whispered.

"Have you had that done to you?"

"No, but like I've said before. I enjoy the reaction. To see you come so hard for me is amazing, Lauren. It's an unbelievable feeling to know I can produce that for you. I can arouse you so much you come apart around me." His voice had lowered to a whisper, and I could have sworn I saw tears in his eyes.

He lay beside me, wrapped his arms around me, and held me tight. He kissed me so gently, so, dare I say it, lovingly.

"Thank you," he said.

We lay in silence for a while.

****

We seemed to be able to move around the kitchen in sync, there was no awkwardness; no 'I don't belong,' feeling. Mackenzie cooked steaks and I set the breakfast bar.

I'd taken a shower earlier, while he got on with some work and we'd decided on an early dinner. I liked watching him cook. He clearly knew what he was doing as he tenderised the steaks, added seasoning, and turned them briefly in a pan before placing them under the grill. I chopped salad; it was as much as he'd allow me to do.

We sat and chatted as we ate. He told me about his home in America. He hated LA and wanted to sell it, he had a dream of living somewhere less populated but still on the beach.

"I'll take you to my mum's, you'd love Cornwall," I said.

"That would be nice. I'd like to meet her and your brother."

I sipped on my cold white wine. "Can I ask you a question?" I said.

"Sure."

"Is that the hardest you'll hit me?"

"I wish you wouldn't use the word *hit,* but yes, for now."

"Is that the hardest you *spanked* Veronica?"

"No. She liked it a lot rougher. Which is why I stopped all that a long time ago, Lauren."

"What does she do now?"

"You remember the hooded guy? That's her partner."

"What was he doing to that woman?" I remembered her being tied up with intricate knots.

"Kinbaku, it's called. It's Japanese bondage."

"What does she gain from that?"

He shrugged his shoulders slightly. "I guess it's the ultimate restraint. She can't move one muscle unless he allows it. He's a master at what he does. He doesn't speak and other than tying them, then comforting them, he doesn't touch them either."

"So what does he gain from that?"

"Control. He's in complete control of her. I guess that's where he gets his kicks. It's not all he does, of course. With Veronica, he's more intense. It would frighten you if I told you what they did."

"I think you might be right," I said.

"I know it would. It's not something I'd be willing to let you experience, and I'd *never* want to watch you with another man, Lauren, *ever.*"

"I don't want to be with another man. What I want is with you. It's because of you. I'd have never thought of any of those things had it not been you putting the question in my mind initially."

"Do you regret that?"

His question took my by surprise, "Not for one minute. Like I've said, I'm scared that I won't know when to stop, how far I'll go, and what happens when it's all over."

"What happens is entirely your decision, it always has been. You read about your Doms, which is all bullshit by the way, and you've seen a very, very small part of that life. But you need to understand, women are the ones in control, Lauren. You say how far you go, you decide what I can and can't do. *You* control every aspect of what I do, whether you realise that or not."

"Are you a Dom?"

He laughed; in fact he nearly choked and had to take a sip of his wine.

"God, no. It's a lifestyle *choice*, Lauren. I might be a dominant male but that's through being a businessman and genetics, I guess. I'm a very sexual man, and there are elements of it I enjoy. I like to control your body, I like being the one encouraging you to explore. Maybe I am the way I am because of what I've been through."

"She hurt you, didn't she?" I said softly, as I laid my cutlery down.

"She did. It was the ultimate betrayal. Daniel and I were best friends, Lauren, when we were young. If she'd fucked a stranger, maybe it wouldn't have hurt as much, but to have an affair, something that lasted a while, with my best friend? That's unforgivable in my book."

"Was she going to pass off the child as yours?"

"I guess so. I should have been honest with her in the beginning, but like I said before, I hoped something would have happened, medically, and it would all be okay."

"Does it still affect you? Not having a child."

He thought for a moment before he answered. "It did, then I came to terms with it, now it's on my mind. But I'd rather not talk about it right now."

"Okay, I'm sorry."

"Don't be sorry," he said with a smile.

"When did we stop playing the game?" I asked, gently.

He didn't answer immediately. Right then would have been the perfect opportunity to bring up the *us* subject, but I didn't, and neither did he. I stood and cleared the dishes. He reached out and grabbed my wrist as I went to talk away.

"I was never *playing*, Lauren. I'm deadly serious," he said.

I smiled over to him, and then stacked the dishwasher.

****

We spent the evening watching a movie. I curled into his side, and it felt good to just sit together and do something so normal, like a regular couple would.

It felt even better to curl up naked, beside him, in bed and have him stroke my hair until I fell asleep. I wasn't going to compare him to Scott. They were poles apart in everything.

Chapter Seventeen

I woke before him. He was lying on his side, facing me. I'd had the best night's sleep I'd had in ages but had woken as the sun was rising. At first, I just looked at him. His dark eyelashes and hair, his slightly olive skin, made him look more European than American. I wondered what his heritage was. I gently climbed from the bed and put on his shirt. I walked downstairs and stood in front of the scariest coffee machine I'd ever seen.

Can't be that hard to figure out, I thought.

After several attempts and many buttons pushed in the wrong sequence, I managed to make two cups of black coffee. Not that black coffee was my drink of choice, but I had yet to figure out how to add the hot milk. Instead, I added a splash of cold to mine. I took them back upstairs.

As I sat on the edge of the bed, he stirred. He rolled to his back and opened his eyes.

"Good morning, I managed to tame the coffee machine into submission," I said, raising the cups.

"Dressed like that, I'm surprised it didn't fall to its knees and worship you," he said, as he pushed himself into a sitting position.

I handed him a cup of coffee. "Now this is something I could get used to," he said as he took a sip.

"Being brought coffee in bed?" I asked.

"By you dressed only in my shirt. Do you have any idea how hot you look?"

I laughed. My hair was a tangled mess, and I was sure I had mascara smudged under my eyes.

I placed my coffee on his bedside cabinet and took his from his hands. I gently pulled back the sheets and straddled his lap. He held my hips.

"I want to fuck you," I said.

"Then go ahead, I'm always ready for you."

I reached between my thighs and wrapped my hand around his cock, which hardened at my touch. I used the fingers on my other hand to tease myself. I loved that his pupils dilated, his eyes darkened. I loved to see his tongue gently swipe over his lower lip and his nostrils flare as he breathed in deep. For everything he'd said previously about his satisfaction at my reactions, I felt the same.

His chest expanded, and he closed his eyes as his arousal took over him.

"Look at me, Mackenzie," I whispered. His eyes focussed on my hand.

I rose slightly and inserted two fingers inside me, he gently moaned at what he saw. It wasn't long before my fingers were coated, and I positioned his cock at my entrance. He hissed as I lowered.

He grabbed my wrist pulling me forward slightly while he sat up. He sucked my fingers into his mouth, and I rode him hard.

When he released my fingers, I placed both hands behind me, on his knees. He met my thrusts with his own, growling out my name as he did. I reached down and rolled his balls in one hand. The pace of his thrusts increased.

"Come for me," I whispered.

I wanted to see if he could. If he could give in to his release when I asked. He did.

His back arched off the bed, and I watched as his stomach muscles tightened, showing defined abs. I loved the body beneath me; I loved the man.

I smiled as he slowly opened his eyes.

"Fuck, Lauren. You didn't come," he said.

"I don't need to, I got as much pleasure watching you as you do watching me."

I slowly raised myself from him. I walked to his bathroom and grabbed some tissues, cleaning myself up before walking back and handing him some. He laughed at the gesture.

"I didn't want to drip all over your floor," I said.

He reached out his hand and pulled me down on top of him.

"Listen to you now. Would you have said that a few weeks ago?"

"No, I guess you've awoken something in me."

"Do you like it?"

"I love it."

He gently slapped my backside. "Move, I need my coffee."

I laughed as I rolled to the side. We sat side by side and drank.

"I'm going to miss this, when you're gone," he said.

"So am I."

"You don't…"

"Mackenzie, can we do one thing?" I asked, cutting him off. "I really want this weekend; in fact, I don't want to wait until the weekend. Then we need to sit down and talk."

He looked at me and slowly nodded. I wasn't sure on the meaning of the expression that flashed over his face. "I'll call Veronica, we'll go this afternoon."

I smiled. "Thank you. It's the last thing on my list. Well, second to last. There's one other."

"And that is?"

"I'm not telling you yet."

I tried to disguise the wave of sadness that rolled over me. *One more night.*

****

Mackenzie was a little quieter than normal as we each packed an overnight bag. I was both sad and excited. I was going to tell him I'd fallen in love with him, and then it was his choice what to do with that. I'd resigned myself that whatever we had might be over, and I'd have to assure him that I could still work for him and not let my feelings get in the way. Or that was the lie I was trying to convince myself of.

What I did do, and whether this was for purely selfish reasons or not, I sent a quick email to the solicitor and asked her to put forward the proposal to Scott. She hadn't discovered who had sent the money, but would investigate via the banks. I wanted my divorce to be concluded quickly. I wanted to move on with my life, whatever path that was about to take. But I still wanted to know who my benefactor was.

"You're quiet," I said, as we drove to Surrey.

"Am I? Just thinking, that's all."

"Anything you want to share?"

He turned and smiled at me. "It's been amazing to see you change so much."

Was that the start of our parting? "You've done that, Mackenzie."

He slowly nodded his head. "What an idiot," he whispered.

"Who?"

"That car, behind us."

I looked at him as he glanced in his rearview mirror. The side mirror wasn't positioned so I could see if there was a car behind us.

"Will you make these couple of days special for me?' I asked.

"I'll make them the best you've ever had."

He focussed his attention on the road, but he did take one hand from the steering wheel and clasp it around mine. I held on tight and looked out the side window so he wouldn't see my tears.

The journey was too short and I soon noticed the house come into view. I wanted just a little more time alone with him. As before, the valet stepped forward and retrieved our bags from the boot and the car keys from Mackenzie. Veronica opened the door. She smiled in greeting.

"It's good to see you again," she said. "I have the cottage ready for you."

She handed over a key and gestured with her arm for us to lead the way. The valet followed behind with our bags. Mackenzie opened the cottage door and allowed me to step through first. I felt immediately at home.

"I have what you requested set out for later. Shall I reserve a table for dinner first?" Veronica said.

"Yes, an early dinner, six o'clock," Mackenzie answered in clipped tones.

Veronica frowned ever so slightly.

"Is there anything else I can get you?" she asked.

"No," he replied.

She nodded at him and turned to walk away. "Thank you, Veronica," I called after her.

"I think I'll take a shower," Mackenzie said stripping off his shirt as he walked to the bathroom.

As Veronica closed the door, she looked at me; I shrugged my shoulders.

I decided to open the wine that was cooling in an ice bucket, I needed a little Dutch courage, the enormity of what I'd asked for, what I was about to witness and receive started to dawn on me. Maybe Mackenzie was *off* because he was getting in 'the zone.'

I sat on the sofa and twirled my glass between my fingers. It wasn't long before Mackenzie walked back in with just a towel around his waist.

"Are you okay?" I asked.

He smiled at me, "Yes, do you want to pour me one?" Maybe his shower had washed away his sour mood.

He sat as I did. I handed over his wine and he turned slightly towards me. He raised his glass, clinked it with mine.

"No sleep, Lauren. For the next twenty-four hours you are completely mine, every minute, every second. You'll only do as I say, not ask, say."

My stomach did a triple flip, worthy of a score of ten, had it been off a diving board.

"Are you ready for that?" he added. It was all I could do to nod.

"Do we need a safe word?" I asked; my voice had raised an octave.

"I'll know when you can't take anymore. If I miss that, which is unlikely, you just tell me to stop."

I nodded again. "What are you going to do?" I whispered.

"Everything I think you can handle. I get this one opportunity, Lauren, this *last* opportunity, to tick it all off my list, and yours."

He rose and strode towards the bedroom, not giving me a chance to answer.

"He's in the zone," I whispered to myself, trying to account for his aloofness.

I sipped on my wine. If he wanted me to stay awake for twenty-four hours, perhaps I shouldn't drink the wine.

It was a half-hour later that he returned, dressed in a white shirt and dark trousers.

"There is a red dress in the closet that I'd like you to wear," he said.

"Okay, will it fit?"

"Of course it will fit."

"How did you know my size?"

"I checked your shirt," he said with a chuckle. His mood swings were going to give me a headache.

I looked at my watch; it was an hour before dinner. "I might take a bath," I said.

"Okay, I'm going to check on some things, I'll be back here to collect you."

He left without another word. I sighed. "Not sure I like your *zone,*" I whispered, as he closed the door behind him.

I opened the closet door to see a full-length, red silk gown. It was backless with a low neckline. Two thin straps looked as if they went over my shoulders and under my arms, other than those, I had no idea how it would stay on. It was a beautiful gown though. I let the silk run through my fingers. On a shelf in the closet was a tissue paper wrapped item. I opened it to see the most flimsy, crotchless, red lace panties. I wondered when he'd organised those.

I ran the bath and when it was full, climbed in and sank down in the warm water. Anticipation flowed through me, and I found myself aroused at the prospect of what was to come.

I closed my eyes and rested my head back. I parted my legs and placed my fingers between my thighs, letting the tips just brush over my clitoris. It throbbed at my touch. I sighed. I raised my hips a little pushing one finger inside me. I released a small moan.

A splash of water startled me. I quickly opened my eyes to see Mackenzie beside the bath. He'd put his arm in, his hand covered mine, stopping me from withdrawing my finger.

"This is mine," he said, inserting his finger alongside mine. "Every orgasm is mine. You do not pleasure yourself," he growled out the words.

"What...?"

He covered my mouth with his. I held on to the side of the bath with my free hand, fearful I might sink under his weight.

He kissed me hard; his finger fucked me harder. It was the most erotic feeling to have his finger and mine inside me at the same time. I mirrored his movement as he stroked inside, at a place that had me writhing.

Water splashed everywhere, covering his clothes and the floor he knelt on. He used his free hand to cup my throat. His thumb kept my chin raised as his tongue fucked my mouth. There was no other word for what he was doing. It wasn't a kiss, it was claiming.

When I felt my orgasm building, I let go of the bath and gripped his bicep instead. I dug my fingernails into his skin and braced my feet on the end of the tub. I arched my body until I was out of the water and even through his kiss, I screamed out as I came.

With closed eyes I slumped back in the water and he pulled his head away. I gasped for breath.

"I'm sorry," he whispered.

I looked at him, "You're soaked," I said, then laughed. That laughter turned to tears.

He reached into the bath and lifted me out; he cradled my dripping body against his as he rested his back against the wall. He lowered his head to mine.

"Please, don't cry," he said.

"I'm not sure why I am," I lied.

He held me for a while longer then lowered me to my feet. He reached for a towel and wrapped it around my body. His shirt was see-through and it clung to his body. He wrapped his arms around me again and pulled me against his chest.

"Why did you come back?" I asked.

"To apologise for being an ass. I saw you and…"

"Why are you being an *ass*?"

"Tomorrow, I'll tell you tomorrow. For now, I want to give you the best experience I can."

"You've made a good start," I said, and then chuckled.

He stepped away holding me at arm's length. He gave me a beautiful smile. "Shall I delay dinner?"

I looked in the mirror. I hadn't wanted to get my hair wet but it was plastered to my head. There was no time to wash it clean though.

"No, I'll be ready in time. And when did you organise the outfit?"

"When you told me you wanted a weekend here," he said.

"I take it you have fresh clothes," I said.

He laughed, "Thankfully, I do." He unbuttoned his cuffs and pulled his shirt over his head.

We walked into the bedroom and he deposited his wet clothes on the floor. He picked up the telephone and called housekeeping; informing them he had some laundry he'd need back in the morning. He grabbed the towel from my body and dried himself off before throwing it back to me. I wrapped it around my chest and sat at the dressing table.

263

While he redressed, I dried my hair, opting to tie it in a tight bun at the nape of my neck instead of spending ages curling it.

"I like that," he said. "I can get to every part of your neck."

I shivered at his words and smiled at his reflection in the mirror. He walked from the bedroom while I applied my makeup.

I dropped the towel on the chair I'd sat in and walked to the closet. I pulled the panties on; it felt strange to wear them, not having my crotch covered. I then pulled the dress from its hanger. I slid it over my head, careful of it touching my face. The material glided over my skin. It was about the most luxurious thing I'd ever worn.

I turned to the mirror and looked at myself. It was a perfect fit, if a little long, and it was only when I turned back to the closet to shut it I saw the shoe box. I hadn't thought about what to wear on my feet.

I pulled it out and opened it. "Wow," I said, as I pulled out an impossibly high-heeled red shoe.

Red was obviously his colour.

I slipped them on, knowing they were going to kill my feet by the end of the evening. I then walked into the living room.

"Fucking hell, Lauren," he said, standing from the sofa.

I smiled, twirled for him.

"I love it, thank you. And the shoes!"

"It reminds me of one of the times when we first met," he said, quietly.

I'd worn a red dress to the conference. Was that only a little over a month ago? It felt like a lifetime.

He offered his arm. "Shall we?" Together, we walked to the main house.

There were many diners already seated and I guessed an early dinner was the norm. I didn't suppose they wanted to engage in their activities with a full stomach.

I chuckled at the thought as a waiter seated us.

"What's funny?" he asked.

"I just thought of the reason why everyone eats early. Got to let it go down before they go down!"

He laughed and pulled a bottle of champagne from a bucket that sat on a plinth beside him.

"Laurent Perrier, for Lauren Perry," he said, while he poured.

"Maybe I was named after it, but it was mispronounced," I said, raising my glass to his.

I took a sip and the champagne fizzed on my tongue. We were handed menus that we promptly laid on the table. I took a moment to look around the room. I didn't recognise anyone from my previous visit, and like before, they all looked 'normal.' The room resembled a high-end restaurant.

Mackenzie reached over and placed his hand on mine, he turned it over as if inspecting my palm. He traced a pattern using the fingers of his other hand.

"This is your life line," he said, following the path of a crease. "And this is your love line."

"What does it say?" I asked.

"It says you're going to fall in love, marry, live a long life."

"Does it? That would be nice."

He looked up at me. "I have no idea, I just made that up."

I laughed as I pulled my hand away. "Let me look at yours."

He laid his hand down, palm up. "Now, that one is your life line, the one that runs from your wrist to your thumb. It looks like you'll have a long life. This finger..." I placed the tip of mine over his middle finger, "Is the finger of Saturn, although I'll rename that Satan," I said. "And this is your love line." I traced my nail over his palm.

"And what does that say?" he whispered, his voice gravelly.

"It says, if you allow it, you'll have a long love life."

"Did you make that up?"

"No, funnily enough, it's one of those things I just remember. You're health line is a little bit shit though, so it's not all good news."

We laughed, "You'll be the death of me, I'm sure," he said.

I caught sight of a hovering waiter and picked up my menu. I let Mackenzie order first, opting to scan a little longer. When he'd finished, I told the waiter I'd have the same.

A bottle of red wine was opened and left to breathe, and our champagne glasses were refreshed.

"If I drink too much, I might not make the twenty-four hours awake thing," I said.

"I'll let you doze for an hour," Mackenzie replied, with a wink.

"I had the best night's sleep last night."

"So did I."

"Did it feel odd for you, to have me in your bed?"

"No, it was the most comfortable thing in the world."

Duck liver paté and small pieces of crisp bread were placed in front of us. I watched as he smeared some on the bread and popped it in his mouth. Even the way he ate was sensual and masculine at the same time.

A rare fillet steak followed. I managed only half of mine. As the evening wore on, my nerves began to kick in. The waiter cleared the table and it was noticeable that I'd grown a little quieter.

"Nervous?" he said, taking my hand once again. I nodded. "Don't be, I'll take good care of you, Lauren."

"I'm nervous about what I'm going to see," I said.

"You don't have to do that. It's not something I'm comfortable with."

"I still feel like I need to, before you do it to me."

"Know that I'm doing it only for you, not because I want to."

"I understand that, and I appreciate it, I do."

"Then it's time to go," he said.

My legs were a little shaky as I stood. He held out his hand, and I noticed a couple of glances from diners as we walked past. One woman smiled at me, I offered a smile back.

He led me to the stairs and we slowly ascended, then along the corridor. He released the catch on the concealed door and we took the flight of stairs to the attic rooms. My mouth had dried and I ran my tongue over my lips, hoping to moisten them. I paused as we got close to the last door down the hallway.

"Turn back if you want to," he whispered.

I looked at him; his face was full of concern. "Turn back, Lauren, please," he said. I shook my head and took a deep breath.

I closed my eyes for a moment, and when I opened them, I squared my shoulders and gave him a small smile.

"If you want me to turn back, I will, for you," I said. "We talk so much at cross purposes, Mackenzie, I don't know what you want most of the time."

"I want you to experience this, I'm just worried; that's all."

"About what?"

"I'm gong to inflict pain on someone because that's what they need from me. I'm not, and I need you to understand this, I'm *not* going to do the same to you. You're not going to see the full extent of what I did to Veronica, just a small part but, if this fucks things up, I'll be devastated."

"I get it, I do. Now open the door, Mackenzie."

He went to say something, and then closed his mouth. He turned and opened the door. He let it swing wide and stood so I could enter.

The room wasn't as well-lit as before, a blind had been pulled. Wall lights gave a subtle glow over the room and somehow instead of making it pleasant, it looked a little sinister. Shadows were created on the floor. I walked to the center of the room and looked around.

"Where is she?" I whispered.

"She'll be here."

Mackenzie removed his suit jacket. He slowly rolled up the sleeves of his white shirt. The muscles on his forearms bulged and his tattoo was on show. Whether it was the light or lack of, I wasn't sure, but his eyes had darkened and his features had hardened. His body visibly changed, he became taut, and like before, I watched every muscle tighten.

He walked towards me and grabbed my wrist, a little roughly.

He led me to one side of the room and sat me down on a red velvet chaise. He stood to one side.

"You do not move from that chair. You do not pleasure yourself in any way. You do not speak unless it's to ask me to stop."

I raised my hand. He frowned at me, I indicated towards my arm with my head.

"Why do you have your hand raised?"

"I need to ask a question."

"Then ask the fucking question."

"You said not to speak."

"Ask the question," he said with a sigh.

"What if I need to pee?"

"Are you kidding me?"

"No."

"Use the fucking bathroom, over there. Jesus, Lauren, you are not going to be any good at this."

"It was just a…"

"Enough," he said sharply as the door to the room opened.

The man I'd seen wearing the hood walked in first, holding what I could only assume was a lead rope attached to a collar around Veronica's neck. I wasn't expecting that. He wasn't wearing the mask, and without it he looked so young, Adonis like.

He led her to the center of the room, where he flicked the end of the leash at her stomach. She was completely naked, with not a hair on

268

her body. I tried not to stare. He flicked her again and she fell to her knees.

He stood in front of her and, as I'd seen before, he stroked her hair. She murmured, it wasn't a moan just a soft mewl. His gentleness was gone in a flash when he yanked on her lead, dragging her to her feet. She didn't take her eyes from his.

I felt Mackenzie's hand on my head; he stroked my hair as I watched the man secure Veronica between two stainless steel poles. He placed a leather cuff around one wrist and clipped it high; then he did the same to the other. When she was secured, he unclipped the lead from her throat. He stood in front of her. Nothing was said by anyone in the room.

I could feel my heart hammer in my chest. Mackenzie ran his hand down the back of my neck; his fingers gently stroked the skin.

The crack of leather as the man flicked the leash against Veronica's thigh startled me. I covered my mouth to contain the shriek. A red line instantly appeared on her skin, she opened her lips and gasped, closing her eyes at the same time. She slid that leg across to the pole. He repeated the process with the other then crouched and bound both ankles.

"She's defying him," Mackenzie whispered. I hadn't realised he'd lowered his head.

I knew not to answer. And I didn't want to. The air in the room was so highly charged it crackled. I didn't want words to break the spell we seemed to have been sucked under.

The man stood, he took her chin in his hand and raised her head to look at him. He stroked the back of his fingers down her cheek and she mewled again.

He turned and stared at us, or rather directly at Mackenzie. I felt a little lost when he stepped away from the chaise. The man walked towards him, and it was as if I was witnessing the squaring up of two men before a fight. If I could see and smell the testosterone, it would have overpowered me. Two very alpha males stood face-to-face. Then one deferred. The blond man handed over the leash to

Mackenzie, he lowered his head slightly, although I caught him glance very quickly my way.

"Don't you fucking dare look at her," Mackenzie growled, his voice had the hairs on my arms stand to attention. The man bowed his head a little lower.

I was instantly reminded of two lions about to fight for territory. Mackenzie was most certainly leader of the pride in that room. The man moved to one side, and he didn't look at me at all. Mackenzie walked towards Veronica; he hooked his finger in the silver loop on the collar and pulled her forward. I could see her legs tremble, and I hoped that was with excitement and not fear.

I was stunned into paralysis, not entirely sure what I was witnessing. Mackenzie was a different man, his body rigid as if about to fight. His features were hard and emotionless.

He circled her. When he returned to face her, he flicked the leash far more aggressively than the man had. I heard the swish and the crack as it hit her stomach. She moaned out loud, arching her body back a little and rattling the chains that held her cuffs.

He stared at her until she stilled. He held out his hand without looking behind him. I watched the Adonis walk forwards and place something in Mackenzie's hand. Veronica sighed. It was as he stepped to one side that I noticed two small silver objects clamped to her nipples. They were connected by a silver chain.

He walked away and to a wall that held a rack. Hanging from that rack were all sorts of implements, he ran his hand through them. The clanking of wood on wood and leather was like a distorted wind chime.

"What's it to be, Veronica?" he said, even his voice was different. Whereas he'd have a husky tone when aroused, it was just harsh.

She didn't answer and I didn't suppose she was allowed to. But she watched him, he watched her. I watched them both. As he slowly drew his hand across the implements again, he hovered over one, her eyes had widened her breathing had become rapid. That was the implement she wanted, she'd told him with her body.

He took down a leather-clad object. It had a handle and wide leather strap that double backed on itself. He slapped it against his hand and the noise echoed around the room. He reached up for a second one. That one had two single leather straps protruding from the handle. Her eyes widened further.

He walked back towards her. I was surprised at how slow everything was, how measured and controlled. I guessed that was what Mackenzie meant by anticipation. Veronica's lips were parted; she ran her tongue over the lower one.

"Did I say you could do that?" Mackenzie said.

Before she had the chance to even shake her head, he flicked the slapper against her lower stomach. She cried out. He slapped her again, and again, each time harder than the last. Her skin was raised and red. She wrestled against the chains holding her, and I swallowed down the panic that was starting to rise in my chest. I had no idea if she was enjoying it or not.

He aimed short flicks all the way down her stomach and across her thighs, trailing the leather back up and over her pussy. It glistened with her juices.

He continued to flick her skin, fast and hard, all the way down her legs. Sweat formed on his back, soaking his white shirt. The smell of him, of her permeated the air, it was cloying, arousing, electrifying. I could feel the wetness between my legs, and I wanted to desperately clench my thighs together. Mackenzie walked around Veronica, continuing to flick the slapper against her skin. He very briefly looked over to me; it was the first indication he'd remembered I was in the room.

He paused. "Spreader," he said to the man.

"Mac…" I heard Veronica say. Mackenzie slapped her into silence.

I looked at the man as he walked towards me; he held a metal bar in his hands. I looked over to Mackenzie; I guess the expression on my face told him all he needed to know.

"Trust me," he whispered.

The man knelt at my feet. He lifted one and gently removed my shoe.

"Do not touch her unnecessarily. She is mine, and mine alone," Mackenzie growled in a completely different tone of voice to the one he'd just used.

I wanted to be outraged at what he'd said but I couldn't. I guessed without realising I'd fallen into the zone myself. I wanted him to take complete control of me. My stomach clenched at the thought, my pussy throbbed with want.

A strap was placed around one ankle and then the other. The bar was extended until my thighs were too far apart for me to use them to gain any relief. I looked at Mackenzie; he gave me a very brief smile and a gentle nod of his head. I could tell then. At that moment, I knew. He would treat her as she wanted, demanded; he would treat me as I needed. He was capable of switching between the two personalities, and I was so thankful for that.

The man sat back on his heels, he looked at me then quickly to my feet. I shuffled them back a little as he licked his lips. I wasn't sure if he wanted to lick them or not.

Mackenzie made a noise not dissimilar to a growl and the man moved away. He stayed on his knees in the center of the room. It dawned on me then. Mackenzie had control of everyone in the room, me included. The man wanted to be dominated by Mackenzie. The power Mackenzie held over the people in the room had my stomach clench even tighter. I was surprised at how arousing it was.

He dropped the slapper he held and transferred the other one to his dominant hand. He trailed it over Veronica's body, and when she moaned, it was clear that time it was a moan of pleasure.

"You need to come, don't you?" he said. She nodded her head.

He walked behind her and brought the slapper down on her backside. He trailed it down her back, alternating between giving her very gentle flicks, to hard whacks.

Each time she moaned louder. I saw the black leather slide between her thighs, he rubbed it slowly back and forth over her. She writhed, and I could see the sweat run down between her breasts. I could feel a bead of my own sweat run down my back.

I gripped the chaise, my fingers dug into the material. I shifted against it, trying to gain some friction and then realised the point of the silk. All I did was slide, the dress having no purchase against the velvet material.

I moaned as I watched, and I saw a ghost of a smile on Veronica's lips. She glanced at me and gave a subtle wink.

Her smile was lost as Mackenzie slapped her pussy. What I saw after had my jaw drop. She came, instantly, and it gushed down her legs. At the same time Mackenzie removed the nipple clamps and she screamed out, writhing against her restraints.

"Fuck," I whispered. The man looked up at me.

Mackenzie walked back to stand in front of her. He drew the end of the slapper through her cum then raised it to her mouth. She opened and extended her tongue, he placed the leather on it, and she sucked it clean.

I struggled to control my breathing. I broke a fingernail as I clawed the chaise. The sound echoed around the room.

"Remove the spreader," Mackenzie said, without looking at me.

As soon as my feet were free I wanted to clench my thighs together, he held my knees apart. I placed my hands over his and tried to push him away. I saw, from the corner of my eye, Mackenzie stride over.

"Release Veronica," he said, the man immediately scuttled back and away from me.

Mackenzie held out his hand and I stood. Without a word he slid the straps of my dress from my shoulders, it fell and pooled around my feet. I wasn't remotely embarrassed about standing there in just my panties. I was beyond that with what I'd just seen.

He led me to the poles, turned me to face him. He ran his fingers down my flaming cheeks. His features had softened, but my body shook from head to toe.

"Shush," he whispered.

He took one wrist and cuffed it; he did the same to the other. He knelt before me.

"You have all the power," he said. He looked at my ankle then back at me, as if waiting for my consent. I nodded.

He cuffed both ankles then stood.

The man was knelt on the floor, he had Veronica in his lap and he was stroking her hair, comforting her. He was gentle, whispering to her. He stood and carried her to the chaise. He laid her down. I watched as he reached underneath for a basket. He opened a tube of liquid and spread it over his hands; he gently ran those hands over her body.

Mackenzie walked to the wall and selected a flogger. He strode back to me and ran it down my chest, over my breasts. His shirt was soaked through, his fringe stuck to his forehead. The heat in the room had turned humid; sweat glistened on my body and ran down my back.

He kept eye contact with me even when he flicked the flogger against my stomach. I took a sharp breath in. He flicked again. Each time my clitoris throbbed. I was desperate for touch and relief. I let my head fall back as his flicks moved up my body. I moaned as they rained down on my breasts. It wasn't like any sensation I'd ever felt before.

The strands of the flogger hit my body at different times, split seconds between them, prolonging the sting, the heating of my skin, and the transfer of energy to my nerve endings underneath. Static coursed over my body, my skin felt alive. My mind was a mass of sparks as impulses of desire and pain fought to travel down the same pathways in my brain.

I needed to come. I needed to feel Mackenzie inside me. I needed more.

I cried out in disappointment when he stepped back. He chuckled.

He moved behind me and I raised my head. It was then that I saw Veronica looking at me. The man had his head between her thighs licking her skin, her pussy. We shared a moment that could never be repeated. A look of understanding flew between us. Although not to the same extreme, we were two women who willingly gave ourselves to the men we loved. She enjoyed watching what Mackenzie did to me, as much as I enjoyed watching what he'd done to her. Although I had no doubt what I'd witnessed was nowhere near what she'd normally experience.

I heard long before I felt the flogger on my back. It was harder than the flicks I'd received before. I cried out, and as the sting made its way to register in my brain, I felt his mouth on my neck. He kissed as if to stop the message arriving.

His hands were on my hips and as he lowered himself, his tongue trailed down my spine. He licked the pain away. He reached under me and dragged his fingers over my exposed pussy. The relief I felt was instant. I wanted to come there and then. I moaned when he, once again, pulled away, denying me his touch.

He walked back to the wall and selected a wooden paddle, I knew what it was; I'd seen a plastic version online. It was wide and I hoped the wider it was, the less painful. Without warning, he wrenched my panties down and slapped the paddle on my arse. It was a similar sensation to when he'd used his hand, and I liked it just as much.

I tried to control my breathing, I could feel myself falling towards that abyss, and I struggled to keep back from the edge. I wanted more, I wanted longer.

Veronica rose from the chaise and walked towards me. Mackenzie grabbed her wrist before she could place her hand on my breast. I watched his knuckles whiten as he gripped her hard.

"She just needs a little more," she whispered, not taking her gaze from mine.

I looked at Mackenzie and his face displayed anger. I smiled at him and nodded. "Please?" I whispered. Without a word he released her wrist.

She held my hips and lowered slightly. Her tongue flicked over my nipple and as Mackenzie brought the paddle back down on my arse she bit, hard. I heard the paddle fall to the floor, the sound only marginally louder than my moans.

My body ached from being held in one position. I felt myself sag a little, letting the poles and the chains take my weight. While Veronica transferred her attention to my other nipple, I felt the strands of the flogger run down my back. I closed my eyes and tensed with anticipation as it was pulled away and then brought down on my backside.

"Again," I said. He complied. I did, as he'd told me, have all the power.

"Harder!" I screamed out the word.

I think I received two more before my body gave in. I screamed out his name. I writhed and tried to wrench my arms from their restraint. Veronica moved away, and I felt his hands on my thighs and his nose run over my clitoris. That was my undoing. I came so fucking hard, so brutally that my stomach hurt, my body shook, tears coursed down my cheeks, and he licked and sucked.

My orgasm was his, every blissful, awful second of it, belonged to him. He totally claimed me then.

****

I was disorientated when I opened my eyes. I wasn't sure where I was. My last memory had been of an orgasm so intense it made me feel nauseous.

"Hey, baby," I heard.

"Where am I?"

"Back at the cottage, hold on. Shield your eyes."

I covered my eyes with my arm, while he turned on the bedside lamp. I was in the four-poster bed, the muslin drapes closed around us. I rolled to my side, to face him.

I placed my hand on his cheek and he turned to kiss it.

"I'm so sorry," he said.

"For what?"

"I didn't expect you to come so hard, to pass out like that."

"Wasn't the first time," I said. My voice was croaky, my throat dry. "I need a drink."

He rose from the bed and strode to the kitchen. He returned with a glass of water. I winced as I sat up.

"Sore?"

"Not sore enough," I said, as I took a sip.

He chuckled. "You...I don't have words, Lauren. I can't find the words to tell you how amazing you were, how you made me feel."

"It was an experience," I said, with a chuckle.

"One you'll never repeat?"

"One where I need a little more control over my orgasms. I loved watching you, Mackenzie; that turned me on more. You controlled everyone. As much as you don't have words, neither do I."

It was his turn to chuckle.

"So your list's complete," he whispered.

"No, there's one more. One that's far more important to me than anything we've done so far."

"I think we need to let your body rest before we get to that. Is there anything I can do for you?"

"I guess I should shower," I said.

He shook his head. "I cleaned you, it's my job, Lauren, to care for you after."

"You cleaned me?"

"I washed your body, soothed the redness with lotion."

"Now that's something I *could* get used to. Can you pass me my phone?"

He frowned at me, but reached over to the dressing table and retrieved it.

I sat and half turned my body away from him. I sent a text. It was time.

My last request, Mackenzie, and I pray it's something you'll agree to. Make love to me, like you mean it.

I pressed send and placed the phone on the bedside cabinet. He looked towards the open door and into the living room where we heard his phone ping. He then looked at me. I let a tear roll down my cheek. He placed his thumb under my eye and caught the next.

"Am I going to hate what I read?" he whispered.

"I don't know, Mackenzie."

He closed his eyes and sighed before climbing from the bed again. I slid from the bed and stood; surprised my legs were as stable as they were. It was a while before he returned.

He walked towards me and cupped my face in his hands.

"I can't do that," he said. I couldn't stop the sob that left my mouth. I bowed my head so he couldn't see the sadness.

"Look at me. Look at me, Lauren, please," he said.

When I raised my head, I saw a man whose face mirrored mine, full of sadness.

"I can't do that because…I want so desperately to make love to you. I want to give you my soul, Lauren, but you'll fucking break me when you walk away tomorrow."

I blinked, not understanding.

"I…I don't understand."

"I love you. If I do this, if I give you my soul, because that's what I'll do if I make love to you, you'll break me when you walk away."

I sobbed again. I let the tears roll down my cheeks and saw the same on his. I placed my hands either side of his face.

"Oh, Mackenzie. Can't you see how much I fucking love you? Do you think I'd have done any of this if I hadn't?"

His smile was slow to form and then he shook his head and chuckled.

"You love me?"

"Yes!"

"Then why the fuck didn't you say that?"

"Because you kept telling me you didn't want a relationship."

"I've never said that, did I? It's about children, Lauren. At what point will you start wanting children and then hate me because I can't give you that one thing?"

"Mackenzie, I want you. Just you. I don't know what will happen with regards to children. Right now, I want us to just be us. You can't have children. I'm going into this with my eyes wide open and with that knowledge. It doesn't make me love you any less. And I could never hate you."

He shook his head again. "I…"

"You said you'd do anything I asked, right?" He nodded his head. "Then do one thing for me, trust me."

I silenced his response with a kiss.

Chapter Eighteen

Mackenzie didn't make love to me once, or twice, in fact I think I lost count. He was tender and gentle. He took his time to pleasure every single part of my body. He kissed me, slow and fierce. He gave himself to me, and I did the same: mind, body, and soul.

I watched him sleep. I wanted to laugh; we weren't supposed to sleep, not for twenty-four hours anyway. I was half tempted to wake him. I'd cried when we'd made love and he'd held me. He'd told me he loved me over and over, and I'd done the same. In the short time I'd known him, I was stunned at the depth of feeling I had for him.

"If you think you're going to abuse my body again, Miss Perry, you have another think coming," he whispered. He slowly opened his eyes.

"Are you turning me down, Mr. Miller?"

"Never, but I'm not making love to you again here. Up and dressed, we're going home."

"That's a shame."

"Here is for fucking, and I intend to do that to you, a lot. We'll be back, often. Home, with you, is where I want to be right now."

"So we don't fuck at home?" I teased.

"We make love and we fuck, and I spank you, and I will claim your ass. You may have finished your list, Lauren, but I haven't."

"Can you build one of those playrooms?"

"I can do whatever the fuck you want."

He rolled from the bed, and despite my protest, pulled the duvet from my body. I laughed as he struggled into the same clothes he'd worn the previous night. It appeared we had no time to wait for his laundry. I quickly dressed and shoved all our things in the two overnight bags. With one last check around the rooms, we left.

It was way too early for anyone to be up except security. Mackenzie requested his car be brought around, and we waited on the steps of the manor house watching the sun rise.

I winced at the sound of the engine as the valet drove to the steps, sure it would have woken people. Mackenzie tipped him as he threw our bags in the boot, and then we roared off down the drive, kicking up gravel as we did.

We arrived back to his house in record time.

****

"I'm going to give you one last chance, Lauren. You'll break my heart, but I'd rather you did it now. Think hard about whether you can be with me and not have children."

"Don't you think I have already? We could adopt, we could seek out some consultant and see if anything can be done. If it can't, then we can love each other even more."

He stared at me. I knew I was going to have some more convincing to do at a later date, but I meant what I'd said. I wanted him and if that meant forgoing children, then so be it.

"How soon can you move in?" Mackenzie asked as he placed two coffees on the breakfast bar. "Damn, forgot tea," he added.

"Is that you asking me to live with you?"

"Isn't that what we're supposed to do?"

"You know, when I first met you, you answered every question I asked, with a question. It was annoying."

"And when I first met you, you evaded every question I asked, it was annoying."

"As soon as I can pack up my flat, I guess."

He smiled. "I'll call a moving company tomorrow, you can rent it out."

I took a sip of coffee.

"So, who won?" I asked.

He looked over the rim of his cup and frowned.

"The game? Who won?" I asked.

"I was never playing but…me, Lauren, me. I won you."

The End

Mackenzie Miller and Lauren Perry will return. Afterall, The Facilitator has a list of his own to complete.

Printed in Great Britain
by Amazon

45648593R00165